THE DISTANT *Lighthouse*

I0744519

DONALD F. AVERILL

COVER ART BY MARY STEBBINS

INK START MEDIA
5710 W Gate City Blvd Ste K #284
Greensboro, NC 27407

FOR OTHER BOOKS BY
THE AUTHOR PLEASE VISIT:

www.authordfaverill.com

CHAPTER 1

The End of May 1957

I hadn't thought much about it until the end of my freshman year in high school, but my best friends, Millie Harris and Jerry Morgan, were going to graduate a year ahead of me. They had just finished their sophomore year. We were attending a party for the Crafton High graduating seniors and Nancy Brewster, the valedictorian, was talking to me, Rocky Linfield, the lighthouse kid, Millie and Jerry. I had been the lighthouse kid for the last five years. I didn't mind. Why would I? It wasn't a tease or derogatory, it was a fact.

Nancy was not a typical senior girl, kind of quiet, had short blonde hair and was barely five feet tall. She was dynamite in the classroom. She was telling us to start planning for college. She looked at each of us saying, "Rocky, you've got three more years, Millie and Jerry, two more years to plan." Those words stuck in my mind and got me thinking. I hadn't taken study hall as a freshman, so I signed up for typing and had already accumulated more credit hours than usual. If I kept adding an extra class or two each year, could I finish high school in two more years and graduate with my best friends?

I wasn't much of a party goer, said goodnight to Millie and Jerry and walked home at eleven that night. I sat at my bedroom desk to plan the next two years of classes after making sure I could earn enough credits to meet the minimum standard. It looked good on paper, but I had to get permission for one circumstance. I could foresee a problem, taking junior and senior English simultaneously. I understood that senior English was a requirement for acceptance into college. I'd have to talk with the Principal, Mr. Oberst, but before I did that, I had to discuss it with Mom and Dad.

The next morning, I had a brief discussion with my parents and I explained my reasoning. Dad was all in favor, but Mom was a little reserved, especially about taking two English classes simultaneously. I told her I was going to talk to Mr. Oberst about it.

I went by the school later in the day after mowing a lawn and asked the principal if he would okay my plan. While I waited patiently in his office, he looked at my grades over the last four years.

I watched his poker face as he reviewed my transcript. After about five minutes, although it seemed more like half an hour, he leaned forward and said, "I'll give my permission if your parents agree. Have them send me a note."

I was elated, jumped to my feet, approached his desk and shook his hand saying, "Thank you, sir. I'll get a note from Mom and Dad." I left his office with the best feeling. I wasn't going to be the odd man out. I would be graduating with Millie and Jerry if everything went as planned.

That evening after dinner, I told Mom and Dad that Mr. Oberst would allow my curriculum if they agreed and sent a note of support. Mom was hesitant saying I would be missing some of the important activities of my senior year, but she somewhat reluctantly joined with Dad and signed the note.

I kept the plan to myself during the summer of 1957. Millie and Jerry had no idea what I was doing, but after three weeks into the fall semester, Millie figured out what was going on. She was excited for me and my plan. Even though we dated occasionally, I had quite a few late nights of studying because of the extra class. Most of our dates that school year were telephone visits which we called homework. I always enjoyed hearing her voice on the phone and she told me she looked forward to my calls. Ever since she and I travelled to the Bahamas when we were ten years old to help rescue her parents from kidnappers, she seemed to have an intuitive sense of what I was up to. I tried to keep little secrets, but Millie was like a military decoding machine for classified messages. Mil kept it quiet for a few days and then we told Jerry what I was doing. Millie and Jerry told me they had discussed the coming breakup of our trio when they knew they were graduating a year ahead of me. Well, my plan worked out with only a couple of hiccups and we graduated together at the end of May 1959. I was anticipating a summer of relaxation before starting college in the fall. But I didn't sit on my tail for long.

I guess a description of us is in order. Millicent Harris is about five-five and very pretty, has shoulder-length dark-brown hair and is very bright. Her parents own a furniture store. She and I are the same age but she's a year ahead of me in school, but that's another story. Jerry Morgan is an inch taller than I am, has blond hair, although it has been getting darker the last couple of years, and is a well-built physical specimen. His stepfather repairs engines of all kinds. His real dad, a Russian soldier, was killed in the war by Germans. His mom runs the hospital lab. I sometimes envy Jerry's muscularity. I'm not quite six-feet tall, have reddish-brown hair and weigh about one eighty-five. I've broadened out in the last year and put some muscle on my arms and shoulders.

As the 1959 summer progressed, I mowed some lawns and worked with Dad at our store, Crafton Crafts, saving every penny for college. Right after Independence Day, Sunday evening, something unbelievable happened. Dad, Mom, Susan, my thirteen-year-old sister, and I were finishing dinner when we heard a banging at our door. Dessert was on our minds and the loud knocking interrupted our thoughts. Then, I recognized Millie's frenzied voice, "Rocky! We have to talk!"

I pushed away from the table and stood up, but I was too slow, Suz had already reached the entrance, unlatched the screen door and let our visitor in. As I approached Millie, I heard her gasping for breath. She uttered, "Finally! I have something to tell you."

Suzy stepped aside and said, "Jeez, Millie, are you pregnant?"

Millie, gasping to get her wind, shrieked with laughter and said, "No, you goof ball. Whatever would make you think that?"

Suzy didn't have time to answer before I grabbed Millie's left hand, pulled her into the living room, and said, "Sit down and catch your breath. What are you so excited about?"

We sat on the sofa, but Suzy wormed her way between us. I pinched her butt and said, "Scram! Mil and I want to talk."

Suzy stalked off muttering, "You guys never tell me anything."

I adjusted my position on the sofa, looked at Millie and remarked, "Don't mind her, she says stuff like that all the time. She wants to know everything that's going on." I leaned back and asked, "So, what's so important for you to run over here at top speed from your place?"

Her eyes twinkled and she smiled, "I think you're gonna like this." She took a deep breath, exhaled and began to explain. "Dad got a message from a furniture manufacturer in Sweden. Mr. Svensson owns a company called Nordic Wood Products in Stockholm. He wants to sponsor a month-long visitation program for three high school age students from America. He's trying to get more young Americans into marketing his company's products. It's kind of a plan for the future."

What she was trying to tell me didn't register. I needed further explanation. I just looked at her, waiting for more.

She slapped my knee, gazed at me and said, "Didn't you get what I just said? He wants three high school age students to visit Sweden and tour Scandinavia!" She looked at me expectantly.

Finally, the light came on. She was thinking of Jerry, me and her. "Jeez, Mil. We all have summer jobs. If we take off to Sweden, how are we going to have enough money to pay tuition for college?"

Ignoring my reservations, Millie answered immediately as she sandwiched my right palm between her hands, "We don't have to enroll this fall. We can start school next year in the spring."

I recognized this would be an excellent opportunity for the three of us. I had never even considered going to Europe before and it was going to be a nearly free trip . . . and for a month. "Yeah! That would be okay with me. What about Jerry?"

"I thought I'd better get your take on it first. If you didn't want to go, then I wouldn't go. I haven't even talked to Jerry yet. I was so excited about the offer, I had to tell you about it."

I couldn't commit to it until Mom and Dad agreed to let me take off for month, so I had to go to the kitchen to explain why Millie was so excited. I hoped they had heard what was going on. I had gotten up from the sofa when they both came into the living room smiling. They had overheard Millie's excited explanation of the visit to Sweden.

Dad spoke first, "If you want to visit a Scandinavian country for a month, it's all right with us, Rocky. Your Mom and I think the trip would be good experience for you to have before going to college."

Mom chuckled, "Rocky, you'll have to bring us some souvenirs from Scandinavia." She shifted attention to Millie and said, "We're about to have some dessert, Millie, would you like to join us?"

"No, thank you, I've got to get back home. I was helping Dad shine my car out in the garage when he told me about Mr. Svensson's offer. I had to run over here to tell Rocky about it. I couldn't wait until tomorrow. I'm so happy Rocky can go with me."

Millie stood up and gave me a hug. "We'll talk it over some more. Thank you Mr. and Mrs. Linfield."

I held her right hand, "I'm glad you came over. We need to talk to Jerry. His parents will have the last word on him travelling to Scandinavia for a month. Let's talk to Jerry tomorrow and see what he thinks. His dad might not want him to go. Jer is his dad's right-hand-man at the engine repair shop. I'll call him in the morning before he goes to work."

"Okay. When should I come over? We can go together."

"No, I'll give Jerry an early call and tell him we're coming over to give him some exciting news."

"You're not going to tell him when you call?"

"Nope. I want to do it together. I'll come to get you at eight o'clock."

Millie raised an eyebrow and gave me a stare. "That early?"

"Don't you have to work tomorrow?"

"Yeah, but not till nine o'clock. The furniture store opens at nine."She moved toward the door and I was right behind.

"I'll walk you home, Mil."

She grabbed my left arm and said, "That's okay, I don't want you to be kept from dessert. You might blow away before the trip is arranged." She giggled, opened the door, blew me a kiss and took off jogging the six blocks home.

The next morning, I was getting goose bumps from a cool ocean breeze as I walked the nearly half mile to the Harris'. I ran the last block to warm up but not be breathless. Millie was sitting on the front porch waiting. She was dressed in khaki shorts, a white sweatshirt and thongs. She had nice, tan legs from riding her bike to school and work since spring. She still had the bike I drooled over when we were ten. Her dad had it repainted and it looked almost new. It leaned against the porch waiting for a rider.

It took us about five minutes to walk to Jerry's house. Mr. Morgan's pickup truck was sitting in the driveway. A dirty, oily car engine took up half the bed. Jerry knew we were coming from my call to him earlier and he opened the door before we had a chance to knock. He came outside and we sat together as Millie told him about the proposed trip to Sweden. Before he had a chance to say anything, his mom asked us to come in the house.

She still worked at the hospital laboratory and was now the supervisor. She was curious about our early morning visit. We sat at the breakfast table and I took over for Millie. I pretty much repeated what she had said to Jerry and Natalie reacted, "I think it would be a good experience for you, Jerry."

"But Mom, I would be losing money for school."

Mrs. Morgan glanced at me. I thought she wanted my support, so I said, "Millie and I will start school in the spring semester. We'd be home to work during the holidays. Jerry could do the same, don't you think?"

"Sure. I don't think Leroy would mind getting a temp for a month. He'd probably enjoy bossing someone new around for four weeks. It would give him some relief from telling Jerry what to do for a month."

"Jeez, Mom, Dad doesn't always tell me what to do anymore. I know what he wants most of the time."

"Well, if you want to go with Rocky and Millie, it's fine with me. I'll talk to your father. The only thing I want you to remember is this. If you visit Finland, don't get close to the Soviet Union border. I don't want you to get into trouble with USSR border guards."

Jerry replied, "Don't worry, Mom. I'm guessing we'd only be in Helsinki for a brief time."

Millie grinned and added, "Rocky and I will see that he stays away from the Soviets."

Natalie laughed, "Jerry will need to get a passport. What about you and Rocky?"

"I talked with Rocky's grandmother last night and she said normally it would take four to six weeks to get our passports renewed. They haven't been used in seven years. But with her connections, we could have our passports ready in about a week. So, Rocky's grandmother's old FBI contacts and Rocky's mom's recommendations are all we'll need to get our passports ready. We should be able to travel by the end of July."

The Morgens agreed to Jerry accompanying Millie and me to Stockholm and in the last two weeks of July the three of us met almost daily to discuss our travel plans. Dad took us from Crafton, a small town on the coast of Maine, to Boston for a flight to London on July 30.

We didn't stay in London for long, only enough time to get a bite to eat and make sure our luggage was transferred. After an hour in the UK, we were back in the air for about three more hours. We arrived in Stockholm and were met by the Svensson family: Mr. Svensson, Lars, his wife, Anna, and their daughter, Carina. Lars was clean shaven and tall, several inches taller than Jerry. I estimated he was at least six-four and wore a dark-blue suit, almost black. Anna was good looking, about five-seven, blonde and wore a heavy light-brown coat over a brightly colored house dress. Carina, also blonde, a bit taller than her mother, was dressed in jeans and a heavy light-gray sweater. Jerry was captivated and poked me, whispering, "Look at that!" I had to admit she was slightly short of gorgeous.

Lars owns and operates a furniture factory and has a small export business to Scandinavian countries. He hesitates to export to more European countries because of all the different currencies and licenses required. However, he has been thinking of exporting to the United States and Canada because of the large population and simpler currency exchanges.

We spent a month in the Scandinavian countries with Carina Svensson as our guide. Millie and Carina hit it off as soon as we arrived in Stockholm, during the first week in August. Carina is more wholesome than beautiful and at least an eight out of ten. Jerry made a comment to me after we had followed her around in Denmark the first week of our tour.

"Damn, Rock, Carina is sexy. What a tour guide to have for a whole month. I can't seem to concentrate on the architectural stuff she points out. I keep looking at her architecture."   "Yeah, I know what you mean, but I still like Millie. I like the way she's built. And you have to agree she's so damn cute . . . and smart."

"But Mil is more like a sister, don't you think?"

I replied, "When I was ten, I thought that way, but not anymore. By the time I turned thirteen, I changed my mind."

"That's when testosterone started taking over, Rock."

"Yeah, but I can control my mental processes and not let the physical urges take over." Chuckling, I punched Jerry in the arm.

Carina wasn't just taking us around Scandinavia treating us to all the sites and food of the Nordic countries as a treat for her visitors. While she was our tour guide, she was working for her father. During the hours she was conducting business, Millie, Jerry and I were normal tourists, purchasing cool but usually overpriced souvenirs, making our way by occasionally getting help from English speaking citizens, although most clerks understood and spoke adequate English. We learned a few handy words and phrases as we shopped.

CHAPTER 2

The First Week of September

The night before we left Stockholm to return home, the Svenssons gave Millie, Jerry and me a sendoff party. The neighbors we met while living with our sponsor family presented us with mementos that varied from Scandinavian coins to wooden objects such as backscratchers to present to our family members. We had lots of laughs, great food and our Swedish friends bombarded us with questions about our small hometown, Crafton, in coastal Maine. We were sad to be leaving such gracious hosts, but we did want to return home; to be with our families for the holidays and get ready for college.

Millie, Jerry and I got up at dawn and were packed, fed, and waiting for a taxi to the Stockholm airport by six o'clock. The previous night, we packed just about everything we had except toothbrushes, and poked them in our backpacks at the last minute. The Svenssons had made sure we were dressed warmly and gave each of us a small bag of snacks for the trip. Our goodbyes were tearful for the women and we gave hugs and handshakes before climbing in a van to transport us to the airfield.

On the tarmac, we carried our own luggage to the plane and were helped aboard by a middle aged man in a light-blue uniform who we thought was a steward. About five minutes later, we discovered the gentleman was actually one of the pilots. This flight was almost entirely cargo, except for Millie, Jerry and me. The Nordic Wood Products logo was stenciled on the cartons that occupied most of the space in the cabin.

Four passenger seats were available in front of the cargo, but they looked like they had been lifted from another plane at the last minute. Two of the seat covers were repaired with duct tape. Millie got on first, made her way past long sealed boxes in the center of the floor and took the front seat on the left. Jerry climbed over the boxes and took the seat behind her. I sat in the seat across from Jerry on the right. When the two engines were starting, the fellow that had assisted us boarding came back from the cockpit and opened the fuselage hatch. He flipped the hinged steps out and lifted a large suitcase into the plane. Then a fourth passenger appeared. We were pleasantly surprised when Carina Svensson climbed aboard.

The noise from the engines drowned out our voices, but Jerry got up and motioned me to take his place behind Millie. When Jerry stood up to move into my seat, Carina stepped over the knee-high cartons and took the seat behind Millie. I shrugged my shoulders at Jerry and we sat down on the right, Jerry behind me. It occurred to me that the difference in the weights of the girls and us might affect the balance of the plane. When the hatch was slammed shut and locked in place, I asked if our seating was all right. The pilot nodded and gave me a thumbs up, then disappeared into the cockpit. The engine noise increased and the DC-3 began to taxi.

I had only flown three times before. The first time was in a small seaplane in the Bahamas in 1952. Then with my dad and a pilot in a Cessna when we visited a navy buddy of Dad's in the hospital in Boston. That was in 1953 and it was a short trip. I don't recall any details, but I wasn't scared because I was with my dad. The third flight was a month ago when coming to Stockholm in a large four engine passenger plane. The accommodations a month ago were far superior to what we now had, but this was a cargo plane, not fitted for paying customer comfort.

The roar of the engines made conversation difficult but once we were airborne, the noise lessened a bit. We had to be within a foot of each other to be heard without misunderstanding and asking for repeats. Fortunately, Millie, Jerry and I had done some investigating when we found out we were returning from Scandinavia via a DC-3 cargo plane. We didn't expect any premium service.

Jerry leaned over my left shoulder and asked, "How long will we be in the air?"

I had no clue so shook my head. "Ask Carina, she should know." I wondered if he was getting airsick.

Jerry leaned over the long cartons stacked in the center of the plane to talk with Carina. I could barely hear their words. He retook his seat and almost yelled, "She said we'll be in Stornoway in about four hours. She'd explain why she's with us then."

I laughed, "Where the heck is Stornoway?"

Jerry smiled and said, "I don't know, but we'll find out in four hours."

I glanced at Millie and Carina. They had turned so they could talk more easily. They were facing Jerry and me and their heads were nearly touching. I could see their mouths moving but I've never been able to read lips. I couldn't hear a word they said. I leaned my head against the fuselage and could feel the engine vibrations. Trying to relax, I closed my eyes. The night before, in anticipation of riding in a cargo plane across the north Atlantic, I hadn't slept well.

I guess I was dreaming. When I felt Suzy shaking my left shoulder, I pushed her hand away, saying, "Cut it out, Suz."

"It's Jerry, Rock. You've been sleeping. Carina wants you to eat something. She brought some things her mother prepared for us in addition to the snacks."

With my right hand, I wiped my face and blinked my eyes a few times. "Uh, okay, I'm awake now."

Jerry put something wrapped in wax-paper in my left hand. I blinked again and focused on it, still a little groggy. It looked like a donut without a hole in the middle about the size of a squished hamburger bun. I took a mouthful and found out it contained a mixture of egg and ham. I never would have known until I took a bite. The only things I could smell were new shipping boxes and aviation fuel. I must have had a funny expression because Millie pointed at me and laughed. I looked at the girls, gave Carina a thumbs up and yelled, "Thanks."

A few minutes later, the pilot we had seen before came back and announced, "We'll be landing in about thirty minutes." Apparently, the girls heard the announcement and gave him a thumbs up, Jerry gave him a salute and I laughed at the gestures. I glanced out the window and could only see clouds. I thought we'd be flying over land and I wanted to see how the countryside appeared from almost two miles up.

The clouds cleared somewhat and I saw brief glimpses of land below for about ten minutes, then water. My ears began to plug up and I reached in my jacket pocket for some gum but couldn't find any. I suddenly remembered putting gum in my suitcase. How dumb was that? I'd have to suffer for a few minutes as pressure adjusted. Not a big deal.

We must have descended over water for fifteen minutes or so before I could see land again. I felt more secure when we were above land masses. I hated the thought of having to ditch a plane in the North Atlantic ocean. I began wondering what the water temperature was north of the British Isles. I'd ask someone at the air terminal when we landed.

Millie got up from her seat, leaned across the cartons and motioned for me to come closer. I assumed she didn't want to be yelling at me. I strained to hear her words but understood, "When we land, I need to use a bathroom. Find one for me as soon as you can."

I grinned and replied, "I need to go, too. Let me know if you see a toilet. Ask Carina if she knows the slang word for toilet."

Nodding, Millie dropped back into her seat and reattached her seatbelt, talked to Carina, listened attentively and laughed. I'd ask her what she found so funny when we landed. I could hear the wheels being lowered as we passed over land and in less than a minute we were on the ground. The plane came to a stop about twenty yards from the terminal, a long, one-story freshly painted building with cars parked on one side, planes on the other. A fuel truck approached us and the engines were shut down.

The other pilot appeared and told us we'd have enough time to have a meal inside while the right engine was being checked. He didn't inform us of any problems, so we were not concerned. I looked at Jerry and he noted, "Probably the oil pressure is running low. It's not a big deal."

Millie and Carina were up and followed the pilot to the rear hatch. I watched him open the door and lower the stairway. He descended first and guided the girls down the stairs to solid ground. Jerry and I followed and caught up with the girls as they quickly walked the short distance to the terminal. We didn't have to show our passports as long as we remained on the airport premises. Jerry and I followed the girls into the terminal and saw Millie and Carina making their way toward the clearly marked toilets beyond the dining tables and chairs. Millie glanced back at me and pointed at the signs indicating the different restrooms for men and women.

By the time we got to the hallway, the girls had disappeared. Jerry and I used the men's room, washed and returned to the dining area where the girls were seated at one of the tables for four. We joined them and I asked Millie, "What were you laughing about after you talked with Carina on the plane?"

"Oh," she snickered, "Carina told me the slang for toilet is cludgie. I thought it was a strange and funny name." Carina grinned and nodded.

I had to agree with her, cludgie was kind of a funny word. I wondered how it had originated. Jerry said he remembered hearing it before when he flew with his parents to Canada from London after the war.

I asked Carina why she had joined us and she said, "Dad was sending Hans Karlsson, but he got the stomach flu. Dad asked me if I thought I could do the job and I said yes. Also, I thought it would be fun to make the trip with friends."

"Well, we were sure surprised when you came aboard."

Jerry quickly added, "We're glad you came with us." He looked at a menu and said, "I wonder if I can get a burger?"

Millie and I laughed. Millie said, "You might have to wait until we get back to Maine. I don't think burgers are available here or in Iceland."

Jerry scanned the menu and said, "Our next stop is Iceland? How far is that?"

Carina replied, "I think it's another three and a half hours. We'll eat again in Reykjavik while they gas up the plane." She glanced at the menu and closed it. "I'd like to take a nap on the plane but it is so uncomfortable."

Jerry suggested, "Maybe we can get some pillows and blankets. Let's ask the waitress."

When the middle-aged server heard us talking, she commented, "Americans, yes?" Carina pointed to Millie, Jerry, and me and answered, "These three are, I'm from Stockholm. We are all students on our way to the United States." What she said wasn't quite true, but three-fourths was. Knowing what we had eaten today, Carina ordered cakes and tea for all. Carina also knew what we had in our packs from her mother, so we would have things to eat if we got hungry before we reached Iceland. When the lady returned with our tea and cakes, Carina asked about purchasing some pillows and blankets.

"Oh, yes. How many would you like?"

Carina surveyed us and we all shook our heads. I think none of us wanted to spend any more money on the trip than was absolutely necessary. A little discomfort was not much of a price to pay. We'd be home in about half a day but a pillow would supply us with another souvenir of our trip.

Carina asked, "How much is a pillow?" When she found out, she glanced at us again and said, "I can put it on my expense account. Are you sure you don't want pillows or blankets?"

We thanked her for the offer but still declined. I figured Millie and Jerry were thinking the same as I was, Mr. Svensson's company had already done enough for us. Carina got up, went to the sales counter and paid for her pillow. It was about half the size of one of the pillows on my sofa at home. It was covered in plaid material, mostly in two shades of green with a yellow stripe.

When Carina returned to our table I asked, "How much were the cakes and tea?"

She grinned, replying, "Free for the three American tourists."

Jerry leaned over to me and said, "She wants to pay for us. Let's let her do it. We'll pay when we eat at Reykjavik. Okay?"

I nodded and replied, "Sounds good to me."

Jerry and I left a generous tip on our table and we all went outside for fresh air before reboarding the plane. Our uniformed pilots were standing under the right wing talking to one of the ground crew. I recognized one of them as the man who had assisted us boarding the plane. I hadn't seen the other one before, but he was tall and had to duck to walk under the wing. They shook hands with the crew member and walked toward us. The pilot we had seen before introduced us to the other pilot and said, "This is our substitute pilot for the flight to Reykjavik, Captain Ron Stoddard. I'll remain as his copilot. I'm Miles Allen."

Curiosity forced me to ask, "What happened to our original pilot?"

Mr. Allen replied, "He had to go to hospital, abdominal problems.

Captain Stoddard has made this trip hundreds of times. He's from New York and I'm from Vancouver, Canada, just so you know. We've flown together many times in the last five years."

Millie inquired, "I'm curious, sir, when do we depart for Iceland?"

"We're about ready to take off. Another ten minutes should do it. The right engine was using excessive oil, but the ground crew got the problem fixed."

Captain Stoddard was already in the cockpit and started the right engine. The powerful motor spun the prop slowly and then faster until the propeller blades were just a blur. Then the engine was shut down. The captain emerged from the plane and gave us a thumbs up. I was ready to board and continue our trip home. I think the others felt the same way 'cause they started walking quickly toward the plane.

CHAPTER 3

Off to Iceland

Millie, Carina, Jerry and I climbed into the plane and latched our seatbelts before the pilots boarded. The captain commented as he passed by, "We'll be in the air in a jiffy. Make sure your belts are secure." We heard the hatch close and Mr. Allen scooted passed us saying, "We'll be in Reykjavik in time for dinner. Hang onto your hats!" We all laughed, he smiled, waved and disappeared into the cockpit.

The engines roared to life and the plane began to move slowly onto the runway. The powerful motors revved, turning us into the wind. We could feel the DC-3's speed increasing. As we lifted into the air, I heard the landing gear fold into the wings beneath the engines. The plane began climbing and turned to the west toward Iceland for our next stop, fuel and dinner.

I watched the girls on the other side of the passenger compartment and saw Carina pass something to Millie. Millie unfolded what appeared to be a brochure and spread it out on her lap. It took her about a minute to read the item and refold it. I watched her glance at me and wave the pamphlet indicating I should reach across the boxes to get it. I followed her gesture, released my seat belt and grasped the item. I sat back in my seat and focused on the folded paper. It was a tourist brochure for Reykjavik, Iceland, illustrating city streets with restaurants, museums and other points of interest marked in red. I studied the city layout for a few minutes, refolded it and handed it to Jerry.

I saw Millie watching me, so I gave her a thumbs up and mouthed thank you. That was the last I saw of the pamphlet. After I passed it to Jerry, I remembered I had a book in my carry-on luggage and retrieved it. I had bought it in Denmark at a used bookstore when Carina was meeting with some of her father's customers. I opened the cover and saw that it had been published in London and was recent. The reason I bought the book escaped me, but I started reading A Separate Peace by John Knowles. I'd read about half the first chapter when I heard Jerry snoring. At first, I thought he was just goofing around, but I swiveled in my seat and took a closer look. He was sawing logs. As I turned back to my book I noticed Carina was also asleep with her head against her Scottish pillow. Millie glanced at me and smiled.

When we were two hours from Reykjavik, Captain Stoddard came back to the passenger/cargo area and squatted down after stretching. He must have noted that Millie and I were the only ones awake. He motioned for me to move next to Millie. I presumed he want to discuss something with us. I stepped over the cargo boxes and sat with my left bun on Millie's seat. She was squeezed against the fuselage wall but didn't seem to be under any distress.

I grinned, "You okay?"

She replied with a grin, "Yeah, but these seats aren't made for one-and-a-half butts."

Stoddard smiled and declared, "We just received a message from Reykjavik. It's fifty-three degrees and overcast. It looks like some bad weather is coming in from the north. We might have to stay overnight if the weather gets worse. I thought you should know the situation. Please tell your friends. Sorry we don't have anything to drink or peanuts to eat."

Millie responded, "That's all right. We have some things to munch on but we'll wait for dinner in Reykjavik."

Stoddard nodded and said, "Well, there's a nice restaurant at the airport and they have rooms to rent for layovers. Do you have any questions?"

I was interested in our next stop after Iceland. I thought we would be landing in Canada for our next refueling, but Captain Stoddard surprised me.

"Our next stop after Iceland will be in Greenland. You'll find Narsarsuaq an interesting place."

I watched his eyes shifting to look behind me at Jerry. I turned sideways and twisted my neck to see if my best buddy was still asleep and saw him waking up. When he sat forward, his folded jacket he used as a pillow fell to the floor. Jerry looked a little dazed, "What's been happening? What'd I miss?"

I thought he might have been talking to Captain Stoddard, but when I rotated my head, the captain was going into the cockpit. All I could see was his back.

I turned to Jerry and updated him, "The captain told me we'll be in Reykjavik before long. It's overcast and the temperature is in the low fifties. We might have to stay overnight."

"Good to know. I'll room with Carina; you can sleep with Millie. Okay?" Jerry grinned knowing those arrangements would never take place, at least not on this trip.

All I could say was, "Fat chance, Prince Morgan." Jerry was dreaming big but not in his sleep. When I mentioned the Reykjavik temperature to Jerry, I began to feel cold and unrolled a sweatshirt and slipped it on, then my light jacket. I noticed Carina was talking to Millie and they were both wearing jackets. Jerry was still wearing a T-shirt, but he had always been more accustomed to chilly weather than I was.

It was getting cold on the plane and I wondered if he was just showing off, trying to impress our Swedish friend with his manliness. In my case,

I just wanted to be comfortable.

I asked, "Jerry, aren't you getting cold?"

He grinned, "Just a little. I didn't want to unpack my clothes to get a sweater and I'm using my jacket for a pillow."

"You don't need a pillow now; you've been asleep for over two hours. Put on your jacket."

"You sound like my mother."

I had to laugh. I watched him put on his wrinkled jacket and said, "I think I'm going to have to watch over you like I used to with my sister."

He grinned and as I watched him scanning the girls, he said, "I've been wondering when you were going to start taking care of me."

His comment was better than him telling me to shut up. I decided to leave him alone for the rest of the trip. Being a year older than me, he knew what he was doing and he was certainly more worldly than I was. He had lived in Russia, England, Canada and now the United States, I had lived my entire life in Boston and in Maine at the Crafton lighthouse.

I redirected attention to my novel and was beginning chapter three when the copilot, came back to tell us we would be in Reykjavik in about ten minutes. He asked us to fasten our seatbelts and store anything that might become airborne during a rough landing. I didn't bother checking with Jerry, but I observed the girls following instructions. I could feel the plane descending and heard the clatter of the landing gear being lowered.

I took a look out the window and saw water below and numerous small buildings off the right wingtip. A few seconds later, we touched down on a smooth runway and taxied quite a distance before stopping. After the engines were shut down, Mr. Allen appeared from the cockpit and slipped past us to the hatch. There was a flood of cool humid air when the cabin was opened and the stairs flipped down to the ground. Jerry was the first to reach the tarmac and assisted Carina and Millie down the steps. I followed, looking at the terminal and commented, "Let's get in there and warm up. I'm hungry, too."

As we made our way inside, I saw the pilots carrying our luggage into the terminal. Apparently they were going to stay the night so we had no other option.

Carina touched Millie on the shoulder and said, "I need to go to the bathroom, too much tea. Maybe the boys can find us a place to eat and stay for the night."

Millie looked at me to see if I would agree to her suggestion and I replied, "Okay, Jerry and I will scope things out. We'll come and get you when we find some accommodations."

The girls disappeared in the direction of the bathrooms. Jerry and I approached the nearest official looking courtesy desk where we thought we could get information and directions. It wasn't occupied but there was a service bell.

Jerry suggested, "Let's ask about a good restaurant and a cheap place to stay overnight." He reached out and slapped the shiny bell. A door opened and a tall, nice looking, middle-aged blonde stepped up to the counter and asked, "May I help you gentlemen?"

Jerry paused as he checked out the woman and inquired, "Could you recommend a restaurant and lodging for the night? We're on our way back to the states from Sweden."

"I thought you sounded American. Where do you live?"

"We're from Crafton, Maine. It's a small coastal town. You've probably never heard of it."

She smiled and said, "I am also from a small city. It is called Skagen. It is the most northern town in Denmark. It is also on the coast."

I stepped forward and inquired, "When did you come to Iceland?"

"My husband is in the military. After the British left, he was sent here by the Danish government to help manage and improve the airfield. It needed much work after the war." She smiled and continued, "You will need to go into town to stay overnight. It is not too far, about two kilometers. You can take a taxi."

Jerry remarked, "There are four of us. We're here with two girls."

I saw Carina and Millie returning from the bathroom and pointed, "There they are."

The service agent, Anna, looked at the girls and asked, "Are they your sisters, or girlfriends?"

I chuckled, "Neither, just good friends; travel companions."

"Well, let me give you a card with location and services available. I know the owner. She runs a very reputable place to dine and rooms for rent. Her rates are quite reasonable."

Anna handed me a small business card, "Here you are. I'll call you a taxi." She picked up a telephone from below the counter and spoke to an operator. A few minutes later a car arrived and the driver came to get us and our luggage.

Carina said something to Anna but I couldn't understand the language. I assumed they were speaking in Danish, a language in which Carina was fluent. We left the terminal, waving to Anna and saying, "Thanks for everything."

The vehicle looked like it had been an official United States Army vehicle, but it had been repainted light-blue and a sign added in Danish, "Taxa." Jerry grinned and I smiled; there was no confusion about the use of the car. Apparently, Anna had informed the driver of our citizenship and he spoke in accent-free English. "Hop in, youngsters. I'm taking you to a night of paradise." He chuckled and opened the back door. Jerry climbed in, then Millie, followed by Carina. I walked around to the other side and got in the front passenger seat.

We waited a couple of minutes while the driver loaded our luggage on top of the vehicle. He climbed in, rubbed his hands together and we pulled out of the parking area onto the highway to the city for the short ride. I was glad to see that the vehicles drove on the right, just as we did in the states. The familiarity somewhat lessened my anxiety.

The two kilometer jaunt was over in about two minutes. I was just getting used to watching traffic when we pulled up to a large house. It looked like a B&B in the mountains of northern Maine.

As the back seat emptied, I offered the driver payment, but he declined, waving his hands. "No. It was my pleasure. Enjoy your meal and overnight stay." He told me Anna and the B&B owner would pay him. They had a deal that was beneficial for all.

I thanked him for the ride and asked if we would see him in the morning for our return to the airport. He replied, "You will have a different driver in the morning. I work at the hospital until noon."

"You have two jobs?"

He shrugged, "Yes, taxes are very high, but the country is very beautiful."

We were up and dressed by seven o'clock in the morning. Breakfast consisted of coffee, orange slices, and Danish pastry. Jerry and I crammed a pastry into our mouths like we hadn't eaten in a week and got seconds; they were that good. After settling our bill with our proprietor, we piled into the taxi and in about five minutes to eight we were at the terminal ready to board our trusty DC-3 cargo plane. It must have been about forty degrees out because we could see our exhaled vapors.

We expected to wait for our pilots but didn't see them board the plane. The engines started and the props turned slowly for a couple of minutes before speeding up, the blades turning into blurs. I figured they were warming the motors and checking gauges before loading passengers. The hatch opened, the steps dropped to the tarmac and Mr. Allen jogged to the terminal. He entered rubbing hands together, glanced at us, smiled and said, "Boarding for Greenland. Last one on is an ice cube."

We all laughed and grabbed our belongings.

CHAPTER 4

Next Stop: Greenland

We barely had time to fastened our seatbelts before the plane was on the runway and picking up speed. When we were eating breakfast I made a mental note to ask the pilots how far it was to our next stop. But I had forgotten about it upon arrival at the terminal. I thought Carina would know, so I leaned across the boxes and asked, "How far to our next stop?"

I guess I surprised her and she gave me a funny look as if I had spoken a language she didn't understand. Then she smiled and said, "Twelve hundred thirty nine kilometers."

I think I gave her a blank look because she put her right hand to her mouth, paused and said, "About seven hundred seventy of your miles."

"Thanks, Carina."

I sat back in my seat and did a quick calculation assuming we were flying close to two hundred miles an hour and after closing my eyes and concentrating, I got three hours and fifty minutes. We'd be having lunch at another airport, but I didn't know where we would be in Greenland. That was going to be my next question.

The girls were busy reading from magazines and books, so I didn't want to bother them with another question. They might not know the answer anyway. Jerry rarely knew the answers to my questions, so I didn't bother him either. I sat there thinking about doing more reading, but it came to me that I was always asking questions about places and distances, and the others rarely seemed concerned. I decided to start acting as my own shrink.

Did I have some underlying fear of not knowing where I was going? Maybe I enjoyed doing calculations in my head to determine the time of my next meal. That was a long shot, I can't remember ever being very hungry and worrying about my next meal. Perhaps I should just chalk it up to being inquisitive. Mom and Dad used to tell me I asked too many questions. I don't think they were being critical; they always made that comment when smiling or laughing. So much for self-analyzing. I'd better leave it for the professionals. I opened my book, turned to chapter three, found where I left off and continued reading.

I was in the middle of chapter four when the plane shook like a car going over a road littered with fist sized rocks. The shuddering only lasted a few seconds, but its effect lasted in my mind much longer. Once again, I thought of what I would do if we had to ditch the plane in the ocean. I wondered what the water temperature would be at this latitude and how long we would have before hypothermia caused major problems. I had never worried much about being in the ocean water near Crafton and had never seen chunks of ice in home waters, but this far north icebergs roamed for long periods of time.

Millie's eyes were as big as I had ever seen them and she yelled, "I hope we don't have any more of that!"

I glanced at the cargo to see if it had shifted but it seemed glued to the floor. I shouted to Carina, "Can you tell me what is in these long boxes?"

She gave me a quick smile and called out, "Ja. They are full of bed frame sides. That is why they are so long . . . almost two meters."

"And the other cartons?"

"Oh, sure. They have parts of chairs and end tables for assembly into high quality furniture. They require an experienced worker to fit the pieces together properly. I'm not positive but there might be some lamps included. I'd have to see the bill of lading to make sure."

Jerry was listening intently and yelled, "What about the headboards and footboards for the beds, are those included?"

Carina nodded and leaned across thee cartons, "They're in the back behind the smaller boxes. My father wouldn't ship incomplete beds." She added, "There is also a box of glue, screws, hardware and dowels. I don't think he forgot anything. His workers are very thorough and pack everything."

Jerry smiled and commented, "That makes sense. You seem to have all the details of your father's business. He should be proud of you and happy that you are representing his company."

She nodded and replied, "I understand much about Northern Europe, but little about Canada and the United States. Maybe you can teach me?"

"I'd be happy to. We all would, but we have specialties. Mine is motors, Rocky's is about lighthouses, and Millie knows lots about everything. Her stepsister works for a company that contracts with the FBI so we refer to her as an FBI agent."

Carina laughed, "I must be very careful to not break any laws."

The plane shook, more violently than before and for a longer duration. I think we all held our breaths for a moment, gripping tightly to our seats.

Millie looked across the cartons at me and said, "Boy, we're going through some rough air."

I nodded in agreement. Our copilot, Mr. Allen, appeared from the cockpit and reassured us, "Don't worry about the rough air we're passing through. We've got a very sturdy plane. As we approach the shore of Greenland, there's always some turbulence. But keep your seat belts on . . . just in case." He smiled and asked, "Do you need anything?"

I guess none of us indicated any desires, because he said, "All right. Please stay in your seats until we land in Narsarsuaq. It's only in the forties there, so be prepared for the cold." He scanned us for a moment longer and returned to the cockpit.

Jerry leaned forward and poked me on the shoulder. "Have you ever heard of the place he mentioned?"

I turned around as far as I could without releasing my belt and said, "Never heard of it. I wonder how it's spelled. Let's ask the girls." Jerry and I both tapped on the cartons in the aisle to attract the girls' attention and they turned to look at us. I said loudly but without actually yelling, "Where is the airport in Greenland, our destination?"

Millie shook her head, not knowing, but Carina answered, "It's in the south of the island where a glacier has left lots of soil and rock. I believe it's built on a moraine. That's what the debris from a glacier is called."

I replied, "Thanks. So, it's right next to the water?"

She nodded, "That is correct. I'm bored, would you like to play a game of chess?"

That was an unexpected idea, but she would have to have a chess board and pieces. I knew that Millie, Jerry and I didn't have a set. Then I thought the chess pieces would get tossed around during the next encounter the plane had with turbulence. I expressed my doubts about playing chess on the plane.

She smiled, reached into her travel bag and withdrew what looked like a small book about an inch thick. She glanced to see if the rest of us were watching and unfolded a hinged half displaying a chess board. She smiled again when we saw what she had and began placing miniature pieces on the board. She grinned and said, "They're little magnets!"

I had seen a travel chess set before at my dad's store, Crafton's Crafts, but he had ordered only one and after he sold it, I didn't see another. There didn't seem to be much interest and it was quite expensive. I proposed, "Let's have a tournament. Maybe we'll have a winner by the time we arrive at the Greenland airport."

Carina set the board on top of the cartons and looked at Jerry. I had never played chess with Jerry and didn't know if he had played before, but he reached over and moved a pawn. The game was on. I hadn't played chess in some time and felt that I probably wouldn't do very good but I would give it a try. The worst I could do is come out fourth. I figured Millie would be better at the game than I was. She had undoubtedly played against her parents and for sure her much older sister, Elena, the secret agent.

I had played checkers with Elena years ago when she looked after Susan and me. Elena let me win. That was when I was ten and in love with Elena.

The opponents for the last game were Millie and Carina. The game was played very rapidly and I thought Millie had an advantage, but just as our copilot announced we would be landing in Greenland in a few minutes, Carina moved her queen and said, "Checkmate!" I saw that Millie would have said the same thing on the next move but Carina was one move ahead.

The girls started laughing and Carina said, "I was lucky, Millie, that was a close one. Good game!" The contests had lasted for nearly two hours with Carina the winner, Millie second, Jerry third and as expected, I came in last. I decided to start playing again at home against Mom and Dad to improve my skill and then take on Millie and Jerry. My game needed improvement so when I get to college I won't be humiliated by other students.

I watched Carina put the chessmen back in the case and fold the board to retain the magnetic pieces. The latch snapped shut and she put the case back in her bag. The next sounds I heard were from the landing gear locking into place. We would be on the ground in Greenland shortly. I didn't know about Carina, but I was sure Millie had never been in Greenland before. Jerry might have passed through Greenland when he was a little kid. It was another new experience for me.

When I looked straight out my window, I viewed a cloudy sky and the plane's right wing. If I looked back and down, I could see the ground below, but for only a moment. The right wing lifted and the plane made a sweeping turn to the left and I watched the ocean when we leveled off for about a minute before the right wing dropped slightly and we started a slow right turn. I felt like I was on an amusement park ride and had lost my sense of direction. As the plane skimmed over the water, I wondered how the runway was aligned with the compass. I thought we were going south to north.

The next thing I knew for sure was that we were on the ground. I couldn't see much but I was glad to be back on terra firma. As the plane taxied off the runway, I noticed there were no tall buildings in the proximity of the airport. Usually, the control tower is an obvious tall structure. Maybe I'll get a better look when we deplane.

When our plane's motion stopped and the engines were shut down, all four of us got to our feet, gathered our belongings and began moving to the exit hatch. I figured we were all anxious to get on the ground and stretch our legs. We were joined by Mr. Allen, who popped the door open letting in fresh, though humid and noticeably cool air. I guessed the temperature to be in the forties. I think we all shivered when we felt the brisk southern Greenland coastal air.

We followed our copilot into the little terminal building, where there was a small cafeteria. I jockeyed myself over to Mr. Allen and asked, "Where is the airport control tower, I didn't see it. Is it nearby the airstrip?"

Allen shook his head and replied, "There is no tower here, we follow VFR. That's visual flight rules. In actuality, this airport is closed for commercial traffic. We just have permission to refuel. We'll be on our way in about an hour. You and your friends should get something to eat."

The four of us sat down in one of the three booths. An older woman approached and asked, "What would you like for lunch?"

Millie replied, "Do you have menus?"

"Oh, I am sorry, no. I just make a few things for lunches. The restaurant is not really open for business. Your pilot asked me to make you something for lunch but I don't work here. My husband is a member of the temporary airport service crew. We live nearby. We moved here after the Americans left last year. They didn't need the airport for the war activities and the long range aircraft available now don't need to refuel here. Denmark is now in charge of the property."

CHAPTER 5

Next stop: Canada

We had a quick lunch of sandwiches, a Danish and a choice of tea or coffee. As usual, Jerry and I had a second Danish which we ate as the four of us walked on the tarmac, waiting for the plane to be readied for the next leg of our journey home. With multiple stops and the monotonous roar of the engines, I kind of wished we were travelling by ship, even if it would take a week rather than twenty-four hours. I was beginning to like travelling with Jerry and the girls.

Fifteen minutes before we were to board the plane, our pilot, Captain Stoddard, met with us and asked if we would like to go to Goose Bay, Labrador, or Gander, Newfoundland. We would spend an hour less time in the air going to Goose Bay than Gander. Millie and I discussed the difference for a few moments and together announced, "Goose Bay." We wanted to be able to get off the plane as soon as possible to stretch our legs and eat dinner before the final portion of our return trip to Maine. Fortunately, Carina and Jerry agreed with us. Later, on the plane, Carina mentioned that she didn't mind either way, she was used to taking long uneventful trips on trains making many stops.

Captain Stoddard commented about the weather, "If we encounter stormy, rough atmospheric conditions, we can turn south if necessary and go for Gander." We accepted his explanation of a possible deviation from Goose Bay and started boarding the plane. When we had been eating,

Jerry asked Carina if he could sit with her on the left side and Millie assured Carina it was all right with her. So, Millie and I waited for Carina and Jerry to get seated before we climbed aboard. The girls occupied the front seats and Jerry and I were behind them.

Mr. Allen checked to make sure we were buckled in place as Stoddard started the engines. He spent extra time checking each of our seat belts and I began to feel a little uneasy. A passing thought occurred to me. Did he know more about the next four hours to Goose Bay than the captain had let on?

The unpressurized interior of the plane was pretty cold and we all donned our heavier coats. The takeoff was uneventful and my initial uneasiness waned as we climbed to Mr. Allen's announced eight thousand foot altitude. It wasn't long before the engine heat warmed the air in the plane and we all unbuttoned our coats. I wondered why the cabin hadn't been heated before but there was probably a reason. After a few minutes in the air, we all had the same idea, 'cause when I checked my friends, they were all reading. I followed suit, turned to the page with the folded corner and continued with my novel.

I must have been reading for about an hour when the plane encountered more turbulence, shaking violently. Millie, sitting in front of me, cried out, "Wow, that was a big one!"

I glanced at Carina and saw that her eyes were scanning the cargo. I assumed she was checking to make sure everything was still tied down. I surveyed the cartons and they all looked in decent shape, nothing had shaken loose.

I heard Jerry yell, "Is it okay?"

Carina replied, "Ja."

When I peered out my window, it was obvious we were in a rainstorm and the sky was darkening. I wondered at what time the pilots would turn south to avoid the rough weather and make for Gander, Newfoundland.

The plane seemed steady, so I resumed reading, but each time I finished a page, I checked my fellow passengers and found they were snoozing, apparently feeling secure in the plane, in spite of the nasty weather outside. I finished a chapter and a half, marked my place and closed my eyes.

I don't know how long I was asleep, but Millie tapped me on the shoulder and asked, "Rocky, do you think we'll ever get out of the rain?"

I didn't have a chance to answer her before the sky suddenly lit up like the sun suddenly came from behind a cloud. There was an extremely loud bang and the plane shook violently. I had never heard a stick of dynamite explode, but that's what I imagined had occurred.

Jerry yelled, "I think we just got hit by lightning!"

"I think you're right, Jer. The engine noise has changed." I pressed my cheek against the window and tried to see through the rain streaming across the glass. There was lightning far off to the right and for a brief second, I could see the propeller wasn't turning. We were flying on one engine. Millie was watching out her window and said, "The right engine isn't running, the propeller isn't moving."

Carina squeaked at Jerry, "Can this plane fly with only one engine?"

Jerry looked at me for help just as our copilot, Mr. Allen appeared from the cockpit.

"May I have your attention?"

I'm sure we all noted his concerned expression. Millie had leaned forward, her hand on my shoulder. I turned to see her face and saw she was biting her lower lip. I had never seen her so worried but we had never been together in a plane struck by lightning before.

Mr. Allen continued, "The plane was struck by lightning as you probably figured out. We lost our right engine, but we can still fly with one, just not as fast. We're about a half-hour from land and might have to make an emergency landing. I'll keep you informed every five minutes unless I'm too busy. If you get worried, one of you can come to the cockpit." He turned toward Jerry and pointed, "I want you to come forward if we have any more trouble."

I didn't know the reason our copilot selected Jerry for communication purposes but maybe he felt Jerry was the strongest of the passengers. At six feet and nearly two-hundred pounds, Jerry was about an inch taller and ten pounds heavier than I, but when we wrestled, no one ever was a clear winner. I always thought I was a tad faster than my buddy, but in track competition, like in a hundred yard dash, Jerry won by a yard. I could beat him at sixty yards though.

In case we had to exit the plane in an emergency, I was closest to the hatch, so I felt responsible for opening the door. I hoped that would never happen. I noticed the left engine sounded different. I wondered if the prop was turning faster so the plane could maintain altitude. But then I thought if we were just going slower with one engine, we wouldn't be losing altitude. I decided to ask about it when Mr. Allen returned with more information.

A minute later, Mr. Allen appeared again, but only for a few seconds to say, "Everything seems all right, we're getting closer to the coast every second." I started to ask my question, but I blinked and he was gone. I wondered how many miles we were away from land. I'd be relieved when we were no longer over the ocean; I was quite sure the plane wouldn't float long, maybe only minutes. I was convinced ocean water was not going to be our friend if we went down, hypothermia would be our worst enemy. I looked around at the cartons full of wood products, they should all float. I began constructing a raft in my mind.

Carina unbuckled her seatbelt and stepped over the cartons separating her from Millie and me. She crouched beside Millie and said wide-eyed, "I am very afraid we will not make it to land. What do you think?"

Before Millie had a chance to answer her, we heard an extremely loud crashing noise, almost like an explosion and then nothing but rain striking the fuselage. It was noticeably quiet . . . no motor noise.

Jerry yelled at me, "Rock! We just lost the left engine! The prop is gone!"

I reached out, grabbed Carina around her waist and told her, "Take my seat and buckle up!" I moved across the aisle and sat in front of Jerry. "I think you should go forward, Jer." As I sat, he was already unbuckling and standing up to go forward. I watched as he moved toward the cockpit. I could see him talking to the pilots for about half-a-minute. Then he returned and said, "We're going to glide as far as possible. Captain Stoddard thinks we can make it to the coastline in fourteen to fifteen minutes. He's changed direction to intersect land at ninety degrees. They think we'll be able to land a bit north of a lighthouse called Point Basilleton. He wants us to get our things ready to rapidly exit the plane in an emergency."

I looked across the cartons at the girls and saw Millie stuffing all her things into her backpack. Carina came to me and said, "Please move back with Millie. All my things are here."

I got up and stepped over the cartons in the aisle and put my book into my backpack. I didn't have much to move around or store. I glanced over at Carina and asked, "What can we do with the cargo?"

She gave me a surprised look and stated, "Don't worry, it is insured. We are more important."

The plane lurched and rolled from side to side for a few seconds then regained stability. We could hear the thunder roar, some awfully close booms but most rumbles were far away. Lightning would occasionally illuminate the sky but it wasn't possible to see anything through the rain except an occasional brief glimpse of the wing.

Mr. Allen suddenly appeared from the cockpit and reported, "We've dropped about two thousand five hundred feet in altitude and at this rate, we should just make it to shore. We might not be able to select our landing site, so make sure you are buckled up for the rest of our flight. We'll try to warn you when we're going to touch down, but we'll be pretty busy up front, so don't be surprised if we have a rough landing." He checked the aisle cartons to see if they were securely tied down. Satisfied with what he found, he returned to the cockpit without any more comment.

I didn't want to alarm Millie any further by talking about a potential crash landing, but It was foremost on my mind. I looked back at the hatch and imagined where I would be stepping to reach the lever to pop the door open and push out the stairs. I figured we should all be out of the plane in fifteen seconds. I wasn't counting on the pilots; they would be the last people out.

Another couple of minutes passed and Mr. Allen appeared, hanging on to the bulkhead leading to the nose of the aircraft and the cockpit. He spoke slowly and calmly, "Our altitude is now about three thousand feet and Captain Stoddard thinks he saw the coastline during the last burst of lightning. Until we touch down, stay put and keep your seatbelts fastened. We should be down in five to ten minutes. Any questions?"

None of us said anything and he pointed at me. "You're responsible for getting the hatch open. Try to get your friends out without injuries. We shouldn't have any fires but get everyone away from the plane in case a spark of some kind ignites the remaining fuel." He took another look at all of us and went to join Captain Stoddard.

Jerry snapped his fingers to get my attention and said, "I'll get back to you as soon as I can to help with the door, Rocky."

I glanced at his smiling face and grinned, "You're responsible for getting the girls to the door, Jer." I checked my watch and we would be landing in a couple of minutes if Mr. Allen was correct. I watched the seconds tick off for a minute or so and then heard Captain Stoddard cry out, "I see land. Hang on tight!"

I squeezed the armrests so hard that my knuckles turned white. That was the last thing I was aware of before I heard one of the pilots yell, "Oh, shit!" Then a loud crunching noise occurred.

The sudden quiet was kind of spooky. The lack of noise was strange. I blinked my eyes and became aware that I was upside down. How did I get in this orientation? I didn't have time to question what had happened, I had to check on Millie and the others. I grabbed my seatbelt with my right hand released the buckle and swung down to the cabin roof, now the floor.

I could tell by her voice that Millie was a little shaken up when she said, "Help me down, Rocky." I told her what to do to release her belt and when her body swung down, I grabbed her waist and hips and lowered her to the floor. She was rubbing her midsection where the belt had stopped her from hurtling forward when we crashed. She seemed otherwise unhurt, so I said, "Move back to the hatch and see if you can open it. I'll be right behind you."

I glanced at Jerry. He had just helped Carina down from the ceiling and was moving forward towards the cockpit. I guessed he was checking to see if the pilots had any instructions for us. Carina looked at me, frowned, and ducked under the cartons still attached to the ceiling. "I'm coming with you, Rocky."

CHAPTER 6

Awkward Exit

By the time I got back to Millie, she had the hatch open but the stairway was in her way blocking the exit. I was able to fold the steps through the opening but had some difficulty holding them up so the girls could get out. There was water below us, but it didn't appear too deep. Water was moving up and down and sloshing into the opening. I could barely see rocks on the bottom and warned the girls. I wasn't sure where dry land was, but when I glanced out over the water to my left, I could see the tail assembly jutting from the ocean, partially submerged. The wing was tilted with the tip several feet in the air, the leading edge above the rocky shoreline. I assumed the nose of the plane was damaged and also on dry land. It was going to be difficult for us to get to solid ground; the wing was tipped down but we might be able to crawl under it.

I couldn't hold the stairs up any longer so I told the girls to step back into the plane. They moved and I lowered the steps back down.

Millie and Carina had looked out into the water and Carina said, "What are we going to do?"

I didn't want the girls to jump in the water and I didn't have any answer to her question. Jerry came up behind us carrying a large canvas bag and a small metal box. He said, "Hey guys, I found a life raft and a medical kit. Sorry to tell you but Stoddard and Allen didn't make it."

I explained to Jerry the problem with the stairs and he pulled out his pocketknife and cut open the end of one of the large cartons. I watched as he slid one of the side boards of a bed frame out of the box and we propped open the stairs so we had easy access to the outside.

Millie and Carina spoke to each other but their words were garbled. I couldn't make out what they said. "Mr. Allen told us if we crashed to get away from the plane because the fuel might ignite," said Millie.

I replied, "If you jump in the water, you might go under or slice your legs open on the rocks. Let's get the raft out the door and inflate it." I looked at Jerry as he pulled the raft out of its canvas container. Carina must have thought Jerry and I were acting too slowly, 'cause she grabbed the raft and pulled the inflation tabs, the rubber raft exploded to almost full size before we had it completely through the hatch.

When I realized what she had done, I shoved the raft out the door before it had fully inflated. Jerry dropped to his knees in the water rushing into the cabin and held onto the lifeboat as Millie and Carina tossed in their belongings and clambered aboard. Jerry gave Carina the medical box and we joined the girls in the raft as water began to surge through the hatch.

I hadn't noticed the rain as we exited the plane, and as soon as we were safely out the door, I began to look for oars. I became aware of the rain as it hindered my vision and the near darkness didn't help. I reached up and when almost standing, grabbed the trailing edge of the wing. Jerry must have realized I wasn't very secure so he moved beside me and still sitting, reached up and grabbed my belt.

"Thanks, I needed that."

He chuckled and said, "Walk us down the wing and away from the fuselage with your hands. I've got you."

While Jerry and I were working the rubber boat along the trailing edge of the right wing, I saw the girls locate the short oars and start rowing as best they could. The water was choppy and the wind was trying to blow us back, but I pulled us the length of the wing. When I reached the tip of the wing, I could see the rugged shoreline about ten feet from us. I yelled at Jerry, "Help the girls with the oars and move us toward those rocks." I pointed with one hand as I held onto the wing to keep us from losing our position. "That way."

Jerry took Carina's oar and we began to move closer to solid land, so I let go of the wing and dropped to my knees beside Millie. She gave me her oar and said, "Here, Rocky, you're stronger than I am."

I paddled as hard as I could and Jerry seemed to be doing the same. We got the raft to the rocks in about a minute and the girls were able to get ashore while Jerry and I kept the rubber boat against the jagged coastline. I called out to Jerry, "I'm gonna get out and pull the raft onto solid ground; keep rowing."

He nodded and yelled, "Go for it, Rock!"

I didn't know what was hidden below water level ready to break my legs, so I jumped onto the largest rocks I could see, reached back and grabbed the rope that encircled the outer edge of the raft. I gave a mighty jerk on the rope and pulled about a third of the raft onto the rocks. Jerry climbed out and we pulled our little lifesaving boat completely out of the water.

Millie and Carina had climbed a slope around four feet higher than Jerry and me. I could see them pointing away from us as Jerry said, "Let's carry this thing up there and flip it over. It will give us some shelter."

"Yeah, let's make a lean-to so we can get out of the wind." We would have to pile a few rocks to hold one side of the inverted boat high enough so we could all get under it. Jerry and I dragged the raft up the slope towards the girls and battled the wind to invert the boat.

I told the girls what we were planning and we all began finding football sized rocks for two make-shift posts. I think it took about fifteen minutes to build two rock piles for supports. All four of us were soaked and if we hadn't been working, we would have been getting cold. We got the raft tilted up without too much effort and climbed underneath. The rain had slowed to a drizzle but the wind seemed to be blowing at a constant rate. I think we were all beginning to feel uncomfortable.

Carina and Millie looked like they had taken a shower with their clothes on. I suppose Jerry and I looked the same.

I looked around at my friends and said, "We're in one hell of a mess. What's for dinner?"

Millie gasped, "Are you kidding us?"

I laughed, "Well, yes. If we're isolated, we'd better figure out what food there is and conserve what we have. I don't think any markets are nearby."

Carina spoke up rather slowly, "Millie and I were looking around as you were getting the raft ashore. We think we're on an island, not the Labrador mainland."

"That's right, and there doesn't appear to be any trees or wood. But we could have missed seeing some things. There seems to be a structure of some sort in that direction." Millie pointed to the north.

Jerry added, "We're going to need something to burn to keep warm and the only place I know where there's any wood is on the plane. We'll have to get some of those crates. What do you think, Carina, your father's manufactured products are in those cartons."

"Those things will make very good firewood," Carina replied.

I hadn't thought much about going back to the plane, but now the return for wood could be especially important. I crawled to the opening of our lean-to and looked at the sky. We had maybe thirty minutes of daylight left. I looked at Jerry and said, "Let's get those long boxes out of the plane before it gets too dark to see what we're doing."

Millie looked worried and said, "I hope you have something sharp to cut the twine lashing those boxes to the ceiling. Are they heavy enough to hurt you if they fall?"

She had a good point. I glanced at Jerry and he held out his pocketknife. I knew how sharp his knife was. He helped me open cardboard boxes of supplies for Dad's hobby store in Crafton. Those boxes were sliced open like they were made of butter.

Carina volunteered, "There are four large cartons, each one weighs about twenty-five kilos . . . that's more than fifty of your pounds."

I asked about the other stuff behind the long cartons, "Should we try to recover any of the other boxes?"

"Whatever you can bring back might be useful to us, but I don't know what each box contains," said Carina.

I thanked her for the information and took another look outside of our shelter. The rain had stopped, but the wind had increased. That would assist our return to the plane but hinder coming back. Jerry and I would have to deal with whatever we encountered. I offered a suggestion to the girls, "If you have any dry clothes, you might change while Jerry and I are gone, but we'll try to make it as short a trip as possible. Since it's getting dark, I don't recommend leaving this area. We don't need any sprained ankles or broken bones."

"Jeez, Rocky, we're not stupid," Millie replied.

Carina laughed and said, "Yes, Rocky, we are not stupid."

Jerry and I both laughed and Jerry addressed the women, "Better get out from under our lean-to, our little boat's going back in the water." We got out from under our temporary roof, Jerry grabbed one end of the raft and I lifted the other end and we carried it near the wingtip and launched it. The wind helped us get to the hatch quickly and I noticed water was higher than before. Either the tide had deepened the water or the plane had moved slightly with the tail fin sinking deeper. I began to wonder if the weight of the boxes we remove would make the DC-3 more buoyant and the current would affect the orientation of the crashed plane. I guess we'd find out in a few minutes.

We tied the raft to the fuselage at the hatchway and stepped into the plane. The water was cold and about eighteen inches deep. The slightly sloping ceiling didn't cause us to slip and we didn't have to stretch to reach the cartons. Jerry warned me, "I'm going to cut only one of the cords. The cartons should be loosened so we can slide them out one at a time. I don't think we can handle over two hundred pounds all at once; we might slip."

"Good idea, Jer."

His knife cut through one of the tight cords and the cartons sagged enough so we could slide the top one out of the bundle. We had to wrestle it into the raft but it wasn't too difficult. Each carton was harder to load because we had less space to move. It was going to be a chore getting back to land but I was prepared to do the hand over hand routine again. When the fourth carton was loaded, Jerry ducked back into the plane, leaving me alone with our cargo.

He reappeared with a small container about the size of a shoe box and climbed in the raft.

"What's in the box?"

"It's something to eat. Let's get out of here, Rock. It's almost too dark to see where we're going."

We reached the edge of the wing with less effort than before and I found it easier to pull us with our cargo even though having to fight the wind. The wing was dry now and I was able to firmly grip the metal. Jerry was on the other side of the raft using an oar and we made rapid time getting back to land.

The girls were waiting for us and helped pull the boat to shore. Jerry swung out of the raft and gave the shoe box to Carina.

"What is this?" She said.

Jerry and I had grabbed one of the heavy cartons and he answered, "Something for dinner."

Millie held the rope attached to the raft as we unloaded three more boxes. We carried everything, including our lean-to roof to our previous location and collapsed under our temporary shelter. We piled the big cartons under the northern side of our shelter to prevent the cold north wind from causing any great discomfort. The stacked cartons caused the pitch of the lean-to to be at a smaller angle than previously, but we all hoped no more rain would come during the darkness. We had little choice but had to keep the wood from getting wet. We all recognized a fire was going to be an essential element for survival.

Carina took inventory of our food provisions and gave us bad news. We were going to have to deal with subsistence levels of nutrition until we could somehow reach civilization. She asked an important question: "Did anyone hear the pilots radio our position?"

We all answered in the negative. She focused on Jerry as if he might know something the rest of us were unaware of but he shook his head and said, "I didn't hear either pilot say anything on the radio. Sorry."

I asked, "So what can we afford to eat so we don't become ravenous?"

Carina told us what our provisions were and followed up with, "Does anyone have anything else to contribute?"

I noticed she had kind of a strange look on her face, a look of suspicion, and I thought she might expect Jerry, Millie, or me of holding back food. There was a slight pause and then Jerry said, "Oh, I forgot." He reached into his jean's right front pocket and pulled out a package of Juicy Fruit gum and tossed it to Carina.

She missed catching the little package and laughed, "I never played baseball."

It was now so dark that we could barely see each other and I asked, "What can we eat tonight? We don't have any water to drink. We'll have to figure that out in the morning. We'll need to collect rainwater but we don't have any containers."

Millie suggested, "Maybe we can use something on the plane. Let's all go back and see what we can find."

"I know!" said Carina. "There is a box full of screws and other devices in plastic containers. We can use them for cups and collection devices after dumping out the hardware."

I said, "Okay, we have plans for the morning. Let's eat a small amount and go to sleep. We'll need our rest so we'll be alert tomorrow."

I don't think any of us snored during the night and I couldn't recall dreaming. Perhaps I was too tired. We were all awake at sunrise. Carina was the only one of us that knew the time, two after six. She had adjusted her watch as we crossed time zones.

It was cold and we were all shivering when it was light enough to see each other. I think we all looked several years older than the day before, but maybe that was just due to stress. Jerry broke open one of the big cartons and began slicing off slivers of wood for kindling. I took another of the long boards and started breaking it into smaller lengths by smashing it with large rocks. There were plenty of them around our encampment. I began to take stock of where we were on the rocks and I realized the girls had been correct when they said we were on an island. But I could see there was some type of structure about fifty yards to the north. I wondered how the girls were able to see it in the rain. Then I recalled bright flashes of lightning would have allowed them to make out the structure.

We each had a quarter of a sandwich, a bite of Danish and a stick of gum for breakfast, then we planned what we would do in the plane. Each of us had a goal. Millie contributed a pack of matches to start a fire and we were able to warm our hands and feet before taking the raft to the water. Millie instructed, "We're going to get our feet wet, so don't wear any socks."

The sky was clear, and only a slight wind came from the east, so getting to the plane was easy. Millie and Jerry searched the forward part of the cabin. Jerry had warned us about the appearance of the pilots, so we decided to keep clear of the cockpit. Carina and I borrowed Jerry's knife and cut the boxes loose from the rear cargo area and searched for the containers she had mentioned. There were twelve boxes and we found the canisters in the fifth box we opened. We dumped the screws, nuts, and bolts out and resealed the plastic holders so they would be sure to float. Each of us would have a cup and two units would be used for water storage.

Carina commented to me as we had searched through nearly half the boxes. "Rocky, what is behind the remaining boxes? They don't go all the way back to the tail."

"I don't know, let's take a look."

We moved three more boxes so we could get behind the rest of the cargo and were mildly surprised. A small bathroom was present. Carina was more excited about our find than I was and she brushed past me to check out the facility.

"There is something useful in here, Rocky. Give me one of those dry cartons. Dump out the contents. I need an empty one."

I was a bit perplexed at first, but when I saw the contents of the box she gave back to me, I appreciated her perseverance. She had found six rolls of toilet paper and a tube of toothpaste in the little lavatory. I wondered if there was any water and when Carina came out of the cramped space, I squeezed in and found a five gallon container of potable water which I detached. A sign had been posted saying the water was limited, but five gallons were good for now, at least for a couple of days. God was watching over us.

Millie and Jerry found a small box of tools and some maps. They used one of the wrenches and a screwdriver to take apart two of the passenger seats so we would each have a substitute pillow. They put their loot in another of the dry boxes Carina and I had searched through. Six of the cargo boxes had been sitting in water all night and were useless. They were floating due to their wood contents.

Millie and Carina got into the raft first. Jerry and I passed boxes to them. Jerry got in next and I, somewhat forlornly, looked back at the other boxes of wood thinking we should get all the dry wood possible from the plane. It looked like there was room for another box. I grabbed an unopened one, handed it to Jerry and climbed into the life raft.

I think the current had caused the tail structure of the plane to move during the night because the wing had shifted away from the rocks towards deeper water. However, it didn't cause me any problems as I guided the boat along the trailing edge of the wing. Jerry and Carina used the oars and helped us move away from the plane to shore.

We unloaded the items we had retrieved from the aircraft and rebuilt our shelter. Once we had everything we could salvage from the plane we could investigate the more remote structure as a possible refuge. I wanted to move to higher ground but decided I should consult with the others. So far nobody was chosen as our leader and we were acting by consensus. Jerry suggested we investigate the remainder of the curved land mass to ensure we actually were on an island. We all agreed and set out in pairs.

Jerry and Carina started moving north along the ocean shoreline and Millie and I started walking up the western side of the suspected island. Before we had gone twenty yards, we lost sight of the others, the land had risen above the sea rapidly. A few more paces further and our friends came back in view; we had just gone past a small hill. There was a curve in the land and we began to move to the northwest as we scoured the shoreline for useful objects.

As we walked along, avoiding some sharp rocks, Millie asked, "Do you think someone will soon be searching for our plane?"

I wanted to be optimistic and replied, "I'm sure there will be a search but it might take some time for one to get started. I don't know anything about the airlines or government of Labrador . . . if that's where we are. I'm guessing that it might take forty-eight hours before a search begins. I hope Goose Bay will realize our flight is hours overdue."

Then, I heard Jerry yell at me. "Hey Rock, do you see that building about sixty yards ahead? Maybe someone lives here!" I had been watching the water slapping against the rocky coastline a few feet from where we stepped and hadn't looked far ahead, but he was right, there was a building. But it didn't look like a house, it seemed to me to be the remnants of an old lighthouse.

Jerry and Carina joined us and we picked up our pace a little, but we had to watch where we put our feet to keep from turning an ankle. It must have taken about five minutes to reach the structure. My first observation was that it was octagonal and no more than twenty feet tall. Jerry and I walked around the base of the structure and saw a door was ajar on one of the western octahedral walls.

When we returned to our starting point, the girls were gone. Jerry yelled, "Carina!" and I called out, "Millie!"

Jerry and I glanced at each other. Jerry said, "What the hell. Where did they go?" There was only one possibility, they had entered the building. I went to the door and squeezed through the opening. Although the light was dim, I saw Millie and Carina sitting in two old wooden chairs, smiling.

Millie invited me, "Come into our new home. Where's Jerry?"

Jerry followed me after I disappeared through the opening and replied, "I'm here. Can you turn on a light?"

Carina responded, "Sorry, we neglected our electric payment." We all laughed. Then I said to Jerry, "Let's see if we can push the door open. The rain seems to have expanded it against the threshold. We can probably force it open wider . . . or even fix it with the use of your knife."

Together, Jerry and I forced the door open as far as it would go. It made a loud screeching noise that could probably have raised the dead. When we succeeded at opening the door, Millie called to me, "Rocky, there is a trapdoor over there, but Carina and I can't open it, maybe you can." She pointed at another wooden door, opposite the entryway, that looked as if it might lead to a cellar.

Whoever had installed the door had done a crude job. The door was only about three-feet wide and maybe four-feet long and would be easily tripped over if a person was unaware of its existence. It was raised about an inch above floor level. I thought it probably had never been a regular door but was made specifically for this place. A shiny metal handle was attached to the middle of one side, obviously for lifting.

I took a look around the interior of the structure, checking out the walls up to the ceiling. There was evidence of a set of stairs to the top, remnants of bolts protruding from the walls, having been cut with a torch and now rusting. It was still too dark to see any details, but it looked as if there was a small nearly square door at the highest point of the roof, something for us to investigate later if we weren't rescued in the next day or two.

Millie asked, "What do you think, Rocky and Jerry? Can we move in here to be out of the weather?"

Jerry glanced at me to see if I was agreeable. I nodded and he replied, "I don't see why not. Let's start moving our stuff here from our lean-to. It will take several trips, some of our things are pretty heavy to carry far."

Up to this time, Carina hadn't said much but she made an important suggestion. "We can use the raft as a cargo ship and pull it through the water, can't we?"

That was a great idea, but not without at least one potential problem. Someone would have to be on board with an oar to guide the boat away from hidden sharp rocks that might rip the raft open. I mentioned it and Millie volunteered; she was the lightest of us. So, we set off to rig the raft for towing.

Jerry made another suggestion, "Let's go back to the lean-to, but I think the eastern shore is better for walking; the ocean water has done its job on the shoreline rocks." The walk back to our previous home was fairly easy. Jerry had been right about the rocks being less dangerous. Having walked the shore on the east and west, I never detected anything growing. The island was devoid of kelp or sea creatures, it was as if the island had been irradiated. I hoped we would be able to catch some fish though.

CHAPTER 7

Our Island Home

As we pulled the raft, loaded with mostly heavy materials including the canister of water, the boxes of wood and Millie, I began to notice bird poop on rocks along the water. I hadn't seen it before. I figured we weren't too far from the mainland. As we began pulling the raft on our first trip, we all heard a rumbling, scraping noise and at first I was surprised. I looked around and noticed the plane's right wing was now partially below water level. The current had pushed the tail of the plane into deeper water rotating the wreckage. The sound was coming from metal being scraped on the underwater rocks. I figured by tomorrow, the plane might be gone, completely submersed. Rescuers would not see an obviously downed airplane, but maybe from the air it would still be noticeable if the wreckage were not too deep.

I think we all recognized the fate of the plane but there was nothing we could do about it. We had to carry on with occupancy of what I thought was a partially built and abandoned lighthouse. It took us nearly twenty minutes to get the raft to our new, hopefully temporary, structure. After unloading, we boarded the raft and let the current take us back to our previous site.

We rapidly loaded the life raft for the second trip to the lighthouse. Carina wanted to ride in the raft and Millie gladly agreed to let our Scandinavian friend take over the guidance with the oar. Jerry and I had an easier job of pulling the raft with Carina in it because the total weight of the cargo was much less than in our first trip. Millie, bored being just an observer, began calling cadence as Jerry and I tugged on the rope. If anyone had seen and heard our crew as we walked along the shore, I'm sure they would have found it very funny. Carina was singing a rhyme in Swedish as Millie called out, "One, two, three, pull!" Jerry and I didn't pay much attention to the girls antics and we laughed most of the way back to the lighthouse. We were rarely in sync with Millie's counting and a few times we were laughing so hard we couldn't pull the rubber boat.

While we were unloading the raft from the final trip, Carina inquired, "Can we catch some fish to supplement our meals? We've got to have more to eat if we're going to do any work around here. None of us have much extra weight to lose."

Jerry thought for a moment then opened the toolbox from the plane. He found a nail and bent it into a primitive looking hook. "Anyone have some string?" he asked. I think we must have displayed some dumb looks 'cause he took one of his socks, cut into it with his knife and started unraveling it. Six feet of thread was not enough because it was too weak. When he had three strings, he gave them to Carina and requested, "Weave these into a single line and I'll attach the hook. Maybe we'll catch a fish." He grinned and said, "That sock had a hole in it."

When the line was ready but before Jerry had attached the hook, Millie took a lipstick and coated the line with the light-red waxy material. Jerry and I watched and he looked at me confidently and said, "I was going to ask her to do that."

I slapped him on the back and replied, "Yeah, Jer, good thinking." We both chuckled, knowing the idea was entirely Millie's. Then he glanced at me and asked, "Do we have anything shiny that might attract a fish?" I sat there thinking and suddenly remembered the inside gum wrappers were shiny.

"Yeah, a gum wrapper. Get Carina to give you a gum covering."

As Jerry and I were talking, the girls had begun to move things inside the building. They were having a tough time picking up the water container, so I had them step aside and I got a good grip and hauled the heavy load inside. In the meantime, Jerry and Carina had moved the raft to the shoreline and shoved it in the water. Millie and I watched them climb in and paddle out about thirty or forty feet and drop the line. Jerry had the line tied around his right forefinger.

Millie stood next to me and asked, "Think they'll get anything?"

"I sure hope so. We need some protein in our sumptuous meals."

"I've never heard you use a word like sumptuous before. Is that a novel word for you?"

"I suppose. They tend to come out when I survive a plane crash."

Millie started laughing and I generated a big smile. I said, "If they get a fish, we'll need to cook it, so let's make an outdoor fireplace." Millie had no problem with my idea but she asked me for more details. I told her what I was thinking and we started looking for rocks we could assemble into some kind of a camp stove. As we collected various stones, Millie asked, "Don't we need some metal for a cooking surface? We don't have anything to wrap the fish in as it cooks."

"Good point, Mil. Let's go back to the plane and see what we can find for a cooktop, there aren't any metal items around here." I looked at the water and made a half-assed suggestion, "We don't have the raft but we could swim to the plane. The current would assist us."

Millie was quick with a reply, "And we'd have hypothermia, wouldn't we?"

"Yeah, bad idea. Let's walk, but we might need tools. Let's take a wrench and a screwdriver."

I got the tools from the box Jerry had found in the plane and we set off along our previous path avoiding sharp rocks. The sun was rising higher in the sky and kept us warm. I didn't see a cloud anywhere in the atmosphere; I couldn't hear any airplanes either. I noticed one bird fly over us but I didn't see it land on the island. It probably saw nothing to eat. But seeing the bird gave me hope; we might be closer to the continental landmass than I thought before. I had another idea: if I could climb to the top of the unfinished lighthouse, maybe I could get a better idea of where we were. If we aren't too far from land, maybe we could try to row the raft to the mainland.

When we were about halfway to the plane, Millie inquired, "You've been awfully quiet, Rocky. What have you been thinking about?"

I told her what I was considering and she asked, "How can you climb to the top of the lighthouse? I didn't see any steps inside or out."

She was right. Maybe Jerry and I could carve some steps and fingerholds into the surface of the bricks, rocks and mortar constituting the walls. I'll see what Jerry thinks when we get back to the lighthouse. For a few minutes, Millie and I discussed what we planned before going to college in spring semester. When we arrived at the plane, we noticed it had moved into deeper water than during our earlier visit. The hatch was nearly half underwater.

Without the raft, we were going to get soaking wet getting into the plane but we had no choice. Maybe water in the plane's interior would be warmer than outside. The fuselage would probably be hot from the sun's rays, the metal helping warm the interior ocean water but I didn't expect much. We grasped hands and waded to the hatch. The water was up to Millie's neck when we got to the hatch. I sloshed into the plane and pulled Millie in. She looked good in wet clothes but we had to find something we could use as a cooktop, no goofing around.

She waded towards the cockpit and I shoved floating cartons of wood products out of my way as I struggled toward the miniature bathroom. The first thing I saw was the metal sink and I jerked it away from its supports. I decided the shallow sink would work if we smashed it flat using rocks as hammers so I exited the restroom and went to the hatch. I called to Millie, "I have something that will work. Let's get out of here."

She answered, "Okay. I haven't found anything useful."

As Millie approached me, the plane shifted and I watched her go under. I prayed that something hadn't dragged her down. After only a couple of seconds, she popped up spitting ocean water and kind of swam to me. I glanced at the hatch and there was barely any room left to exit without ducking under the propped up stairs. I realized we had to get out as fast as possible. If the stairs dropped and blocked the hatch opening, we would be in major trouble.

I guided Millie to the opening and forcefully pushed her out into the ocean. I hoped she wouldn't be mad at me but I had an explanation for my actions. I had to get out with the sink and I didn't want to get hung up on anything, but I wanted her to get out safely first. I knelt and pushed the sink out and then tried to swim through the hatch, but I ended up somersaulting, holding on to the sink as it pulled me to the bottom. I righted myself and when standing, my head was above water. I held the sink in my left hand and the trailing edge of the wing with my right until I could walk out of the water. Millie had stripped off her blouse and skirt and was standing in her wet undies. I was dripping wet and tossed the sink on the rocky shore where it made a loud clank.

"Why did you shove me, Rocky? I didn't need your push." She didn't seem to notice that I was seeing her next to naked. I tried to keep my eyes on her face as I explained.

"I wanted you to get out safely before the whole plane went under and the stairs swung down blocking the exit. If that happened, I would have had to fight to get out and maybe have to leave the sink behind, so I had to get you out and safe first."

"Well, okay. I guess you're forgiven. I didn't understand why you shoved me."

I grinned, "Don't worry about it. I like your swimming suit."

She blushed slightly, turned away, slipped into her semi-wet blouse and stepped into her still damp skirt.

I finished wading ashore and peeled off my shirt but left my pants on to hide my wet, nearly see-through underpants. I picked up the sink and we started back to the lighthouse. Our clothes were almost completely dry by the time we arrived at the pile of rocks accumulated for our camp stove. The sun was unusually warm and we sat in the diminishing lighthouse shadow. I figured it was close to noon and was feeling hungry. I knew we had little to eat but anything would be better than an empty growling stomach. At least we had some water to drink.

We sat in silence for about ten minutes before we heard Jerry and Carina returning from their fishing expedition. When Carina saw us, she yelled, "Hey! We caught some fish!"

Millie's funny bone showed up. She yelled back, "We caught a sink!"

I had to laugh but I was sure Carina and Jerry had no idea what Millie meant. Millie glanced appreciatively at me and said, "Thanks." I had to laugh again; she was in good spirits.

The anglers lowered the raft to the ground and Jerry held up the largest of the three fish. It looked like it must have weighed several pounds. The other two swimmers were small but would probably have enough protein in them for three or four portions. After evaluating the fish, Jerry and I began working on the outdoor stove.

Jerry took a look at the sink to get an idea of the size to make the camp stove walls. While he put rocks in place, I started refashioning the metal sink. Fortunately, the shallow depth didn't require much pounding with a heavy nearly round rock to flatten it. When I quit pounding, the metal was approximately twelve by eighteen inches in size with a somewhat jagged hole in the middle.

Jerry had moved away from his construction site and I laid the metal sheet on top of the u-shaped assembly of rocks. "Hey, Rocky, I'm not finished."

I thought what Jerry had already made was good enough for our use but I went over to see what he was working on. He had a fist-size rock in his right hand and he appeared to be shaping another rock by chipping off chunks of it. As I observed his actions, I was reminded of watching a movie about Native Americans making arrowheads. He collected the smaller broken off wedge-shaped pieces for use to better his small rock structure. I followed him back to the shaped stone assemblage where he did some rearranging and then reached for the flattened metal sink. He placed the metal sheet on top and sighed, "Ready for a fire. Let's gut the fish."

CHAPTER 9

Cooking Fish

I had never gutted a fish before, that was a job for a grocer or someone at a fish market. When I was younger, I wasn't allowed to use a sharp kitchen knife, or any other knife with one exception, a butter knife. As I grew older, I guess I didn't show any interest in cleaning a fish, and neither Mom nor Dad enjoyed fishing. I liked eating salmon, trout and tuna and only on occasion found a bone in the cooked fish. I can't remember a time when Mom or Dad, didn't buy fish ready to cook from a store. I suppose I should learn how to clean a fish though.

This time, Carina took Jerry's pocketknife and got rid of fish guts while Jerry and I prepared wood for the fire. Carina handed Jerry his knife still slimy with entrails and he washed it off with ocean water, then made kindling. I think Carina left Jerry's knife dirty on purpose, because I saw Millie and Carina washing their hands at the shore, laughing, and glancing over their shoulders at Jerry. Of course, the girls might have been joking about something else entirely.

We got the fire started and in a short time the fish were sizzling on the reworked bathroom sink. Jerry had made some skewers when he was slicing kindling from a piece of the wood I had broken off one of the bed sideboards. Without salt or any spices, the fish was palatable and bland but we all appreciated what the ocean had provided. Millie and Carina cut a Danish into small portions and that disguised the aftertaste of the fish; water helped, too.

While we ate, we discussed making foot- and finger-holds on the outside of the old lighthouse. I was the one that had the idea to climb to the top to get a look around and see if I could see a larger expanse of land; maybe a bigger island we could travel to. There was no way to climb the interior walls, only a few short metal posts protruded an inch or two from the concrete and brick. Neither Jerry nor I had the arm and finger strength to climb hanging in the air and the posts were far apart. So far, there had been no sign of any rescuers; we might have to save ourselves. But maybe it was too early to expect searchers, especially by plane; we had only been lost for one day.

Everyone agreed that climbing to the top of the structure was a good idea. Jerry and I began to chip away with the screwdriver at the concrete portions of the wall. The bricks embedded in the concrete seemed to be ornamental and were not in optimal positions. We decided against using Jerry's knife like the screwdriver for fear of ruining it, the sharp edge was too important to sacrifice. The work was slow, awkward and very tiring. We kept from breathing debris by placing a handkerchief over our nose and mouth. Jerry and I started by alternating taking ten minute shifts, sometimes a bit longer. While he and I dug into the steep wall, the girls took the raft and circumnavigated the island, looking for anything to eat or use as a tool.

When the girls paddled away, Jerry and I worked out a routine. One of us would chisel out a depression until we could guarantee a good grip or foothold and then we exchanged places. Digging into the tough concrete wall with the screwdriver had to be accomplished blindly, if we leaned back we would fall to the ground. By the time the girls returned, we had ascended to around twelve feet. Our legs and arms weren't tired but our hands were getting sore. We took a break to talk with the women.

They were excited about something as they lugged the raft ashore, dropped it after getting it free of the water and ran to talk to us. They started talking at the same time, then realized their voices were confusing us and stopped. Carina said, "You tell them what we saw, Millie."

"We saw gasoline, diesel or oil in the ocean water out there about fifty feet or so." She pointed out to sea. "I'm kind of guessing where we were when we saw it. We didn't notice it until we came around the northern end of the island and passed the lighthouse. What do you think is causing it?"

Jerry asked, "Why do you think it's something like gasoline?" Millie replied, "There wasn't very much, but it was on the surface and had different colors, kind of like a film of oil on the surface of a parking lot."

I said, "I think they're right, Jer. We should check it out. Could something from the war be out there? Perhaps there's a sunken ship or one that recently went down. Could be it's a lost fishing boat."

It was obvious that Jerry was thinking similarly, "I'll bet a boat hit this lump of rocks and sank nearby. It might be worthwhile to check it out. I could use a break from pounding concrete with a screwdriver; my knuckles are pretty sore."

"Yeah, mine too. It won't be dark for two or three more hours, let's take a dip in the ocean."

Jerry and I removed our shoes and socks and put our shoes back on to walk across the rough rocks. We each grabbed an end of the raft and carried it to the water. We placed our shoes where they wouldn't get wet and jumped in the life raft. After we paddled out a short distance, I estimated our position with regard to the lighthouse and said, "We need to go south, Jerry. Millie pointed farther south." He agreed and we rowed into and across the waves for a couple of minutes.

Jerry called out, "There. Is that what they saw?" he pointed at the water about five yards from the raft and a bit to the north. Apparently, we had gone a bit too far south.

I squinted, shielded my eyes from the sun, and said, "Yeah, that must be it." I peeled off my T-shirt and slid over the side into the chilly water. I didn't touch bottom so I took a deep breath, inverted, and dived straight down. I didn't want to go very deep. I must have gone down about fifteen feet and was having difficulty seeing much of anything. I turned around, exhaled as I rose to the surface and grabbed the side of the raft.

"I couldn't see anything, not even the bottom. It's a lot deeper out here than where the plane is."

Jerry grabbed my hand and pulled me into the raft. I wiped some of the ocean out of my hair and asked, "You wanna try?"

Jerry pointed at the sky to the north of the lighthouse and said, "Maybe tomorrow, there's some bad weather approaching. Let's get back to the lighthouse."

The clouds looked mean and as we began rowing, I could feel the wind had picked up, blowing from the north. Fortunately, with our low profile, wind was not a problem but the waves were getting higher and pushing us toward shore. We hardly used the oars during our return.

The girls were waiting for us, holding our shoes and socks. When we touched land they tossed us our shoes. We sat on the edge of the raft and slipped them on. Before we had the raft clear of the water, Carina asked, "Did you see what Millie and I saw?"

Jerry answered, "Sure did. Rocky dived down about fifteen feet but couldn't see anything. When we saw those clouds, we decided to try it again when the water is calmer. Rock said it's pretty deep out there."

I followed with, "Let's get the boat secured so it doesn't get blown away in the wind tonight."

As Jerry and I carried the raft close to the lighthouse and placed several heavy rocks inside to keep it from blowing away, I watched the girls talking and pointing at the raft.

Millie approached and asked, "What will happen if the water rises high enough to float the raft?"

"I guess we'd be up shit creek." I hadn't thought that the water could rise so high but big waves could push water clear up to the lighthouse, it wasn't that far above calm sea level. The girls were thinking about important things and had some clever ideas. I mentioned the possibility to Jerry so we added another two hundred pounds of rock to the raft. We didn't have anything to tie the rope to, no posts or trees.

Millie added, "I was going to tell you about something earlier but forgot when we detected the gasoline in the water. The airplane is almost completely submerged. If we get an intense storm tonight, I think the plane will be gone tomorrow. Is there something we should try to salvage from it before it's gone?"

I thought for a moment, "I can't think of anything. We've already recovered just about everything we can use. I've thought about burying the pilots, but I don't think it's possible. It's kind of sad. We have no choice but to let the sea claim them."

Millie nodded, "Okay, I'll tell Carina."

With the sky darkening in the north and the sun getting low above the western horizon, I began to think about dinner. I grinned at what I thought was a bit ridiculous and wiped it from my mind. It was too soon to eat dinner. Jerry had gone back to work cutting grooves into the cement and just completed another handhold a foot above the one we had previously eked out. My mind drifted to what I thought the girls could do before nightfall. I hadn't considered our comfort at night as particularly important until now, but another night of sleeping on an extremely hard surface and without warmth was causing thoughts of escape to be increasingly present in my mind. How in hell were we going to get off this chunk of rock? Were we to just wait for someone to rescue us? Climbing to the top of the tower was going to be important. I was relying on my ability to visually detect some salient sign of human life. But there was high probability of a storm arriving within a few hours. What could I do to prepare for crappy weather?

I stood there below Jerry looking at the crude stove we had made and an idea popped into my mind. If we heated some large rocks and took them in the lighthouse, they would provide some heat, maybe enough to make the interior a little warmer, but not any softer. Jerry was busy so I found some approximately spherical stones of reasonable size to heat on our stove and started a fire. I had no way to measure how hot the rocks were getting but I decided when I sprinkled some water on them and it steamed, I could use my hands like gloves and roll or carry the rocks into the lighthouse.

Millie and Carina were watching me and making jokes about my hot rocks until they realized what I was doing. When they saw me roll one of the large stones into the lighthouse, they gave me a round of applause and brought more wood to feed the fire. Carina was the first to realize that to retain heat in the lighthouse, we would have to shut the door which was stuck open. She got Jerry's knife and began to carve at the bottom of the door so we could close it.

While Jerry chinked away at the wall, he figured out what was transpiring below and was inspired to continue working even though his hands were getting sore. After I had the first batch of stones processed, I asked, "Hey Jer, want to trade places?"

"Yep," was his almost immediate answer and he dropped to the ground. With the screwdriver in my belt, I climbed as far as possible and continued with the next groove toward the summit. A day's work and we were three quarters of the way to the top. I thought I might be able to see something, so I looked around and almost lost my balance. I decided I'd better keep my mind on my job, if I cracked my head on the ground below, it might be curtains.

I felt a few raindrops strike my face, but I continued to work until I heard Millie below. "Better come down Rocky, it's starting to rain. I don't want you to get hurt when the wall get slippery. Besides, we're having fish for dinner. You need to wash your hands."

I started to laugh but held it back; I didn't want to relax and lose concentration coming down the sharply inclined wall. I didn't need any injuries that would prevent going into ocean water or require medications we didn't have.

Jerry had used my technique for moving the hot stones into the interior and Carina was finally able to get the door closed. It still scraped slightly but we didn't have to wrestle it open any longer. She had done a fairly good job. Millie had gotten us something to eat. Her initial thoughts were to give us all equal portions, but she changed her mind and gave Jerry and me some extra fish. She commented that we were expending a lot of energy and needed the calories. Besides, we had plenty of fish and could get more.

As soon as the fish was warmed, we continued heating the large stones, reheating those that had cooled and could easily be manipulated with our bare hands. We all got involved with the process until the rain started coming down so hard it was difficult keeping the fire burning strongly.

CHAPTER 10

A Chimney

We placed the last of the heated stones on the floor and shut the door. Earlier in the day, Millie and Carina had come up with a plan for each of us to know where the others were in near darkness. It wasn't completely black inside due to the ill-fitting door allowing a few beams of light in from outside during the day. But when the storm hit with all its might, we had to rely on the girls' location method if we moved around. Jerry and I let Millie and Carina decide on the sleeping orientations based on their method, the numbers on a clock. Millie was at nine, Carina at ten. Jerry and I were assigned to two and three respectively. The door to the outside was at position six and the trap door at twelve.

We sat and talked for about an hour, occasionally able to get brief glimpses of the others when brilliant bursts of lightning lit up the sky, fleeting beams of light sneaking around cracks at the edges of the ill-fitting door. When I heard Jerry's slow, methodical breathing, I knew he had fallen asleep but the girls were still talking. They were still gabbing when I surrendered to the darkness.

The next thing I was aware of was foot movement and the lighthouse door being opened. It was dawn and cold but I didn't hear any wind. Millie and Carina were going outside, each carrying a roll of toilet paper. I didn't have to guess they were going to use the great outdoors as their bathroom. Jerry and I would soon do the same. We waited patiently for the girls to return, but they seemed to be taking longer than expected.

Jerry and I were standing just inside the door commenting about our bladder pressure when Millie called out, "Hey guys, we're finished, it's your turn." We stepped out into the morning sea air and looked at the raft, expecting it to be full of rainwater. It was sagging as if it had a pressure leak and the inside was practically dry. I squinted and took a second look before calling Jerry to verify what I was seeing.

He looked closely, picked up one of the heavy rocks we had used for weights and said, "What the hell happened? The raft has been punctured and the bottom is sliced open. Someone is messing with us. We must have had a visitor during the night."

I agreed, "Yeah, the girls wouldn't pull a stunt like this. Let's tell them about it."

"Okay, but I've got to relieve myself first."

I walked with Jerry to the shore and we added some yellow water to the ocean. Then

we quickly surveyed the area near the lighthouse but didn't find any other disturbances. We returned to the lighthouse to talk with the girls who were adding kindling to the stove. They were concentrating on lighting thin strips of wood and I interrupted them, announcing, "We had a visitor last night."

Carina reacted, "Oh! Did you see a seal? I'll bet there are lots of them in these waters."

Jerry replied, "This seal carried a knife. There are punctures in the lifeboat."

I added, "And the bottom is sliced open. I'm afraid the raft will be useless if we see land from the top of the lighthouse. We're screwed. We'll have to wait here for rescuers. Can you go fishing today?"

Carina said, "Ja. We will fish while you finish with the handholds."

She glanced at Millie who nodded.

Millie looked apprehensive, a little troubled. I asked, "Did you see something?

She nodded, "I thought I was dreaming last night, but I guess I saw someone with a flashlight."

Jerry asked, "Did you hear anything? A boat?"

"No, just the light swinging like someone holding it while walking."

I had another question, "The light came in from outside?"

She shook her head, "Unh-unh. The light went from inside then out the doorway."

I reasoned there were two possibilities; the visitor came in, looked around and went out, or the visitor was here and left, but Mil didn't see the person return, 'cause she went back to sleep. I mentioned what I thought and there was a chorus of "The trap door!"

I think we all were troubled with the thought of someone sneaking about at night. We might have to post a watch tonight.

Carina put her hand to her mouth, pointed at the floor and said, "My God. Do you think someone is down there?" She gazed at Millie and said, "I think I want to sleep next to the boys tonight."

"Me too. Let's move our belongings . . . if the boys don't mind."

Jerry and I raised our eyebrows, grinned at each other and I said, "It's okay with us." Then I suggested, "Why don't Jerry and I sleep on top of the trapdoor. No one could open it unless they are superman."

Jerry reacted immediately, "Not that we wouldn't like your company, girls."

Millie scowled, "We weren't thinking of sleeping with you guys, just nearby." While they were thinking of it, they carried their belongings over to where Jerry and I had our things. They moved our stuff to the floor next to the trapdoor.

We each had a bite of our last Danish and a couple of ounces of fish for breakfast then got busy working. Unable to use the raft now, the girls made a much longer fishing line from a pair of shorts the girls wouldn't wear during the chilly weather. Jerry and I alternated working on the wall, taking fifteen minute turns making handholds.

An hour after the long fishing line was put into use, several squeals of delight were heard as the fishers migrated along the eastern shore of the island. As we worked, Jerry neared the top of the structure and asked me something I had never considered before, "Could you kill a seal?"

I didn't have an immediate answer, but after I pondered for a minute, I said, "Only if my life depended on it. I've seen trained seals at aquariums that save human beings and I wouldn't want to hurt one. That's a tough question, Jer. What would you do?"

"Good answer, Rock. I feel the same."

He descended the wall and handed me the badly worn screwdriver. After observing the tool, I doubted whether it could ever be used for its intended purpose. The tip was ruined. Jerry made a good suggestion as he watched me inspecting the implement. "I think we should dig out a notch so we can secure a rope to it. It would aid both ascent and descent. It would make climbing up there safer, too."

The rope from around the perimeter of the life raft was at least twelve feet long, so it would come in handy for going up and down the wall. Until now it had only been used to pull the raft but not anymore. I chipped out one more notch and climbed to the top of the lighthouse. There was a convenient spot where the rope could be tied so we didn't have to use the screwdriver any longer. There were four half-inch-diameter bolts sticking up about four inches above the concrete. I assumed a gallery was planned to be attached using the threaded rods.

While I attached the rope, I noticed the top of the building was poorly constructed and I thought I could remove a board to see what was underneath. I had the screwdriver in my pocket and used it to pry up one of the small edge boards. The wood had been waterproofed and was held in place by two rusty nails. It looked to me that the rooftop covering was only meant to be temporary but it was sloped slightly to provide water runoff.

I peered below the removed board expecting to see a closed wooden door beneath me. The sun illuminated the top of the interior ceiling about a foot below. I made out a small trapdoor about two feet square centered in the octagonal ceiling. I had seen the other side of the small door from below; I was very curious. I tried to relate this structure to our lighthouse at Crafton. It was obvious this structure had never been completed. I wondered why. If it had been functioning, would our plane have crashed on this chunk of worthless rock? I wondered if the pilots would have made a different decision. I replaced the wood but couldn't reattach the nails. Using the rope, I dropped to the rocks below very easily. The line wouldn't reach to the ground but it was easy to grab once we climbed about four feet up the wall. Jerry and I each tried the climb before we called a stop to our project.

The girls were pleased with their catch. They returned with five fish, one large one like Jerry had caught before, surely a salmon, and four much smaller ones similar in size to river trout I had seen in Maine. Jerry and I cleaned the fish, a new experience for me, and the girls cooked them. I wondered how long a person could live only eating fish. None of the others knew the answer. As we sat around the fire watching fish cook, we heard an airplane in the distance, off to the west but out of sight. From the sound, I estimated it was more than a mile away, maybe farther if the plane had two engines as most search planes do. Hopefully, a search pattern would include our dinky island. I hoped the crescent shaped rock was on the charts so somebody would take a look. We had only ourselves to attract attention, nothing to create enough smoke to be seen from a distance.

After hearing the engine noise, we sat in silence listening to the sounds of waves lapping against the rocky shores. We were all probably thinking about being rescued, at least I was. Carina whispered something to Millie and then directed a statement to me, "We will probably run out of firewood in another day. Is there any way we can make fires inside the lighthouse? Heating rocks has worked to warm the interior but it isn't very efficient."

I had to agree. I mulled over what I knew of the lighthouse structure. The presence of the trapdoor in the ceiling should have hinted making the tower into a chimney. I felt a little foolish 'cause I hadn't thought of it before. If I could open that door, the smoke and fumes would be exhausted just like a designed chimney. Not much rain would come in because the top board we would remove was off-center. Besides, a few water drops wouldn't bother us. We could move our rock stove to the center of the floor.

I mentioned my thoughts to the others and Jerry said, "Come on, Rock, let's go up there and open the flue."

Five minutes later, while the girls watched, we scaled the wall and I showed Jerry the board I had removed earlier. The top of the lighthouse was an octagon about six feet across, so there was space for two people without danger of falling off. I pulled up the previously loosened board and Jerry dropped to his hands and knees to inspect the space above the trapdoor. He pulled his head up and said, "You didn't tell us there was a rope coiled up here."

"What? No kidding!?"

"Nope. There's a rope. I bet it's long enough to reach the floor."

I dropped to my hands and knees and took a closer look. "I'll be damned." I must have missed seeing the rope in the shadows.

I asked Jerry, "Do you think we could stand on the ceiling structure and kick through the trapdoor?"

Jerry snickered, "I don't think we need to do that, Rock, it's a sliding door. It's not hinged." He reached down and grunted as he slid the door open. "Boy, that was really tight. At first I thought it might be nailed shut." He gradually uncoiled the rope from the circumference of the space, letting the loose end drop below. He pulled his arm back and said, "You want to go down on the rope? We'll have to remove a couple more boards so you can get to the hole. I'm not sure I can get my shoulders through that space, but you're not quite as broad shouldered as I am. You might squeeze through."

"I'll try it, but I'm gonna give it a good pull to make sure it's well attached. You sure you don't want to try it first and surprise the girls? I think you might get through the opening."

Jerry grinned and replied, "No, you go ahead. Take the first crack at it. I'll go down the way we came up."

We pulled up two more boards for access. I dropped my legs through the opening, grabbed the rope with both hands, tried to keep from getting slivers through my jeans and started down, cautiously at first but still having some reservations about my safety. I didn't want to drop freely nearly twenty feet to the concrete. As I descended hand over hand, I wondered how long that rope had been there and how strong it was, but I made it to the floor without falling. The rope was hanging there dangling two feet above the floor like an awfully long noodle. The builders had probably planned to use the rope to lift heavy objects to build the gallery and install the lighthouse electric lamp.

I crept to the doorway to see where the girls were and saw them watching Jerry come down the outside wall. I sneaked behind Millie and tapped her on the shoulder. She nearly jumped out of her shoes, whirled around and would have slugged me if I hadn't stepped back expecting a violent reaction.

"Rocky! How did you get down!"

"Jeez, Mil, you almost clobbered me. I came down on the inside using a rope."

"I thought someone came out of that dungeon door. I expected you to come down after Jerry, thinking you were still up there." She pointed to the top of the lighthouse. "Show me how you got down."

I motioned with my index finger for her to follow me inside. Carina and Jerry were right behind her. When she saw the rope hanging there she said, "I wish we could have spaghetti tonight."

"That's your first thought? I guess you're tired of fish."

We all laughed and Carina commented, "Can we move the stove inside now?"

I grinned and answered, "Sure, but leave the ashes outside." Carina gave me a dirty look. She isn't accustomed to my humor.

CHAPTER 11

Where are the Travelers?

Susan Linfield, Rocky's twelve-year-old sister, was sitting on the edge of her bed painting her toenails with a new shade of bright pink polish when the phone rang. It was ten o'clock in the morning in Crafton, Maine, and Mrs. Linfield, Sandra, had gone to the lighthouse to admit some sightseers from New York. Susan almost decided to let the phone go unanswered, but after the third ring, she ran to the phone and picked up the receiver on the next jingle.

"Hello?"

A mature male voice asked, "May I speak with Rocky Linfield?"

"He's not home from Sweden yet. Would you like to speak with my mother?"

"Yes, please."

"Okay, but it might take a minute, she's out at the lighthouse."

"All right, I'll wait."

Susan placed the phone on the table, put on her flip-flops and ran to the lighthouse yelling, "Mom! Someone's on the phone. He wants to talk to you."

Sandra appeared from the lighthouse door and said, "Who's on the phone, Susan?"

"I don't know, just some guy. He didn't say."

"Okay. Please stay with our visitors and answer any questions. I'll be right back." Sandra jogged the short distance to the residence and disappeared inside. Slightly out of breath, she picked up the phone and said, "This is Sandra Linfield. How may I help you?"

The male's words came over the line rapidly, "This is Hans Svensson in Stockholm. Have you heard from your son? He should have called you from Goose Bay yesterday. My daughter, Carina, is travelling with your son and two of his friends."

"You mean Goose Bay, Labrador, Canada?"

"Yes. They were coming back to the states on a DC-3 cargo plane. My daughter was to call me as soon as they reached Canada. I haven't heard from her and I believe they are a day late. Have you heard from your son?"

Sandra chuckled, "No, I haven't, but Rocky isn't always very prompt about phoning home. I'll talk to my husband in a few minutes and we'll call the Goose Bay airport. We'll investigate and I'll call you back when I find out anything."

"Thank you Mrs. Linfield. I'll be expecting your call. Goodbye."

"Goodbye." Sandra hung up the phone and sat looking at it trying to decide on a course of action. Mr. Svensson sounded worried. She knew she had to call Lee. What if something had happened to the plane? Should she call Millie's parents and Jerry's also? Sandra thought Millie would surely have called home first and told her parents when she would arrive home and where they should meet her. She flipped open the phone book and called Millie's father at the furniture store.

"Harris's Furniture, Leroy speaking. How can I help you?"

"Hi Leroy, this is Sandra Linfield. Have you had any word from Millie?"

"Nothing yet. She's supposed to call when she gets to Canada and then again when she's in the States. Then we'll go pick her up . . . wherever that is."

"Well, I don't want to alarm you, but Mr. Svensson just called and asked if his daughter is here yet. She's a day late from calling home and he's a bit worried."

"Well, Millie called us from Greenland a couple of days ago and said they would be going to Goose Bay, Labrador, and then home to Maine. I'm guessing they had connection problems and had to stay over in Goose Bay."

"But don't you think she would have called? I know Rocky would have and we haven't heard from him."

"Millie is very independent. Remember the incident in The Bahamas? Rhonda and I have given Millie a long leash ever since she turned sixteen and learned to drive. I believe she's all right, just stuck at some airport. Don't forget she's with Rocky and Jerry, Sandra. Those two boys are responsible young men. I don't think we should worry."

"Maybe you're right but I'm going to check with Steve Morgan to see if he or Natalie has heard from Jerry and if they haven't, I'm going to call Goose Bay and find out where the kids are."

"Okay. If you find out anything Rhonda and I should know, please give us a call at home."

"I'll do that. Goodbye Leroy."

Sandra heard a click and hung up the phone. She dialed the operator and asked for a connection to Goose Bay, Labrador, Canada and was told she would be notified when the connection went through. She'd call the Morgans when she had more information.

Susan returned from the lighthouse a bit flustered and said, "Those people from New York thanked me but the lady told me that our lighthouse was small and antiquated compared to the ones in New York. I told her we don't have as many rich people visiting like they have in New York but our lighthouse performs just fine. Ships are warned of the coastline and we've never had a wreck nearby."

Sandra thought for a moment but decided that Susan had handled the situation without saying anything nasty to the woman, so she commented, "Thank you for taking over. You did admirably."

Susan looked at her fingers and said, "I'm going to paint my fingernails. I'll be in the bathroom or my bedroom. Did you hear from Rocky?"

"No, dear. I'm trying to get in touch with him now. I'm expecting a call from Labrador."

"Oh, where's that?"

"The eastern coast of Canada, part of Newfoundland. There's an airbase in Goose Bay. I think your brother is there with Millie, Jerry and a Swedish girl."

Susan continued to her bedroom and Sandra sat uneasily beside the phone looking at her watch as the seconds ticked off. Ten minutes after placing her call the phone rang. She took a deep breath and answered, "Hello."

"Is Mrs. Linfield available? This is the Goose Bay airfield in Labrador."

"This is Sandra Linfield. I'm calling from Crafton, Maine. I wanted to check on a flight from Greenland that was due at least a day ago. Has it arrived?"

"No ma'am. That DC-3 cargo plane is more than twenty-four hours overdue. We've sent a search and rescue plane out. A search of the coast is being conducted as we speak. The missing plane radioed us during a thunderstorm, but we lost contact. They said one of the engines was down due to a lightning strike. I'm afraid that's all we know at the moment. We will call you back as soon as we have more information."

"All right, thank you."

Sandra heard a loud click and hung up the phone with her left index finger. She dialed the machine shop that Steve Morgan owned, Morgan Mechanics, and Steve answered on the third ring, "Hello."

"Hi, Steve. This is Sandra Linfield. Have you heard anything from Jerry?"

"Not a peep. About a week ago, he called me from Denmark, or was it

Sweden? He said something about coming home with Rocky and Millie on a cargo plane. Have you heard from Rocky?"

"No. That's the problem. I just got off the phone with the Air Force base in Goose Bay, and they told me the plane was more than a day overdue from Greenland. They've sent out a search plane to check along the coastline."

"Hmm, that doesn't sound too good. Why don't you have Lee light a fire under those people and have them send out a PBY search and rescue plane to check offshore and look for a debris field. I hate to even think about it, but those kids could be on the ocean in a life raft."

"Okay, Steve. I'll call Lee and give him your suggestion. I'll let you know if I hear anything about our kids."

"Right. Thanks Sandra, bye."

"Goodbye."

She didn't have to look up the number for Crafton Crafts located on the peer. That number was one of a dozen or so that were always recalled with little effort. She dialed the number and her husband answered on the second ring; he wasn't busy.

"Hello, Craft shop, Lee speaking."

"Lee, I'm really worried. I called Goose Bay and Rocky's plane is more than a day overdue. I just got off the phone with Steve and he hasn't heard from Jerry and the Harrises haven't heard from Millie. Steve suggested that you kick some butts and get a seaplane out looking for a life raft. The Air Force said they were checking the coastline, but would they have an amphibious search plane, a PBY?"

"I'm sure they have search and rescue planes." He paused for a few seconds and continued, "This doesn't sound very good. I'll make some calls and see what I can find out. I don't know who's running the show up there and I doubt if they've ever heard of me. However, I'll see what I can discover. Okay?"

"Okay. When will you be home for dinner?"

"About five-ish. Things are pretty slow down here today."

"Promise to call about Rocky?"

"Yeah, as soon as we get off the phone. I'll call Washington."

"Love you, bye." Sandra hung up and sat looking at the phone, worrying a little less but knowing she was not alone with her concern about Rocky, Millie, Jerry and Carina. Hoping she would have more information when Lee came home for dinner, she went in the kitchen and began preparing lunch for Susan and herself although she wasn't very hungry.

Lee almost always took a lunch box to work containing cheese and lunch meat sandwiches prepared at home. Sandra usually added a pickle or carrot stick and included a thermos of coffee. When Lee started the business on the wharf, he had lunches that included fish, but Lee tired of seafood after a month and requested Sandra only make lunch meat or cheese sandwiches. Occasionally he would close from noon to one o'clock during the winter months and eat a burger and fries at a restaurant a block from the wharf. Once in a while when he felt his stomach was prepared to handle it, he would have a chiliburger. He still suffered stomach problems that developed when he was hiding out in Northeast China.

Sandra tried to keep busy all afternoon to avoid intense thoughts of worst-case scenarios, but despite her attempts, she was on edge all afternoon. Every time the phone rang she startled, hoping it would be good news about the kids but most of the calls were asking about the open hours of the lighthouse. She hesitated using the vacuum cleaner for fear the noise would cause her to miss the rings of an important call.

She was finally able to relax when Lee got home from the store. Now both parents were present to handle calls from the Air Force in Goose Bay. Lee came in the kitchen, put his lunchbox on the table and sat down with Sandra. She immediately started enquiring, "Did you get any more information about Rocky's overdue flight from Greenland?"

"I did. The Air Force sent out a Catalina and the Canadians sent out a Canso, that's their PBY, and started a grid search from the position of the pilot's last radio message to Goose Bay. They even sent a car to a lighthouse close to the intended trajectory to see if anyone had heard the plane. The lighthouse keeper said she hadn't heard anything, but thunder that night was very loud and she might have missed engine noises. She also said no lights from a plane were observed."

"So, will they continue to search the ocean? Have they searched on land . . . for a crash site?" Sandra asked.

Susan had spent the afternoon with girlfriends and wandered into the kitchen afraid she might be snooping. She looked at her mother and father and asked, "What are you talking about? Is something going on that I should know?"

Sandra said, "Sit down, Susan. We didn't want to tell you anything until we had more information but we need to tell you about Rocky. His plane is overdue and a search is being carried out in Labrador, Canada. Your dad and I have been on the phone ever since I got that call this morning. We've been trying to get information from the American and Canadian Air Forces. They've been looking for the plane Rocky, Millie, Jerry and a Swedish girl named Carina were on when returning to the states but so far no trace of the plane has been discovered."

Tears began to form in Susan's eyes. She gave her parents an intense look and said, "Do you think Rocky's . . . dead?"

Lee stood up and took Susan in his arms. "We don't know much about what's going on, honey, so don't worry. Let your mom and me do the worrying. You know, every time Rocky has gotten in trouble, he has always gotten out of it all by himself. But he has Millie and Jerry with him. They're a powerful group of young people. I'm sure they'll be fine."

CHAPTER 12

Lights in our Eyes

Before it was time to eat again, I climbed to the top of the lighthouse, replaced all the boards except for the short one on the edge and recoiled the rope. I was sure the smoke wouldn't damage it and the heated gases from our stove would have cooled by the time they passed through the opening in the ceiling. We had plenty of cooked fish, so with no more Danish to eat, we had fish and a stick of gum for lunch. It wasn't much, but we had no choice but to be thankful for what we were able to get from the ocean.

The afternoon passed slowly. What was there to do but seek food and pray that we would be rescued before long? We took turns fishing and walked the shores looking for anything we could eat or burn, but with few rewards. The girls seemed to have the best luck fishing and we had enough fish to eat for another two meals. Jerry's knife had been handy for gutting the ocean catch. We took turns cleaning the fish. Late in the afternoon, Carina found a piece of driftwood on the western shore near where the plane had crashed. It wasn't much, but we could get a little heat from it.

I don't know if she was hallucinating, but Carina reported hearing airplane engines. She thought the noise was coming from the south. None of the rest of us had heard anything but waves breaking on our shores. We all napped when we weren't combing the shores or fishing.

Twelve hours of light was about all the time we had each day and not long after Carina returned with that chunk of wood, I climbed to the top of the lighthouse and tried to get comfortable so I could watch for lights. I figured at the top of the lighthouse I was over twenty feet above ground and adding the elevation of the floor above the ocean, I was close to forty feet above sea level. From what I knew about lighthouses, I estimated I could see a lighthouse beam from at least sixteen nautical miles or about eighteen miles straight through the air. I wondered if eating fish for several meals had improved my eyesight.

Although it was nearly dark, Jerry joined me at my perch. The north star was bright and we used it as our directional aid. We talked about our predicament as we scanned the horizon expressing our frustration about lacking a seaworthy boat. When we talked about the girls, we were careful to do it in whispers for fear they might hear us through the open trapdoor. We were both proud of the girl's determination to make the best of our situation.

We could see an occasional sparkle and yellowish-red light from the fire below. We sat with our feet hanging over the edge of the lighthouse, our heads far from the rising smoke. We didn't want to start coughing. I was surprised the rising smoky air wasn't hot at all, just warm.

About an hour after Jerry joined me, we both noted a light on the southwestern horizon.

At first I thought it might be a star being eclipsed by clouds, but after watching it for several minutes, we decided it was a beam from a lighthouse, it was periodic.

"What do you think, Rock? How far is it from us?"

I didn't answer immediately. It took me about a minute to estimate the brightness. "I'm making a seaman's guess, but I think it's at least ten miles from here."

We watched the light for a few minutes before Jerry asked, "Should we tell the girls?"

"Nah, let's wait until we get ready for bed. If we tell them now, we'll be pummeled with questions. Let's keep checking for more lights. Maybe we'll have something more definite to tell them. Besides, the longer we sit up here in the dark, the better our night vision will be. Maybe we'll have something more positive to report if we see more signs of life."

We discussed trying to swim that distance, but we both decided it would be certain death, so that idea was short lived. In addition, traveling that distance in a structurally sound life raft would be difficult considering the coastline's currents and waves.

Jerry was the first to notice the light we had seen appeared to be getting vertically elongated. When he pointed out the variation in the light, I watched it for ten to twenty seconds. I could see the light varying in brightness and occasionally disappearing for a few seconds at a time.

"I think there are two lights, Jerry. Maybe someone is coming toward us. The second light's almost in line with the first light and us. Jeez, I hope that's a boat coming for us."

"God, I hope it's coming for us. Should I tell the girls?"

"Better not yet. If it isn't on a boat coming for us, they'll be extremely disappointed."

"I guess you're right. Let's keep our eyes on it."

We must have watched the moving light for at least five minutes and then it suddenly disappeared. I had to say it, "I don't think whatever was shining that light is coming here. We're out of luck. Damn!"

"I'm glad you advised me to avoid telling the girls. I think we'd be watching them cry for the first time."

"I don't think Millie would cry; she'd just be mad as hell at us for giving them hope." I sat there dejected, leaned back and looked up at the northern sky. There was a beautiful display of the northern lights instead of the clouds we had seen for the last couple of nights. The curtains of dancing greenish lights distracted my mind from the disappointment of not expecting an imminent rescue. Jerry and I watched for lights near the horizon for another ten minutes and then gave up for the night. We'd try again tomorrow.

Down on the lighthouse floor, the girls kept the fire burning, warming our collective bedroom. They expected a cold night and had donned about every piece of clothing available. Looking like they had put on twenty pounds since Jerry and I had gone on top of the structure, they tended the fire and looked hopefully when we came through the door.

Carina had the more hopeful expression, "Could you see anything?" she asked.

Jerry replied as he moved toward his belongings, "We saw the beam from a lighthouse. Rocky thinks it's about eighteen miles from us, way too far to swim. Without a boat we're sunk."

Millie interjected, "Clever choice of words, Jerry."

I ventured to say, "We thought we saw a boat coming this way, but the light vanished. We watched for a while and then gave up. We'll try again tomorrow night. The northern lights were beautiful though, dancing curtains of green."

"You should have called us, Rocky," said Millie. She seemed a bit irritated.

Jerry saved me from making up something explaining our negligence. "You can still see the aurora, just step outside."

She wiggled around in her overload of clothing and said, "I'm warm in here, it's getting cold out there, isn't it?"

"That's for sure," I said as Jerry and I knelt beside the fire and rubbed our hands over the reddish coals. When our hands were warmed, we moved our things on top of the floor trapdoor and I told the girls, "We'll let you know if someone tries to come up from below."

Carina smiled and warned, "You'd better or you will be in deep trouble."

Millie tossed another piece of firewood on the coals and advised us, "We've only enough firewood to warm some fish for breakfast. Carina and I are going to try to sleep."

I replied, "Okay, Mil, have a good one."

Jerry and I tried to get comfortable on the floor door, but with little success. We used the cushions from our seats in the plane for pillows. There didn't seem to be much difference between the wood platform and the concrete floor, they were both unforgiving to our bodies. I laid back with my hands behind my head looking up at the ceiling and listening to a few tiny explosions from the fire, wishing that someone would arrive in a rescue boat to save us. I knew Mom and Dad were worrying and trying to figure out where I was, or if I was still alive.

I must have fallen asleep, because the next thing I was aware of was a bright light shining in my eyes. Jerry and I both sat up, shielding our eyes from the bright beam and yelling, "What's going on?" All we heard was, "Who are you people?"

Carina called out, "Rocky! Jerry! What's happening? Who has the torch?"

We couldn't see the person brandishing the bright flashlight beam, but a woman's voice said, "I am Hannah. I have come to bring food to my father. Tell me who you are and how you got here."

Jerry was more awake than the rest of us and said, "We were on a cargo plane from Scandinavia and crashed on this barren island two days ago. Our pilots were killed and the plane was swept out to sea. Could you please shine that light on the wall so it's not so bright?"

Hannah reacted, "You must be the people the authorities are looking for. They visited the lighthouse yesterday and were looking for evidence of an airplane. They didn't tell us about the passengers. Are there any more of you?"

Millie answered, "No, just the four of us. You mentioned your father, is he hiding below? Does that trapdoor in the floor lead somewhere?"

Hannah swung the light to the side on the wall and chuckled, "He's not hiding, he's mining for gold. I'm not surprised you haven't met him. He's kind of a hermit and keeps to himself." She walked to the trap door and requested, "Please move your belongings. I will call my father."

Jerry and I shoved our things off the trap door and stood back as Hannah approached it and bent down. She made a fist and pounded on the wooden door three times, waited a second, then rapped three more times.

She looked up at us and said, "It might take a minute or two, he could be working."

Millie asked, "How often do you come to see your father?"

"Every two to three days. I bring food and clean clothing from our lighthouse."

My curiosity had been stimulated, "You came from the lighthouse we can see from the top of this tower? The light from the southwest?"

"Yes, that's right."

Hannah set the flashlight on the floor with the beam on the ceiling but there was enough reflected light so we could all see each other's general features. I noticed that Hannah was about the same age as the rest of us but she could be older, I couldn't tell in the poor light. Almost as tall as I am, her dirty-blonde hair in a ponytail and dressed in greenish jeans and a dark blue sweater, she appeared to be a nice looking woman. Jerry poked me when he noticed I was checking her out; he was doing the same.

Millie and Carina introduced themselves and I introduced Jerry and myself. We were all going by our first names. I detected Hannah's slight accent and wondered what her family name was, it might help me place the accent. I couldn't figure it out, Jerry would probably know. I asked, "Where are you from in Europe?"

She gave me an arrogant smile, "You haven't recognized my accent? I was born in Germany during the war."

It was evident she felt superior. In our situation, it didn't take much for me to dislike this woman, no matter what her appearance was.

Jerry's Russian father was killed by Germans during the war and I wondered how he was going to react. He hadn't lost his cool. He asked, "How old were you when you came to Canada?"

Hannah never answered. Two noises were emitted from the trap door but I couldn't place how the sounds were made. All eyes were drawn to the wooden gate that led below ground. We watched the door swing open slowly and a tall, bearded man wearing metal-rimmed glasses and sweat-stained clothing joined us on the concrete floor. He carried a three-inch diameter metal cylinder in his right hand and was at least two inches taller than Jerry. Millie and Carina moved closer to Jerry and me, slightly intimidated by the large unkempt older man. This guy must have been the person carrying the flashlight Millie had seen at night. I watched him slip the metal object in his righthand pants pocket.

"Ah! It is good to see you are all doing well. I see that you have met my daughter. I am Konrad Schneider. Tell me your names, please." As Mr. Schneider scanned our faces, we stated our names. I figured he wouldn't remember our names long but I was wrong. He directed his attention to each of us, asked about our families and where we lived. We sat on the floor eating sandwiches Hannah handed us from a large wicker picnic basket as he questioned us. As I listened to his voice and ours in answering, I wondered if we were consuming his meals for the next few days. I didn't question what the food was, happy to have something other than fish.

At one point, when there was a lull in the conversation, he mentioned destroying the life raft. "I apologize for damaging your little emergency boat. I believe it was in your best interest. You don't know the waters in this area, they are extremely dangerous in such a low profile vessel. If you were to be capsized, you would not survive in these cold waters."

Carina replied, "I guess we should thank you then. You were

looking out for our welfare, but when we discovered the damage, we were disturbed."

Mr. Schneider abruptly stood and said, "We must be going to our lighthouse, it is about an hour away. We will give you more to eat, bathroom facilities, and a warm place to sleep for the night. Tomorrow we will discuss your future. Get your belongings together and Hannah will take you to our boat. I will be with you in a few minutes."

CHAPTER 13

The Rocky Point Lighthouse

We were relieved to be moved from entrapped existence on a barren piece of rock to a boat over thirty feet long which would return us to civilization. I looked forward to be going where I could call home to let my parents know I was still alive. I was sure Millie, Carina and Jerry had similar thoughts. I noticed a big change in everyone's attitude as we made our way to the boat at anchor about ten yards offshore and about thirty yards from the lighthouse. It was the first time in my life I was happy to be leaving a lighthouse.

Hannah took us, two at a time, in a small skiff powered by a small outboard motor to the larger boat where we were helped aboard by Sunny, a wiry built man about forty years old wearing a heavy sweater, black trousers and gray and orange skullcap. He reminded me of one of the dock workers at Crafton but was without a pack of cigarettes either in his pocket or twisted in his undershirt sleeve. He didn't say much, just made sure we were given blankets and some warm tea.

Carina and Millie were ferried first, then Jerry and me. When we were on the boat with the girls, Hannah went back to get her father who carried a leather satchel. When we were all settled on board, Hannah and her father moved to the cabin and I felt the inboard engine start. Millie sat beside me and hugged my left arm, "Rocky, aren't you happy we're finally on our way home?"

I smiled, patted her hands and replied, "Yeah. I was just about done with that rock. Jerry and I saw a light moving toward us but it shut off, so we thought we were in for another day without being rescued. Our folks will be glad to hear that we're all safe. I think you should be the first to call home. Your dad will pass the word to all our parents. Carina will want to call home also, I'll bet her parents are worried sick. She's probably never been this far from home before."

I was sitting between Millie and Jerry on the aft deck watching Hannah steering, her father and Sunny huddled in the cabin. I wondered what they were discussing. Mr. Schneider seemed to be pleading with his daughter but I was unable to hear their conversation, so he could have been asking why his shirt wasn't pressed. They had an animated conversation for about five minutes and then dispersed, Sunny going below and Mr. Schneider came back to talk with us. Hannah remained piloting the boat.

He was a very imposing figure, standing above us with only running lights to illuminate him.

He looked at us for a second and then crouched in front of Jerry and me. He began asking what I knew about lighthouses and after he had drained my brain, he asked Jerry about his background. He seemed more interested in Jerry's knowledge of motors than he did about the lighthouse in Crafton. That piqued my curiosity.

Mr. Schneider spoke very rapidly, hardly giving us a chance to answer one question before he asked another. We had to concentrate on his words because of the rumble of the engine below us causing interference and his modest accent which seemed more pronounced when he was conversing with several people. He showed little interest to speak with the girls. I suppose they were happy to be ignored, not having to respond to his police-like interrogation.

He abruptly turned away from us when the boat slowed. As he moved toward the cabin, I saw a bright light illuminate the bow and the water in front of the boat. I figured it was the same light Jerry and I had seen far away when we watched from the top of the distant lighthouse. The only reason for the light was we were nearing the coast and the pilot had to watch for objects that might damage or sink the boat. I rose on my knees, looked forward across the bow and saw the bright radiation slowly turning clockwise and rising in the sky as we approached. We were approaching the source of light Jerry and I had seen before. The beam seemed to be coming from high above the water.

The cabin cruiser snaked back and forth to avoid rocky obstacles much smaller than the island we had been marooned on. As we came closer to the bright beacon the boat began to slow. The warning light was so intense it illuminated the surroundings at water level and I caught sight of a wharf apparently attached to a rocky cliff supporting the cylindrical tower enclosing the brilliant light beam. The engine beneath us slowed and idled as the boat drifted toward the dock. I was able to make out a steep set of stairs that we would have to climb to reach the structures high above. The motor reversed the moment we bumped against the wharf and then grew silent. Sunny held a coil of rope, jumped to the dock and pulled us against the floating wooden platform. Mr. Schneider, without words, motioned for us to move off the boat.

Carina and Millie hopped over the gunnel and started up the steps, Jerry and me close behind.

We climbed about a dozen steps to a curved landing that hugged the rounded cliff, then about twenty more steps to the lighthouse foundation. Hannah and Mr. Schneider were right behind me and I could hear Mr. Schneider's labored breathing. I wondered how long he had worked below ground at the distant lighthouse.

The girls slowed to prevent stumbling, as we crept through the shadows for a few seconds before seeing the lighthouse keeper's lighted windows. We took about ten steps to the main building's door and waited for our rescuers. None of us knew whether to knock or try the door, so we just stood there looking at each other.

Millie sighed, whispering to me, "I've got to get warm; I feel like I've been cold forever."

Including the ride on the plane and three days after the crash, it hadn't been that long, but I nodded in agreement. As we stood there shivering, Jerry put his arm around Carina's shoulders.

Mr. Schneider stepped past us to the door, rapped twice and entered into the cozy, well-lit living space. He almost pulled us into the large room where logs were burning in a large fireplace and disappeared through a door close to the hearth. The girls started peeling off their outer layers and moved toward the fire. Jerry and I joined them and took off our jackets. A bespeckled well-fed woman of about sixty years came through the door adjacent to the fireplace carrying a tray of steaming mugs.

"You poor dears. Here is something to warm your bellies. I added just a bit of rum. I will get you more to eat. I think you are tired of fish. Yes?" She stepped back after passing out the mugs, pointed at each of us and said our names. She gave us a big smile and asked, "Is that correct?"

Mr. Schneider must have informed his wife who we were.

Jerry said "Yes," pointed at her and inquired, "What is your name, ma'am?"

"Oh! I am Mrs. Schneider, Ingrid Schneider. I am so happy to meet you young people. We do not get many visitors on our island."

We were all surprised. Carina asked, "We're not on the mainland?"

"Well, It depends on the tides. Sometimes we are on an island and sometimes we are on a peninsula. Most of the time we live on an island." Ingrid smiled and nodded, "You will see when the sun comes up."

Hannah and her father reappeared in a change of clothes and sat with us in front of the fire. Mr. Schneider said, "As soon as you get something to eat, we will show you your lodgings for tonight. We will make more permanent arrangements tomorrow."

Ingrid had retired to the kitchen and returned with soup, sandwiches, doughnuts, and apple and grape juices in large pitchers. As we all ate and talked with our new acquaintances, I kept thinking of Mr. Schneider's words about permanent arrangements. Was permanent a slip of the tongue? I wondered what he had in mind. Was it going to take several days to get transportation for us?

Hannah was visiting with Millie and Carina as if they were long lost buddies and occasionally glanced at Jerry and me. I didn't have much to say and Jerry said even less as we scanned the furnishings. Jerry pointed out the model ship on the mantelpiece and we took a closer look. It was a three-masted sailing vessel carved from a single piece of wood, not made of balsa pieces like ship models Dad sold Crafton's Crafts. This was the real thing. Jerry and I both marveled at the precise workmanship and attention to detail. We wondered about its origin.

Mr. Schneider noticed our interest in the model and joined us next to the fire.

"What do you think of Neptune's Daughter?"

I replied, "Someone spent many hours working on this model. Who built the ship?"

Schneider said, "I wasn't told the name of the craftsman, but he was the captain of the ship, Neptune's Daughter. The ship foundered on the rocks not far from here in 1853. The captain was given another ship and he made this replica of the original Neptune. The crew stayed here while they waited for their new ship to arrive. The new ship was called Seagull's Lair. That is the story I was told." We gazed at the model and Schneider said, "The keepers my family replaced decided the lighthouse should keep the model as a part of the history of the location. We decided to honor the request."

I commented, "Good decision. I was wondering what the script *ND* stood for on the model. I'll bet it would bring a good price at a seafarer's auction."

"Maybe, but I want it to remain part of the lighthouse. Rocky Point is a real part of maritime history of the North Atlantic." Schneider sighed, reached for his satchel and removed some papers. "Since you boys seem to understand craftmanship and motors, I would like your opinion of some of my designs." He laid one of his drawings on the roll-top desk adjacent to the fireplace and invited Jerry and me to take a look.

At first, I didn't know what I was looking at, but Jerry recognized what the sketches were for. He looked at me and I shrugged my shoulders. He whispered, "I think it's the diagram of a powerful motor. It's got seals so it will work submerged. I don't see any electrical connections though."

Mr. Schneider heard us and intervened, "You are close, but it is not a motor, it is a winch with a tremendous mechanical advantage."

I asked, "What is its intended use, Mr. Schneider? Is it to be used to pull ships ashore?"

He grinned, "You are getting close, Mr. Linfield, but I think we all need to get some sleep. It has been a rather hectic day, don't you think? I will give you more information in the morning. I want you to keep an open mind."

Hannah and Ingrid came into the room carrying blankets and pillows which they handed to Millie and Carina, turned around and went back for more bedding. I could tell from their expressions, Millie and Carina wondered where were they going to sleep. Ingrid came back with another armful of blankets and said, "Please follow me."

I didn't know if Jerry and I were to follow. We stood there watching the women walk down a short hallway and through a substantial wooden door. I had lost my sense of direction since coming in the building and wasn't sure where the girls were going. A light came on a second after the girls passed through the door and I recognized the interior of the lighthouse tower.

Ingrid stood in the doorway and motioned, "Come here, boys, you are next."

From Mrs. Schneider's tone of voice, I imagined we were going to be locked behind bars, but Jerry and I followed Ingrid's instructions and entered the lighthouse. What I saw was completely unexpected, the ground level of the lighthouse was furnished like a medium-priced motel room with four sets of bunkbeds, enough berths for eight people and the cement walls were covered with wood paneling. There was a small sink and mirror between each pair of bunks and the circular staircase leading to the top of the lighthouse also led to a small toilet decorated like an outhouse. We stood there looking around and Ingrid pointed out the facilities, indicating we would have to take turns using the toilet. I hoped there would be plenty of toilet paper. I had to assume a shower or bathtub was located in the adjoining buildings.

Mrs. Schneider said, "Make yourselves at home, we will see you in the morning." She backed through the door leaving us standing there as the heavy entrance door slammed shut. I wondered what was next. I imagined hearing a recorded message before the lights were turned off.

Millie asked a fundamental question, "Where do you suppose we can find a telephone?"

Jerry replied, "Yeah, aren't we allowed one call home?"

I was too tired to think of anything to say, so I laughed.

CHAPTER 14

Jerry picked bunks as far from the girls as possible and as I was making my bed, I asked him why he chose to be so distant from them. He said he wanted to be far away if he ripped one off during the night. He felt his stomach was cooking up some gas. I grinned, laughed and then thought he had made a good decision, I might have the same problem. But initially I would have chosen a bunk closer to them in case we had some things to talk over. Like when we could call home to tell our parents we were still alive and safe.

I glanced across the circular room and saw Millie but not Carina. Millie must have seen me looking toward her and she pointed above and said, "Badrum." I nodded, guessing that was Swedish for bathroom. Swedish was rubbing off on Millie. It wasn't much of a guess; I didn't think she was taking the circular staircase to the light high above to adjust her makeup or brush her teeth.

Jerry looked comfortable under several layers of blankets. He had folded two of them in half and crawled under the pile. He was determined to spend the night warm, perhaps sweating, after the last couple of nights freezing his butt off. I wanted to ask him about plans for the winch Mr. Schneider had showed us, but his eyes were closed and as I stood close to him, I could barely hear his slow breathing. He was already sound asleep.

There was one last thing I wanted to investigate before getting in my bunk, so I attempted to open the heavy wooden door. I pulled on the handle but it wouldn't swing on the hinges, it was locked. As I stared at the door, the lights dimmed and went out. I wondered if they were on a timer or if one of the Schneiders had shut off the lights. Then I experienced the same feeling as I did on the distant lighthouse island, trapped and no method of escape being evident. I made my way to my bunk in the semi-darkness, a tiny amount of light from above providing slight illumination, crawled under the blankets and closed my eyes.

I woke up during the night, looked around and saw Jerry was still asleep. My night vision was enhanced so I could make out lumps covered with blankets on the bunks across the floor. The girls were also still sleeping. The next thing I was aware of was hearing Mrs. Schneider saying, "Time for breakfast! Get dressed, go to the bathroom and join us in the house. You can shower after you eat."

As each of us completed our maneuvers, we drifted into the house and waited until the group had reassembled. Hannah appeared and said, "Come with me, please." We passed through a pantry, a large kitchen, and into a dining room where a large capacity table was appointed with seven place settings.

I glanced at Millie and asked, "What time is it, anyway?" She looked at Carina and I heard from our Scandinavian friend, "Almost seven." I figured we had gotten about nine hours of sleep and could probably use even more.

Mrs. Schneider entered the room carrying a large platter with the biggest stack of pancakes I had ever seen. That laid to rest our wondering what was for breakfast. Mr. Schneider followed with two pitchers of what I assumed to be maple syrup. A second later I got a whiff and knew I was right. Hannah was the next server and brought in glasses of water and placed a large metal pitcher of coffee on a trivet near the center of the table. That's when I noticed the small wooden pirate's chest that appeared to be a centerpiece. It was about the size of my mom's jewelry box. It didn't look authentic; it was too small, more like a toy.

When everyone was seated, Mr. Schneider gave a few words of grace, "Bless this food and our new guests." He scooted his chair back a little and declared, "Dig in! I hope you like pancakes, we will have sausages for you in a short while." He started the pancake platter moving clockwise, Carina and Millie each taking two flapjacks, but when it got to Jerry and me, we each stabbed three with our fork. Butter and syrup were added and we were close to taste bud heaven at the Rocky Point lighthouse. I glanced at our tall host and saw him signal his wife with a quick wink. She left the table and returned with another serving dish containing a mound of sausages. She served everyone and returned to her seat, smiling.

Midway through breakfast I pointed at the miniature pirate's chest and asked Mr. Schneider, "Was this chest also carved by the ship modeler?"

He shook his head and replied, "Perhaps. I found it below the Crescent Island lighthouse when I began digging. It was in plain sight, just sitting near the foot of the ladder. There was a note inside, but my wife and I have not been able to decipher what it says. There were also several coins with the note. I will show them to you after breakfast. I think you might find them interesting."

I added more syrup to my half-eaten pancakes and listened to the girls' conversation with Mrs. Schneider. They talked about the tablecloth and some of the other decorations in the dining room, and eventually the telephone topic was raised by Carina.

"Do you have a telephone? I would like to talk to my father in Stockholm. He is probably genuinely concerned about me. He has not heard from me in nearly one week."

"We do not have a telephone, Miss Svensson. We communicate by short-wave radio. I have arranged for you to relay messages at one o'clock through the airbase at Goose Bay. I contacted the base earlier today. The American Air Force has already sent a message to your parents."

I felt a slight sigh of relief silently pass among my friends. Our parents in the outside world had been contacted. I had a question that had been rattling through my mind since last night, so I enquired, "Why were we locked in the lighthouse last night?"

Millie, Jerry and Carina looked at me with a little disbelief at what I was saying. They were not aware of what I knew.

Mrs. Schneider had a big grin and giggled, "I didn't know if any of you youngsters were sleepwalkers. If you went outside at night, you might fall to your death from the cliff. We are quite high above ocean water and jagged rocks below."

I had to smile, realizing there had been a logical explanation of what had bothered me at the time. "I guess I should thank you for doing that. Maybe I was just overtired and thought the locked door was something sinister, so thank you for thinking of our safety."

Ingrid grinned and nodded, "You are welcome. Does anyone need more pancakes?"

Jerry and I requested two more and as we ate them slowly to not appear voracious, we listened to an interesting conversation between the girls and Mr. Schneider.

Apparently, Carina had suspected Mr. Schneider was not just Mr. Schneider, the lighthouse keeper, so she asked, "May I ask what your background education is, sir?"

Mr. Schneider sat back in his chair, wiped his mouth and said, "I was a professor of mining at the university in Berlin. My specialty was in the use of explosives."

Carina replied, "Oh, you are Professor Schneider. We should call you Doctor Schneider."

"That is not necessary. That was too many years ago. I have not had any students or done research in nearly fifteen years." He grinned and said, "I now am professor of digging."

We all laughed and Ingrid interjected, "Konrad, you should show them the message and the coins. Those things might be important."

Hearing he had been a professor, I had more respect for Mr.

Schneider, in my eyes he was Doctor Schneider. I watched as he scanned our dinner plates.

"If you have finished eating, I will show you what I found in the little treasure chest." He got up, helped Hannah and Ingrid clear the tableware, then picked up the treasure chest from the center of the table and motioned for us to gather around. He placed the miniature crafted box on the table in front of him and carefully opened the hinged lid.

Jerry and I moved closer to inspect the hinges. They looked like they might be made of human skin or at least some animal skin and tacked to the lid and the bottom of the box with tiny slivers of wood smaller than toothpick tips. The entire inside of the box looked as if it was centuries old, but why did the outside look so nice?

I would reserve my question for later. We could see about half-a-dozen irregular coins and a rolled up piece of paper, or what resembled paper. The professor picked up the paper-like object with a napkin and carefully unrolled it saying, "This is not paper. Hannah found out it is made from goat skin treated with whale blubber or seal fat. It is incredibly old and has marks that appear to be some sort of written language, but we cannot decipher it. The marks remind me of Egyptian hieroglyphics."

Carina asked, "May I take a look?"

Professor Schneider held the unrolled item and let Carina move closer to inspect the writing.

"Oh!" She pointed at one of the symbols and said, "I believe that mark means riches. Perhaps someone at a museum or maybe a university anthropology department could translate it for you."

Millie remarked, "How did you know about that symbol?"

"In school we studied a unit about ancient languages of European countries."

While the girls were chatting with the professor about the symbols, Jerry and I were eyeing the coins at the bottom of the chest. Jerry nudged me and asked, "Do you think those are Spanish doubloons?"

I shrugged my shoulders and replied, "I don't know, I've never seen a doubloon, but these sure look old, really old."

The professor must have overheard us and remarked, "The coins are from Roman times. They are made of bronze which was used before the time of Christ. Silver and gold coins came much later. I found information about the coins in the Goose Bay library after Hannah and I discovered them."

I asked, "They were in the box with the parchment?"

"No, I found them when I was digging on the island. I do not believe the parchment and the coins are of the same age. I have often wondered how they made their way to Labrador."

I assumed the professor was still looking for more coins below the foundation of the unfinished lighthouse where we had stayed for two days, so I asked, "When was the last time you found any coins?"

He suddenly excused himself and left the room, leaving my question unanswered. Carina and Millie used napkins so they wouldn't touch the parchment and rerolled it. They looked at the coins after removing them from the treasure box and inspected both faces. Carina gave us a short tutorial about the terms used for the front and back of a coin: the obverse and reverse respectively.

Jerry and I grinned and said, "Heads and tails?"

Millie wadded up a napkin and tossed it at us. She might have thrown some food at us if any had been available. Both girls were really into the history concerning the parchment from the miniature treasure chest, more so than Jerry and me. We were more interested in the coins than a preserved piece of goat skin. I've always been interested in codes, but I couldn't imagine the animal skin containing a code.

The Schneiders returned to the room and the professor said, "Please take your seats, I have a story to tell you." When we were all seated, he began retracing his family history to the early years of the Second World War.

"When Germany invaded Poland in 1939, Ingrid and I discussed what might happen to Germany if most of the world opposed the war. One of my coworkers was Jewish and he was sent away. Hannah was just a baby, only a few months old, so Ingrid and I decided she should take the baby to Canada. I knew I could not leave because of my expertise with explosives. When the United States entered the war, I knew Germany was in great trouble, so I began work on a plan to leave the country. In late 1942, I was sent to a German submarine base to work on a new torpedo design, the torpedoes in use were detonating erratically."

He stopped for a moment, checked his watch and explained, "I do not want you to miss the appointed time to make the call to Goose Bay." He smiled and said, "Sometimes I talk too much."

Ingrid said, "Do not worry, Konrad. I will keep track of the time."

Professor Schneider nodded and continued, "Over the years, I was careful and got promoted to Kapitanleutnant by the middle of 1944. I then had more opportunities to carry out my plan of escape to the west."

Jerry and Carina understood the rank Dr. Schneider had mentioned if translated to English and Carina explained, "He was promoted to Lieutenant-Commander."

The professor said, "Yes, thank you, Miss Svensson. One of my coworkers who was a devoted believer in what Hitler was doing needed some help on an experimental submarine and he asked me for assistance. When I discovered what he was developing, I recognized it would be my opportunity to escape, but I would have to be careful to avoid detection."

The professor took a deep breath, a sip of coffee and was interrupted politely by Millie, "Excuse me, professor, but can you tell us what the experimental submarine project was all about?"

I was curious, too, but thought the professor might tell us in his next breath.

He said, "It was a secret one-man submarine to be launched from the top of a U-boat. I was responsible for the explosive charge which was equivalent to three regular torpedoes. It would be enormously powerful and with only one impact would surely sink any ship, even a battleship or an aircraft carrier."

I realized it was a death sentence for the pilot of the sub, so I asked, "You knew the submarine pilot would die?"

He nodded, "Yes, I was well aware of that, so when I designed the explosive, I added an inconspicuous switch to deactivate the device. I had to make it so I was not blown to bits when I encountered a solid object, like a ship or hidden rocks or even the shoreline."

The professor had my complete attention now. "So, how did you plan to get on and pilot the little submarine?"

"Ah, that was the biggest problem I faced. I had to trick my coworker and make sure the regular submarine pilot did not show up when we left base. I had to take his place, so he had to be disposed of at the last minute."

I could tell from the expression on her face what Millie was going to ask next, "You killed the regular pilot?"

He shook his head from side to side and grinned, "No, I made him sick, extremely sick. He was throwing up regularly for two days before he was supposed to leave port. He was so weak, he could not walk and had terrible headaches. He had been assigned to the ship two days before and no one knew him, so I used his uniform and put things in my mouth to change my normal appearance. I worried, but I made it on to the U-boat without discovery of my true identity."

Jerry asked the next questions, the same ones I was thinking of.

"Professor, what happened to the little submarine? How did you arrive in Labrador?"

He looked at Ingrid and she said, "We still have one hour, Konrad."

He nodded, "I am almost finished." He took another swig of coffee and continued, "The U-boat was about eight thousand meters off the coast of Labrador when the captain sounded the alarm and I climbed into my piloting station. Captain Anders had recognized a large American submarine and I was to sink it. As I moved closer to the target, I began to doubt the existence of a submarine, what I saw was some rocks and what looked like a lighthouse. The captain had mistaken the profile of the rocks and lighthouse to be a large submarine. It didn't make any sense to continue, but I couldn't return, so when I got within about thirty meters of the target, I abandoned the submarine and made my way to shore."

I could tell Carina had something on her mind and she waved her hand to the professor. He called on her, "Yes, Miss Svensson. You have a question?"

"When Millie and I were fishing, we noticed some gasoline in the water east of the distant lighthouse. Could it be coming from the submarine?"

"Without a doubt. The sub was not made to stay underwater for years; it was designed to last after only a few weeks in ocean water. Watertight seals around the engine must be deteriorating."

I had the next question, "Professor, is the submarine worth salvaging?"

He paused before answering and then said, "Yes, for two reasons. The first is for the gold."

Jerry was startled and stood up looking at the professor. "How did gold get in the submarine?"

I pulled Jerry back to his seat and said, "Relax, Jer. Let him tell us more about the sub."

Professor Schneider leaned back in his chair and smiled, "I converted all my salaries for more than four years to gold and secretly stored it on the submarine. When I abandoned the sub, I could only escape with a small amount."

Jerry had calmed a little and inquired, "So, how much is still on the sub?"

Ingrid interjected, "Go ahead, Konrad, you should tell everyone."

"All right. It is about eighteen thousand United States dollars. When I escaped the sub, I could only swim with two kilograms of it. It is in small gold bars. I would like to recover the gold. It is our only source of wealth we have except for the amount we get from the government for operating the lighthouse. We don't own anything at the lighthouse except our personal belongings. The stipend is barely enough to make ends meet."

Jerry asked, "Do you own the boat?"

Schneider shook his head, "No, it is part of the lighthouse fixtures, like the radio. We need it to get to the mainland when the tide is up. I, of course, must use the boat for travel to the distant lighthouse to carry out excavations." The professor's eyes slowly examined us and he asked, "Do you have any more questions? If not, I would like to make you a proposition."

Millie quickly responded, "What would you like us to do for you, sir?"

"There are two parts. The first is for the ladies. Take a photo of the parchment and try to get a translation from a university like Boston College or Harvard. I want you to show the parchment to Professor Simmonds at Harvard. Make sure you see him. He is an anthropologist. I would also like to know about the Roman coins. You can show them to him, also. Tell him to send me a letter if he wants to know more about where I found them.

"The second part concerns the young men. I would like their assistance in recovering the gold from the submarine. They would need to remain at Rocky Point. I will pay them one thousand dollars each for their efforts. That would help pay their costs for enrolling at the university."

Millie and Carina looked at each other and nodded. Carina said, "We will do it, professor."

He looked at me for an answer and I said, "We would like to talk it over, sir." Doctor Schneider nodded and Jerry and I moved into the lighthouse for a short discussion. I was not as enthusiastic as Jerry, but if he was willing, I would go along with it. Jerry was thinking the money was much more than he could earn working for his father. When he mentioned that, I realized I had the same interest. Jerry said, "Let's do it Rock. It might be interesting. The professor is really cool."

With our decision made, we returned to the dining area and approached the professor with our hands extended. We shook hands and he said, "Thank you. I will try to make your stay exciting . . . and profitable. I think you will be particularly good assistants."

The Schneiders and the four of us talked for about fifteen to twenty minutes longer before Ingrid announced, "It is time for all of you to call home. Hannah will take you to the radio center."

Millie and I glanced at each other and shrugged, wondering where we were going. "I guess we'll find out soon enough," she stated. We followed Hannah into the lighthouse and started climbing the circular stairway. The steps were made of metal, and slightly wedge shaped, just like the ones in Crafton. As we went higher, nearing the light source, Carina uttered, "I didn't think I had a fear of heights, but I'm afraid to look down. Hold on to me, Jerry."

Millie glanced at me and commented, "I don't think this tower is as high as yours, Rocky." Then she added, "I mean the one in Crafton."

I knew what she meant from her first statement. I agreed, "Yeah, Mil, we're only at thirty feet. I think we'll always compare other lighthouses to . . . ours." I smiled and grabbed her hand as we reached the level below the light. Her fingers were cold, but mine were warm, unusual for me when I was with Millie.

The level below the light was equipped with a desk and a radio transmitter/receiver about the size of a large suitcase. A red light on it glowed and when Hannah flipped a switch, the light turned green. She sat at the desk and moved so she was within a few inches of a large microphone about the size of a fat flashlight. She pressed a button, said some call letters and waited for a reply.

I flinched when the speaker blasted out a reply from the air force at Goose Bay. Hannah pointed at Carina and then at a second chair beside her and said, "Carina, sit here and tell the person who you want to talk to. Be as specific as possible."

We made brief calls. Carina talked with her overjoyed father for about a minute. Millie was next and she was so happy to hear her father's voice, she shed a few tears. She told her dad she would call him again so he could pick up Carina and her in Boston. Both girls told their parent where they were and everyone was safe.

I was next and called home, expecting to hear Mom's voice, but Susan answered the phone. "Hello?"

I said, "May I please talk to your mother?"

"Rocky! I can tell it's you. It's good to hear your teasing voice. We were afraid you were dead. Just a minute, I'll get Mom." I heard the phone clunk on the table and Susan yelling, then a few seconds of silence before I heard Mom's voice, "Rocky, where are you? We have been so scared. When will you be home?"

I took advantage of my time on the call and blurted out as much information as possible until Jerry poked me. My time was up. I had told Mom that Jerry and I were staying at Rocky Point lighthouse for a while to help the keeper with some maintenance. I was careful to avoid mentioning the gold bars or the submarine. I didn't want the authorities to claim the sub and its contents.

Jerry bumped me off the chair, cozied up to the microphone and talked with his dad. For almost as long as I had on the radio, Jerry explained what had happened and we had a job for maybe a couple of weeks at the lighthouse. He avoided the words sub and gold just as I had. When Jerry was finished, Hannah took over the microphone and signed off.

Carina started toward the curved staircase with Jerry right behind but Hannah wanted to talk to us before we descended to the ground floor. She asked us to wait a minute.

"Air Force interviewers are sending a plane for you. It should arrive shortly and will land about a mile offshore." She smiled brightly, "It is a PBY. I will ferry you to the plane, so get your things and prepare to go to the dock below. You need to be ready in about fifteen minutes. Rocky and Jerry will return by helicopter. I will pick you up when you get back unless you can walk . . . that is, if the tide allows passage. I will be watching for you."

It didn't take long for us to be ready for travel. Millie and Carina thanked the Schneiders for their hospitality but weren't sure when they would see them again. Millie mentioned my grandmother, Mrs. Makler, might be able to assist with the coins and the translation of the message on the parchment. She knew many important people in the U.S. government might help. I hadn't even thought about my grandmother's connections. Grandma was as smart as ever and in spite of her advanced age would probably have some good ideas and still have strong connections at Harvard.

I watched as Carina and Jerry listened to Millie and the professor talk. Then Carina told Doctor Schneider she would send her father a wirephoto of the parchment. Mr. Svensson would contact Anthropology Departments at universities in Norway and Sweden for a translation. She would send him the translation by mail. "What is the address? Do I send the letter here?" she asked.

"Yes, just mail the letter to Rocky Point Lighthouse, Labrador, Newfoundland, Canada. We get mail delivery once a week, unless there isn't anything coming our way."

We heard airplane engines pass over the lighthouse and Hannah said, "We should go now. Let's get down to the boat. You four have a plane to catch." We hustled down the stairs to the dock and Sunny helped us get aboard without incident. Hannah swung on board, got seated at the controls and we were off on the short haul to the Canso waiting for us away from the rocky coastline.

It was reassuring when we reached the plane and were helped aboard by men in air force uniforms. Hannah gave us all a hug as we left the cabin cruiser for the amphibious airplane. We didn't see the boat pull away from the plane, but we heard the engine. I was sorry to be leaving our rescuers, but happy to have contacted my family and headed toward civilization. Jerry and I would be back before long, perhaps in only a few hours.

CHAPTER 16

Trip to Goose Bay

As soon as the hatch slammed shut, and we were buckled in our seats, the engines roared and we were skimming across the surface of the ocean. I had a mental image of a duck taking to the air from one of the lakes in Maine, its webbed feet pushing against the water to gain speed. It seemed to take a long time before we were airborne, but it couldn't have been more than twenty-five seconds.

We couldn't see the Rocky Point lighthouse from the air, I figured we were flying north at take-off so it was left behind. After a sweeping turn toward the west, we seemed to be flying southwest. The flight was going to be kind of long, about an hour in the lumbering bird, but Jerry and I had a chance to talk to Millie and Carina. We wanted to make sure they didn't divulge anything about the submarine or the gold when interviewed. Jerry and I were afraid the government would confiscate the sub and its contents. If that happened, Mr. Schneider would have lost all claims to the gold he had earned over a five year period. He would have nothing for his efforts.

Millie seemed a bit annoyed with our comments, thinking they didn't understand reasons for secrecy. She asked us, "Is it all right to show people the coins and the copy of the parchment?"

Jerry caught on right away, smiled and said, "I don't see why not. That stuff doesn't hold any military secrets. What do you think, Rocky?"

I didn't notice Millie's sarcastic question at first, but I tried to lessen its impact. "Good question, Mil. I agree with Jerry."

Carina wasn't troubled and asked a serious question, "I'm wondering if we should say anything about the unfinished lighthouse out there on that lonely rock."

I was on top of that one, "Don't lie about it, just mention how we used the structure." I glanced at Jerry and said, "Do you think we should hide anything from the air force?"

"What's to hide? Someone will undoubtedly go out there to recover the pilot's bodies and they'll want to check out the lighthouse. I hope they don't see any gas or oil where we saw it on the eastern surface of the ocean. That could prove disastrous."

We didn't have much more to talk about and were quiet for the last half-hour to Goose Bay. The plane made a soft landing on the airstrip and we were met by a couple of officers driving jeeps. They escorted us to a terminal building and into an office after asking whether we would like something to eat. The girls wanted salads and hot tea. Jerry and I requested hamburgers, fries and Cokes.

Ten minutes later, we were served lunch, the first real lunch in about four days. I wondered what we would have been eating for a noontime meal at Rocky Point. I could have eaten another stack of pancakes.

When we had finished lunch, the same two jeep-driving officers returned with a female officer. The men were lieutenants with notebooks and the woman in charge was a captain. She asked the first question, "Which of you would like to trace your path across the North Atlantic?"

Millie, Jerry and I eyed Carina, since she seemed to know the most about the place names of the airfields we visited.

"Okay, I will start, but I might forget some details." She scanned us and said, "Please tell me if I leave something out." Carina had a fantastic memory for place names and even remembered the names of people that had waited on us at mealtimes.

I was glad they hadn't chosen me to reconstruct the flights of the cargo plane, it would have taken twice as long as Carina took to get to the plane crash. We hadn't stopped her once as she related our travel from Stockholm to the storm and loss of the engine. When Carina tried to re-create the crash details, she faltered and looked at me for help. She said, "We kind of followed you when the plane crashed. You can explain what happened in more detail. I was a little shaken."

I took over, explaining how we exited the plane. I pointed at Jerry and he related going forward and finding the pilots were both deceased.

The captain asked, "How did you know the pilots were deceased?"

"I checked for pulses and couldn't find any. I checked both of them twice. They were banged up with bad head wounds, too. I think glass had cut them, maybe from the instruments. The windscreens were intact. Their legs looked broken. Water was coming in and we didn't have much time to fool around. We were afraid we were sinking and had to get out. Remember, the plane was upside down. Rocky got the life raft into the water and held the stairs up so we could get out."

Jerry peered at me and raised his left eyebrow. That was his cue to me to finish the explanation of our escape from the plane in the rain. I told of our overnight stay under the life raft and move to the unfinished lighthouse to get out of the weather. I wasn't sure whether I should mention Doctor Schneider's slashing of the life raft but the captain saved me from having to make any more decisions about our island stay.

"So, the Schneiders arrived to do some fishing when you were about out of food?"

"Uh, yes. We were really happy to see them and their boat. We all felt relieved. The night before, Jerry and I saw the light beam coming from Rocky Point but we figured it was far away. I estimated it was eighteen to twenty miles from us."

The captain glanced at the lieutenants and asked, "Any questions?"

They both answered, "No Sir," put their pens in their breast pockets and snapped their notepads shut. All three officers stood and the captain said, "Transportation for you has been arranged. The ladies will fly to Boston and you young men will be going back to Rocky Point in a helicopter." She grinned, "In Air Force planes . . . they are very reliable, even in terrible weather. The plane for Boston leaves in half-an-hour. The chopper is ready to go whenever you are ready, gentlemen."

The officers wished us good luck and vanished down two opposing hallways. An orderly ushered us to a waiting room where we could watch planes coming and going. We had been there less than ten minutes when a different orderly announced, "Rocky Linfield and Jerry Morgan? Please follow me."

When I stood up and grabbed my overloaded backpack, Millie ran over to me and kissed me. Even though it was a surprise, I had enough brains to kiss her back and say, "I'll see you back in Crafton, but I'm not sure when. I really enjoyed traveling with you. Have a good trip home. Bye."

I turned to pursue the orderly and saw Jerry and Carina hugging each other but I didn't hear their words. Carina kissed Jerry on the cheek and he bolted after me. I tried to keep one eye on the orderly so we wouldn't get lost down a wrong corridor and watched Jerry catch up to me.

Jerry stated, "I saw you had a nice goodbye with Millie."

I smiled, "Yeah. That was our first kiss since we stowed away to the Bahamas seven years ago."

"It's good that you're keeping track. She's never kissed me like that."

I laughed, "Yeah, Jer, I guess you and Millie are just good friends."

"Thanks, Rock. Rub it in!"

"Sorry, Jer, but you are an older man. I know you've been watching her fill out over the past couple of years, just like I have. Every time I look at her my juices begin to flow."

"Mine too, but now I have Carina to drool over."

Our conversation was cut short as we exited the building and walked toward something I didn't think existed; a helicopter called the flying banana.

Jerry grabbed my arm and said, "Holy cow! Your dad has a model of that chopper in his store. I can't believe we're gonna ride in that beast."

I couldn't recall ever seeing the model. We jogged to the hatch at the middle of the ship and climbed aboard. One of the airmen shoved us into seats, gave us some earplugs and ordered, "Buckle up!"

I glanced around and saw a dozen serious faces dressed in uniforms; each soldier armed with a rifle.

Jerry poked me and laughed nervously, "I don't think these guys are going with us for our protection." With the earplugs installed, I could barely hear him but read his lips.

I had to agree with his assessment. Apparently the soldiers were going on some sort of training mission. It was fortuitous that Jerry and I were hitching a ride to Rocky Point Lighthouse. The rotors began to whine and we lifted off leaving Goose Bay behind. The eyes of the soldiers seemed to penetrate through my body like x-rays. I felt uncomfortable and wondered if the troops thought Jerry and I had some special connections or were celebrities. It was too noisy to try to talk over the sounds of the engines so I leaned back and tried to enjoy the flight.

We rode in the banana for what I thought was more than an hour with nothing to do but wish we were in cars traveling overland. In that case we would be able to enjoy the scenery and carry on conversations. I could tell when we were about to land because the engines sounds and noise from the rotors lessened. There was a jolt when the dual engine chopper touched the ground. I was relieved to be getting off the noisiest form of air travel I had ever experienced. When the door opened and the sea air rushed in, Jerry and I hopped to the ground and waved as the helicopter blades spun faster and the banana lifted off and swung away from the lighthouse.

Jerry and I began walking towards Rocky Point which was about fifty yards from us. The tide was out and we could see the pathway to the buildings and tower. The circular structure looked like a postcard picture with the ocean water in the background. It was really impressive.

We had only treaded about thirty feet before we saw Hannah greeting us by waving. As she got closer, I could tell she was saying something, but I couldn't decipher what it was. I concluded she was speaking German. I glanced at Jerry and said, "What did she say?"

He started laughing and pointed at my ears. I had forgotten to remove the earplugs we had inserted when on the flying banana. I felt a little foolish but removed the plugs and stuck them in my pocket. "Thanks, Jer, I thought Hannah was speaking German and I couldn't understand her."

"No, it wasn't German, it was English. She said, Welcome back, travelers."

The three of us picked our way across the recently underwater rocks worn smooth by the constant erosion by ocean water. The smooth stones were dry and slipping was not a concern. We climbed a gradual incline to the lighthouse buildings and met the professor at the main entrance to the house. He was smiling and said, "We are glad to see you back, it has been nearly four hours. Are you hungry? Did you have something for lunch?"

I replied, "Jerry and I had hamburgers. Thanks for asking. What's for dinner?" He realized that I wasn't serious and we all laughed.

"Come on in and we will discuss the next steps concerning the submarine recovery."

As we entered the biggest section of the lighthouse lodge, Mrs. Schneider greeted us with, "Welcome back! I am so glad you returned before dark and when the tide was out. I am going to do some laundry. Please give me things you would like washed. You may change clothes in the lighthouse if you like."

Jerry and I had extra underwear in our backpacks but nearly every bit of clothing we owned had been dunked in the ocean when we were on the distant lighthouse island. We carried our things into the tower and chose different bunks than before, but ones close to each other so we could talk without yelling. We decided to give Mrs. Schneider all our underwear, including socks, and redressed in only pants and shirts. I had my mom to thank for putting my initials in my clothes before we left for Scandinavia, so there was no mix-up with Jerry's. We wore the same size shirts but his inseam was two inches longer than mine.

CHAPTER 17

Back to Crescent Island

Jerry and I assembled with the Schneider family and Sunny at the big table in the dining room where we could go over the drawings of the cavern below the distant lighthouse and the professor's equipment design sketches. Hannah had joined us, pushing a cart with six mugs of hot chocolate. The mood was festive. I assumed the upbeat mood was due to Jerry and me returning to help recover the gold.

While going over the drawings of the excavation, a question returned from thoughts I had before we had met with the Schneiders. I asked the professor, "How did the trap door ever get placed in the floor level of the lighthouse." I had never known of such an arrangement before and I had seen at least ten lighthouses in the last eight years.

"Oh! Good question, Rocky, and there is a long answer." He took a drink from his mug and began, "That lighthouse was suggested by coastal defenders during the war, but construction was delayed and began about nineteen fifty. The construction foreman was confronted with a problem. There was a very uneven formation that needed to be leveled but tools available were not suited for a small rocky island. An advertisement was made for a demolitions expert and I applied for the job.

Although my background was in mining, not construction, I had a discussion with the foreman and he hired me. When the rocky pinnacle was being removed, a void appeared beneath ground level. As I inspected the depression, I found those Roman coins. I made a bargain with the construction foreman to frame an opening at ground level, so I could further investigate the depression. At first he wanted to fill it with concrete, but I talked him out of it. I would give up one day's pay if he would allow me to have access to the subterranean void by installing a trap door of my own construction."

Dr. Schneider took another swallow of now lukewarm chocolate and enquired, "Is there anything else I can tell you about the distant lighthouse?"

Jerry asked, "Why wasn't the lighthouse structure completed?"

"That's an easy one," the professor said. "The province had been a part of Canada for only about a year and funds were earmarked for other, more important structures, like bridges and roads. The lighthouse was sealed and left unfinished. Two years later, when Ingrid, Hannah and I took over here as keepers, I began reinvestigating the depression below the structure's floor. That is when I found the small chest containing the parchment. It was extremely dirty, so I cleaned the outside and coated it with varnish."

The professor had answered all the questions Jerry and I had about the incomplete tower on the small crescent-shaped barren island north of Rocky Point. I had imagined the lighthouse hadn't been completed because it was located in a wide bay with little ship traffic. Further analysis of the region didn't warrant a lighthouse that would be expensive to maintain.

Hannah commented, "Once a week I like to take the boat to the island and see how much my father has done below ground. I usually take about five days of food for him. He gets so involved with his work he sometimes forgets to eat so the food lasts for a whole week. I hope he finds more Roman coins. I think they are very interesting. I never thought I would ever see and touch things over fifteen hundred years old. It is difficult for me to imagine what those people were like, even after reading the history books. It must have been a difficult life for women back then."

I added, "For guys like Jerry and me, too. We probably would have been conscripted into the Roman army fighting Christians all over the known world."

Jerry grinned, "No, I think I would have been on a fighting ship chained to an oar with some other stinky fellow like you, Rocky." He chuckled, "I wonder if I would have had a girlfriend to visit on weekends."

Ingrid was laughing and commented, "I think you would have been in the coliseum fighting lions with your bare hands. I think you are very brave young men, like Konrad."

I reacted, "Thank you, Mrs. Schneider, but I wouldn't be very brave when fighting lions, I would probably be trying to outrun them."

The professor slowly rose to his feet saying, "There are some things we need to load on the boat before it gets dark. We need to get everything ready to leave tomorrow at daybreak. Come with me to the dock. Better get your jackets on, there is a cold north wind. We might see some snow tomorrow."

Jerry and I went to our bunks. I put on my sweatshirt and jacket. I believed what Mr. Schneider had suggested, he knew the weather better than we did. The professor waited for us at the door and we followed him into the foul elements. Jerry was right behind Schneider and I followed them closely, hanging on the railing with white knuckles as the wind tried to blow us into the ocean below. I imagined being on the stairs in icy conditions. It would be scary and nearly impossible to descend without falling.

Sunny sat on the dock waiting for us beside three big boxes and two large coils of rope. The boat was lashed to the dock but it rose and fell a couple of feet in the ocean swells. It was evident that more than one person was necessary to load the cargo without accident. Sunny instructed Jerry to join him on deck. The professor and I transferred the bulky boxes from the dock to the outstretched arms of the boat crew. It took some coordination to pass the boxes over the sides of the boat. The professor was stronger than I thought and I didn't have to expend too much energy. It took us about ten minutes to get the boxes onto the upper deck of the boat. The coils of rope were tossed on board in a few seconds.

Sunny and Jerry followed the professor and me back to the lighthouse where we could warm up.

Sunny ate dinner with us and told us some crazy stories about climbing mountains in Switzerland when he was a teenager. He fell into a crevasse one time and was trapped for several hours before being rescued. Ever since that experience, he has never liked being in tight places and doesn't like being covered with blankets when sleeping.

Sunny is about three inches shorter than I am, so stands five feet eight. Jerry and I both noticed his slight accent but he couldn't have said more than a few dozen words in the last two days. His climbing experiences had been quite brief. I wondered where he slept, since he wasn't around when we had dinner last night or breakfast this morning. Jerry said he thought Sunny might be staying on the boat, but I don't think so. The constant motion of the boat even though tied to the dock would be a problem. I don't suppose our knowing where he sleeps is particularly important, just a curiosity of ours.

His swarthy complexion seems to indicate he might be from Greece or a Mediterranean island like Cyprus or even mainland Turkey. I'm guessing he weighs about one-sixty-five. I grinned when it struck me that he might be a gardener. I haven't seen him doing much in the vicinity of the lighthouse except on the boat. I suppose he could be a fisherman.

After dinner we played cards and chess until about nine o'clock then turned in. Neither Jerry nor I saw Sunny take part in any of the games, but Jerry told me when we were getting ready for bed that he saw Sunny go into the lighthouse, but not return. That made me think Sunny was sleeping above us near the top of the tower. He could be responsible for keeping the light shining during the night, or maybe he's just afraid of the dark.

Mrs. Schneider banged on a metal pot with a big wooden spoon at five o'clock to wake us. She gave us our laundered underwear and said, "Pancakes and bacon in ten minutes. Don't be late. Hannah will take you and Konrad to the distant lighthouse at six. Dress warmly and take all your things. You will be there for one week."

Ground level of the Rocky Point lighthouse tower was cold and bare feet on the concrete floor felt like standing in snow. Jerry and I got dressed quickly. We put on two undershirts and Jerry said, "I wish I had a stocking cap. Maybe it will be warm below ground. What do you think, Rock?"

"It's hard to tell. The chilly ocean water will keep the rocks cold, but the three of us working will warm the air around us. Maybe the professor has a heat source to warm our hands and feet."

Jerry replied, "There's no sign of electricity out there, that's for sure."

There wasn't much conversation during breakfast. Professor Schneider kept looking at his watch and seemed to be concentrating on something. Jerry and I stuffed ourselves with hotcakes and bacon and washed everything down with strong coffee. I hoped the boat ride wouldn't be too rough, I didn't want to get seasick. I knew pancakes and bacon bits coming up wouldn't be as tasty as going down. The last time I was carsick was when I was eight, after a pancake breakfast. I've never been seasick, but I've never been in rough water like I'm expecting today.

Sunny was in the boat when we arrived to board. He must have eaten before we got up and rearranged the cargo on deck, probably to balance the load. The skiff was mounted across the stern of the boat. I figured it was considered more efficient than towing it behind us in rough water. Hannah climbed on board, started the engine and we left the dock heading into the north wind and three foot swells.

Professor Schneider yelled, "Lights!" and the bow lamp spread a bright beam across the water ahead of us.

Hannah called out, "Sorry, father!"

That was the first time I had heard Mr. Schneider issue an abrupt command to his daughter. I imagine she was ashamed of being forgetful, I know I would have been. Without the bow light, negotiating through the coastal vicinity rocks might be disastrous. The sun's rays had not yet penetrated the foggy coastal environment and visibility was only a few boat lengths. As the headwind lessened, I figured it was still going to take us an extra quarter of an hour or even longer to get to the distant lighthouse.

When we broke through the fog, the sun was about twenty degrees above the horizon and the wind had almost died. A few minutes later we could see the unfinished lighthouse standing above the sea. We approached the island from the western side where the water was fairly calm. As Jerry and I watched Sunny launch the skiff, Jerry leaned close to me and said, "I overheard the professor and Sunny talking about the gold."

I didn't think that was unusual, so I said, "Was that strange?"

"Well, yeah. They were talking in Russian."

"Not in German?"

"Geez, Rock, don't you think I know the difference?"

"Sorry, Jer. We'd better keep it quiet that you speak Russian. I'm beginning to think something weird is going on. If the Schneiders are German . . ."

Our conversation was interrupted by the professor. "We need to get one of the boxes on the skiff. Sunny will take us ashore one at a time plus a cargo box. When two of us are on shore, we will carry the boxes to the lighthouse."

Jerry whispered, "I hope one of those crates is full of food."

I replied, "Yeah, me too, this island doesn't have anything to offer to eat but rocks."

"You mean you're tired of eating fish?" Jerry grinned and we hustled to help the professor manhandle the largest box to Sunny in the skiff.

Professor Schneider said, "Jerry, you go first. Maybe you can get the big carton to the lighthouse by yourself, but don't get injured if it is too much of a strain."

Sunny struggled to get the cargo centered in the skiff and then told Jerry to join him. I watched them travel about a hundred feet to shore and unload the cargo. I could see that Jerry thought the box was too heavy for one man. He threw his hands up and sat down beside it. I wish I could have seen the expression on his face. When he sat down, it was obvious to me; he was going to wait for help.

CHAPTER 18

Hard-rock Mining

After returning with the skiff, Sunny exhibited a painful expression and disappeared below deck. I think he had injured himself when loading and unloading that heavy box. It took Schneider, Jerry, and me a half hour to get everything ashore and another fifteen minutes to get the boxes and ropes into our island home. Hannah backed the boat into deeper water, turned ninety degrees, and piloted the boat south, this time with the wind at her back. All three of us had broken a sweat and we sat down to relax for a minute before the professor took something from his pocket and made his way to the trapdoor. Jerry and I watched curiously.

Schneider passed his hand over the length of the righthand side of the door. We heard a sliding sound and looked at each other; what had Schneider done? He noticed our gazes and smiled, "Magnetic locks." He held up a flat cylindrical magnet and stuck it back in his pocket.

We got to our feet and slowly approached the trapdoor as the professor exposed the cavity below. He backed down into darkness as we watched from above. When a light came on so we could see where we were going, Schneider called out, "Come on down." Jerry backed into the hole and I followed. We descended a wooden ladder at least twelve feet into a dimly lit cavern about the size of a carousel. We could stand in the center without bending over.

I scanned the interior of the nearly circular cave. There was a half-bicycle in the center. The front wheel was missing. Jerry poked me and said, "He's got a generator attached to four car batteries. I think I know something we'll be doing."

My eyes traced two wires from the bike contraption to a black box which was wired to the batteries on the far side of the underground room. Wires from the batteries ran to a switch connected to several small light bulbs.

Jerry noted, "Nice setup here for lighting. I wonder what else he's got down here."

I answered, "Not much need for refrigeration, it's cold below ground. I guess we can keep warm generating current for the batteries. At least we're used to riding bicycles."

The professor had been listening to us and said, "Let me show you what I have been up to." He motioned for us to join him at the wall of the cave where an open box of tools lay on the floor against the wall. A sealed three gallon bucket labelled Hydraulic Cement sat beside the toolbox. I was aware of compass directions and could tell there had been work on the eastern wall, ocean water on the other side. It appeared to me that the professor was trying to create a hole through the wall. Unless the hole was above the water line, water would flood the cave, shorting out the batteries. I thought I had some important questions for Schneider.

Jerry beat me to it. "Are you trying to create a hole through the rock wall?"

"That is correct. I want to use the winch I designed and pull the submarine closer so the ocean current does not carry it into deeper water."

I had the next question. "How do you expect to tow it closer to the island?"

"That is for you boys to figure out. I cannot go into water that deep, but I think you can. I have some gas cylinders in one of the boxes we carried into the lighthouse."

"But we don't have the necessary diving equipment," said Jerry.

"I have thought of everything you will need. The items are packed in the largest carton. I will show you." He motioned for us to go topside.

Jerry and I quickly ascended the ladder and after the professor turned off the lights below, he came through the trapdoor opening. He stepped next to the large box and pulled a big pocketknife from a side pants pocket. We gave him plenty of room to remove the twine that bound the largest crate, not wanting to get too close to that wicked-looking blade.

Seeing the contents of the box was similar to the excitement of opening a Christmas present and discovering something unexpected. Schneider said, "Unpack everything. I will keep track."

As we took items from the large carton and laid them aside, Jerry and I were surprised by what the box contained, two outfits for diving in the ocean. When the box was empty, Professor Schneider asked, "Are two complete sets of diving gear present?"

Jerry and I glanced at each other and nodded. Every piece of equipment we had experienced in our Crafton SCUBA lessons was present. Whoever assembled the outfits knew what they were doing.

I replied, "It looks like it, but we have never gone deeper than thirty feet. Our instructor didn't want us to experience more than two atmospheres pressure."

Professor Schneider reacted, "I think the submarine is not any deeper than thirty feet, but I could be wrong. The time you would be at greater depths would be minimal; all you need to do is attach a rope to the nose eye on the sub. Then we can use the winch and pull it to shallower water."

Jerry inquired, "Professor, where is the winch? I've only seen a sketch."

Professor Schneider was opening one of the smaller boxes and didn't respond immediately. He looked at Jerry and said, "We need to construct the winch. Hannah will bring us the parts in a few days. I had to get the gears shipped from the United States. They should arrive day after tomorrow. Sunny is making the rest of the parts. He is an expert machinist."

So, Sunny is a machinist, not a gardener. I don't need to wonder about his expertise any longer.

Professor Schneider began unpacking tins of food that looked like tuna fish cans, but when I looked closer at one of the cans, I was pleased to see it was marked chicken, I wanted to avoid eating fish for a while. Larger cans contained corn, carrots, string beans, spaghetti, and several different kinds of soup. Peanut butter, jelly, and five loaves of bread were also packed in the carton. I began to wonder what the third box contained. In less than a minute I found out.

The box was sealed, but not with twine. It was nailed shut.

The professor used his knife and removed a board from the wooden carton then used the board to help pry off the remaining two boards. He tossed the boards to the side saying, "Those will make good firewood for the stove you boys made. We'll burn the rest of the box, too . . . and the packing."

Jerry and I watched with great interest as he withdrew items from the box. He carefully unwrapped a laboratory balance, a Bunsen burner, a cylinder of propane, and a yellow plastic instrument with a dial and a handle. He looked at the materials for a moment and then removed the remaining packing material and a flashlight from the carton, then flipped the empty box upside down. He glanced at us and smiled, "I have changed my mind, we will use the box as a table for the balance."

As the professor arranged items on his makeshift table, Jerry poked me and whispered, "Isn't that yellow instrument a radiation detector? It looks just like the one in the high school physics lab."

"I'm not sure, I didn't take physics. What do you think he'll tell us it's for, detecting gold?"

"Shh, he's looking at us."

To prevent him from thinking we were planning something, I asked, "What's that yellow gadget for? Does it detect certain rocks or metal used on the submarine? If that's the case, it will come in handy at depths where it's dark."

He reacted without hesitation, "It is for detecting gold. That last item is a high beam flashlight that can withstand at least three atmospheres pressure. It might be needed to see at depths below thirty feet.

"We must continue work on penetrating through the rocks to the outside prior to any diving. I have calculated the opening will be fifty centimeters above the water level at high tide."

Jerry and I understood the ropes would pass through the opening and be attached to the submarine. The winch would be fastened to the cave floor and be used to pull the sub closer to the island making the gold more easily accessible. We waited for the professor to give us more information. The pause was short lived. He turned and started toward the trap door as he resumed talking.

"My calculations indicate we have about one meter remaining to puncture through the rock. Come with me and I will show you what to do. Have either of you done any hard-rock mining?"

We answered in unison, "No sir."

When he started down the ladder, we heard his muffled voice, "I thought not."

I glanced at Jerry; he shook his head. The professor was hard to read, at one time he seemed happy to have us with him and another time he appeared to hold us in disgust. But I wasn't going to let his moodiness bother me, I just wanted to get paid a thousand bucks for helping him recover his gold. I'm sure Jerry agreed.

I went down the ladder into the dim yellowish light and Jerry followed. The professor joined us and directed us to stand by the toolbox. He sat on the generator's bicycle seat giving us instructions. We started work with gloves, a sledgehammer and a rock drill. I had never seen a rock drill before. It was a hardened steel rod about eighteen inches long and about three fourths of an inch in diameter. The tip was star shaped. The drill would be struck and then rotated a few degrees and struck again to make a hole for dynamite. We were to break rock without any explosive charges. It was going to be tedious work.

We were slow at first, trying to get familiar with the technique and not hitting anything but the steel drill. Jerry started swinging the hammer and I held the drill, rotating it after each hammer blow. I pictured the hammer striking my gloved hands and the associated pain, but Jerry didn't hit me. It was close a couple of times at the start but soon became routine. While we burned calories and began sweating, the professor pedaled away on the bicycle-generator.

After less than fifteen minutes, we had to take off our jackets and sweaters, leaving only T-shirts covering our torsos. The body heat generated by three working men had caused the temperature to rise enough to make working conditions comfortable, the cavern was no longer cool. At twenty minutes of exercise, Jerry and I switched duties and I started swinging the hammer, working slowly at first so I didn't miss the drill and injure my buddy's hands.

We took short water breaks after each twenty minute shift as we chiseled our way through solid rock. We stopped for lunch after an hour and a half. Jerry mentioned the carbon dioxide buildup was going to be a problem if we stayed in the cavern too long. I hadn't thought of that but I had to agree. Professor Schneider had taken a much longer break after a half hour of pedaling, disappearing up the ladder leaving us to pound away at the rock. While I swung the sledge, I began to have increased respect for the early miners who, like us, did not have mechanized equipment for mining. When we climbed out of the den of toil, as I called it, we discovered what the Professor had done when he left us earlier. He had prepared the entire floor of the lighthouse into a livable support area. His ingenuity surprised us.

I immediately became suspicious and whispered to Jerry, "It looks like we'll be spending some time here, probably more than the week we originally planned. What do you think?"

"Yeah, Rock, but I've stayed in worse motels. Maybe we're not here for gold, maybe something else."

We were careful to not give the professor any inkling of our misgivings, only talking together when we could not be overheard, or about our work when Schneider could overhear us. After lunch we went back to work with the professor assisting by holding the drill or swinging the hammer. We worked for another two hours before taking one more break. Professor Schneider stepped away from the excavation area and said, "Let's break out some of the rock and dispose of it above."

The two holes we had drilled into the rock wall were about two inches apart so by using a metal bar, we broke the connecting rock into fist-sized chunks. With more bashing with the hammer, we cracked and removed more rock so we had a depression in the wall nearly a foot in diameter. Some of the debris had really sharp edges, so gloves came in handy for cleanup. After nearly four hours of taxing physical labor, it was discouraging to have created only about a cubic foot of rubble. The broken pieces of rock were loaded into the smallest cargo box we had and carried up the ladder. Jerry and I were selected for the task.

Professor Schneider followed us to the outside and showed us where to dump the rubble. I thought we would toss it in the ocean but Schneider had us carry it to the other end of the island and dispose of the debris on the high point where our plane had crashed. Jerry and I couldn't figure out why the professor cared where the chunks of rock were dumped. We didn't really care, but we had to walk the length of the island toting that damn box. Being obedient slaves, we followed orders.

When we started back toward the lighthouse, we heard airplane engines and watched a Canso land on the water a quarter mile from us, turn and head in our direction. Jerry was the first to realize what was taking place and said, "That's a Canadian PBY. I'll bet they're coming to check out the wreckage of the cargo plane."

CHAPTER 19

The Harvard Visit

The Canso's engines shut down within fifty yards of the island. Schneider, Jerry and I watched as a life raft was launched and three individuals began steering it toward us. An outboard motor propelled the little boat nearer as we waited to see what they had in mind. As they drew closer, we saw a man in uniform steering, the other two in civvies were waving.

Schneider pointed to shallow water where a safe landing was possible. We watched the men step ashore and introduce themselves to Professor Schneider. Jerry and I heard them say they were here to investigate the DC-3 crash scene and plan recovery of the pilots. Schneider turned to us and said, "These young men were on the plane."

I recognized the military man but we had never met. We had seen him at Goose Bay when we were questioned. He was in the Canadian forces. The other men represented a recovery team and an insurance company. We shook hands and took them to the spot where we had last seen the wrecked plane.

Jerry and I trailed behind the four men, Schneider leading and taking care to avoid turning an ankle on the rocky terrain. We stayed a few yards back and talked in low tones, murmurs but not whispering. We didn't want to draw attention away from the search for the plane or attract the visitors to the lighthouse. We figured Professor Schneider was being very cooperative for the same reason. There would be numerous questions about our activities below ground if the men saw the equipment spread out on the structure's floor. I was positive they would notice the radiation detector. We decided to only answer questions, not volunteer anything. For the first time I wondered if the professor had a gun.

The insurance investigator focused on Jerry and me and stated, "I heard a summary of the crash from the authorities but I have another question. What did you notice about the damage to the plane following the crash?"

Jerry had been in the cockpit immediately after the crash and I let him explain what he had seen. He had told the same story at least three times before. As I listened again, he added nothing and didn't omit any details.

When the visitors finished with their questions, I had one for the recovery expert, "Will you raise the plane and have it rebuilt?"

"Good question. We will have to evaluate the damage, but it will probably be used for parts."

Jerry had the next query. "How do you expect to get the plane out of the ocean?"

"We'll tow a recovery barge up here. That will take maybe a week. It should only take a day or two to lift the plane. The first thing we'll do after raising the plane is recover the bodies. The barge is large enough to land a chopper on it. We'll fly the deceased to Goose Bay and return the bodies to their families."

I had to ask, "How do you plan on locating the plane?"

"That's not a problem, we have experienced divers for underwater recovery. From what you have told us, the plane can't be far from where we're standing."

Professor Schneider hadn't said but a few words to the three men, only pointing out where the plane had flipped over. The officer asked his companions if they had any more questions. They said no and shook their heads. He took a deep breath, exhaled and scanned the water where the plane had disappeared. "Well, it looks like we are finished here. Let's get back to the plane and on our way to Goose Bay." He thanked Schneider, Jerry and me for our assistance and made his way to the motorized lifeboat. They climbed in the little boat, backed away from shore, swung around and headed to the Canso.

Professor Schneider sighed with relief, "That went well. Those men had their minds on one thing, recovery of the airplane. I was surprised they didn't inquire what we were doing here. You boys did a fine job. Let's get more rock removed before we stop for our evening meal."

I asked the professor, "If a crew comes back in a week with a lot of equipment, what are we going to tell them? How will we keep them away from the lighthouse? Someone will be curious and want to take a look."

"I don't expect to be here in a week. Our job will be completed before anyone comes to recover the plane." He looked at Jerry and me for a moment and said, "Come on, let's get back to work. We have some gold to recover."

When Jerry, Rocky and the professor were eating lunch in Labrador, Millie and Carina were entering the airport terminal at Boston Logan International Airport. Millie headed for the telephone to call her father and Carina tagged along to acquaint herself with the busy structure. Carina stuck closely to Millie for fear of getting lost but when Millie's call went through, Carina stepped aside and looked for a map of the city. She didn't see one nearby, so she stepped into another telephone cubical and opened a phone book. Flipping through the pages to Harvard listings, she ran her finger down the page and saw that Harvard was in Cambridge.

Millie hung up the phone and stepped away so another patron could make a call. Carina said, "Harvard is not in Boston, it is in Cambridge. Where is that?"

"It's a suburb of Boston. Let's get a map."

The girls saw a kiosk for car rentals and headed toward it. As they walked, Millie commented, "My father will pick us up here later tonight. He told me to stay here, but we can go to Harvard and return by evening. What was that professor's name?"

"Professor Simmonds in Anthropology."

Another kiosk sold newspapers, magazines, and books. The girls had almost overlooked the display of road maps of all the Northeastern states and the major cities, the maps must not have been big sellers. Millie picked out a map of the Boston area and they located the Harvard Campus. Carina estimated the distance from the airport at twenty miles.

Millie was enthusiastic and suggested, "Let's get a taxicab, it should take only twenty-five minutes."

"Okay, but I'm kind of hungry. Let's get something to eat and then grab a taxi."

The girls had a quick bite and set off to find a cab. Millie had a one-hundred-dollar travelers' check, so she paid the tab for their meal. Carina had some money but it was Canadian and needed to be exchanged.

A half-hour later, they were on the Harvard campus but had no idea where the Anthropology Department was located. They were standing on the sidewalk looking at the buildings when a young man walking beside a bicycle approached, "Excuse me, but you ladies look lost. Can I be of some assistance?"

Carina poked Millie and she asked, "We're looking for the Anthropology Department. Could you please point us in the right direction?"

"Not a problem. I'm on my way there right now. I'm a graduate student in Anthro."

He stuck out his hand toward Millie and said, "I'm Stewart and you are ...?"

Millie shook hands and replied, "I'm Millie and this is Carina."

Carina moved forward, shook hands and said, "Glad to meet you. Thank you for helping us."

They started walking and Stewart said, "You have an accent, you're from Scandinavia?"

"Yes, Sweden."

"May I ask why you are interested in anthropology?"

Carina replied, "I think archeology, actually. We have some Roman coins and a photograph of a

parchment with some symbols we cannot interpret. We were told to see Professor Simmonds."

Smiling, Stewart shook his head. "Doctor Simmonds has taken a sabbatical in Washington. That's D.C., not the state. He won't be back until fall of next year. That's if he comes back, he's a bit of an odd bird."

Millie glanced at Carina and commented, "Professor Schneider said to contact Professor Simmonds. What should we do?"

Stewart suggested, "Well, Doctor Irvine is an expert on ancient coins. How about first seeing if the coins are the real thing?"

Millie and Carina nodded to each other and Millie said, "Take us to the coin doctor."

Stewart and the girls walked to Divinity Avenue and entered an old two story red brick building.

The lobby of the Wilmoore building had an odd, but not offensive odor. Millie remarked, "Stewart, what's that odor?"

Carina chuckled and answered, "I have detected that aroma before. I think it is called old. There is a Stockholm library that has the same smell."

Stewart acknowledged, "Very good description, Carina. This is an old building. It's to be renovated next year. Doctor Irvine's office and lab are in the basement." He pointed to a narrow descending stairway, "Over that way. The steps are worn, use the railing so you don't turn an ankle."

Stewart led the girls down a long stairway to a brightly lit hallway that opened up to a spacious laboratory where a half-dozen large tables surrounded two huge support pillars. Millie could hear footsteps coming from the first floor transmitted through the ceiling. There was a door labeled Dr. Sam Irvine, obviously separating an office from the laboratory. No one was working in the lab.

Stewart walked over to the office door and knocked lightly, "Doctor Irvine? You have two visitors with some questions about Roman coins."

When the door opened, an older woman with gray hair and wearing glasses asked, "Roman coins? Real or fake?" She stepped out into the bright lights and ran her hand through her unruly hair. Millie's immediate thought was the woman could be Albert Einstein's fraternal twin; she had the same hairdo.

Millie almost said, I'd like to talk to Professor Irvine but at the last second she realized this person was Doctor Irvine. Millie stepped forward and said, "I'm Millie Harris and this is Carina Svensson. We would like to get your opinion about some coins that appear to be very old."

Carina dropped her backpack to the floor and reached inside. She extracted a rectangular paper wrapping and handed it to the professor. "The coins are inside."

"I should hope so." She unfolded the paper and found six coins which she took into the lab and placed them on an oversized table that supported a large black instrument. She turned around and announced, "These appear to be cheap fakes, but I will examine further. This will take about an hour. I assume you would like to wait."

Millie and Carina glanced at each other and nodded. Millie said, "Yes, Professor, we'll wait. What is this instrument?"

"It is an arc spectrophotometer. You can't see it working. Why don't you go upstairs to the lounge. I'll call you when I have the results of my investigation." She stared at Stewart and said, "Stewart, please take these young students to the lounge and get them something to drink."

Millie opened her mouth to say something but Stewart took hold of her wrist and whispered, "Don't bother, she probably won't even hear you. She's wrapped up with a systematic inquiry."

Millie shrugged her shoulders, looked at Carina and motioned with her head, "Let's go have a Coke."

As Stewart led the girls up the stairs he commented, "We do whatever Professor Irvine says. No one wants to get on her bad side. She's the queen bee in the department." He waited until we got to the top of the stairs and whispered, "The grad students call her Ms. Relic." He grinned and continued, "The grad student lounge is on the third floor, actually it's an attic, but it's a great hangout."

They climbed two flights of stairs and entered 'The Lair', the graduate student lounge where they found two sofas, half-a-dozen padded chairs, a card table, a coke machine and a telephone marked 'local calls only'. The telephone looked like it was one of Alexander Graham Bell's phones, but Millie could see that it was a modern reproduction. Two students sat on one of the sofas apparently grading papers. They looked up and gave Millie and Carina a cursory glance. The female student said, "Hi Stew." The male had his head in a grade book and looked like he was almost asleep, his red pen held loosely between the fingers of his right hand.

"Want a cold drink?" said Stewart.

Carina and Millie said, "Sure," and he fed three dimes into the machine, extracting cold bottles of Coke. Stewart popped the caps off and handed the bottles to the girls.

Sitting at the card table, Stewart asked, "Tell me how you found the coins."

Carina and Millie asked Stewart for a few moments of privacy and he stepped away from the girls. They leaned toward each other and discussed how much they could reveal about the distant lighthouse and the search for gold by Rocky and Jerry. They decided to say the boys were investigating the lighthouse to look for more coins. Millie motioned for Stewart to rejoin them.

The girls spent almost an hour relating their close call with death when the cargo plane crashed on the rocky island off the Labrador coast.

CHAPTER 20

Back to Crafton

Stewart was captivated by the girls' story. He asked a few questions as they related the events surrounding the air travel from Europe. When they finished he said, "You should write this up and publish it with The Readers Digest. They'd pay some cool cash for that story."

Carina commented, "We don't want anything to leak out until we find out more about the coins and parchment. If they are part of a new discovery, the history of European settlement in the new world could be altered. What if the Romans were the first people to visit North America from the Mediterranean?"

Millie hadn't considered how history would be altered if what Carina said were true. She had been too involved with contacting Professor Simmonds about the coins and parchment to think about potential changes in history.

The odd looking telephone rang twice and Stewart answered.

"Stewart here. Great! You have the analysis. We'll be right down. Thank you Doctor Irvine."

Millie and Carina had overheard Stewart and headed for the stairway after depositing their empty Coke bottles in the crate beside the machine. A few minutes later, they were in the basement at Doctor Irvine's open office door.

"Come in and have a seat, ladies."

Professor Irvine was holding a pencil and standing behind her desk waiting for her visitors to be seated. She appeared to be waiting for a class of students to settle down before she began a lecture. The girls sat but Stewart remained standing.

The professor spoke, "Your Roman coins are all fakes. They might have been given as toys in a package of cereal. They are just cheap imitations, perhaps only a few years old."

Millie and Carina were shocked. Millie asked, "How can you tell? They look so real."

"Spectrographic analysis indicates nearly pure copper and tin were used to make your coins. The real coins have impurities not present in modern refined elements. Under the microscope, real coins show pitting and tiny spots of oxidation. The imitation coins do not show these characteristics. Your coins are undoubtedly fakes." She gave Millie a small envelope containing the coins. "Sorry, ladies."

Millie and Carina stood up and thanked Professor Irvine. Stewart thanked her, too, and the young people went upstairs to the lobby. They talked for a few minutes before Stewart asked the girls for their phone numbers.

Carina gave him her number in Sweden after informing him she didn't have one in the United States.

Stewart responded, "Don't be surprised if I visit Sweden in a year or two. I know I'll be traveling to Europe before long. Maybe we'll see each other again in Italy or Greece, that's where I'll be working on my doctorate."

"Stewart, what is your last name?"

"It's Williamson. My father writes science fiction novels, but I like non-fiction."

Carina said, "Maybe I'll take holiday in the Mediterranean next summer."

"Let's keep in touch. It would be nice to see you again and visit your factory."

Millie crossed her arms over her chest, smiled and said, "Well, I live much closer, in Crafton, Maine. My parents don't have a factory but they sell furniture. We usually vacation in the Bahamas and my sister works for a covert agency that sometimes works for the FBI, so you'd better watch it." She giggled and suddenly realized that her sister, Elena, was married to Lieutenant Nesbitt, an experienced code breaker. The parchment should be shown to him.

Stewart smiled, "Well, that gives me several choices for vacations. I'll call ahead of time to warn you so we can make plans. But you will probably have boyfriends that won't appreciate me showing up out of the blue."

Carina chuckled, "We can always have a good time with old friends, and we can brag that our friend has a Ph.D. from Harvard."

Millie added, "Yeah, an intellectual from an Ivy League school."

Stewart ushered the girls out of the building to the nearest taxi pickup location where Millie and Carina could sit while waiting for a ride back to the airport. Stewart told them to stay put, he would call for a reputable taxi. They said goodbyes and he jogged back to the Wilmoore building.

Less than ten minutes later, a cab appeared and the girls were back at Logan International by four thirty. As they entered the terminal, Millie invited Carina to stay with her family while visiting furniture companies in the northeastern United States. They stopped at a bank at the airport where Carina got five hundred dollars of Canadian money converted to American dollars. She had expressed her uneasy feelings to Millie of being without United States currency. She said it was like not speaking the language.

They sat in a waiting area and watched travelers, a few milling around aimlessly and others knowing their exact destinations. Some people carried their own luggage and others rode in a cart chauffeured by an airport driver.

An unfamiliar voice announced, "Millie Harris, please proceed to a white courtesy phone."

Carina grabbed Millie's arm and said, "Could that be your father?"

Millie stood, swiveled her head looking around, "Do you see a white phone?"

Carina said, "Over there!" pointing at a wall phone next to a snack kiosk.

Millie ran to the phone, lifted the receiver and said, "This is Millie Harris."

"Hi, Mil, where are you?"

"Hi, Dad. We're at a snack kiosk right inside the main terminal."

"Okay. We'll be right there. Don't move a muscle."

Millie laughed as she hung up the phone and looked at Carina, "That was my dad. He said not to move a muscle. I wonder who came with him?"

Carina replied, "That sounds like my father, "He would insist that I 'sit still'."

Millie took off her backpack and fidgeted with the straps as she watched people entering the terminal. Then she recognized her father and mother slowly enter the building, searching for her.

Millie jumped up and down and waved, "Over here!" She dropped her things and ran into her father's arms, Rhonda joined in the hug saying, "You look just fine, Millie. We're so happy you're all right."

Millie shed a few tears, wiped her eyes and turned toward Carina, who was still sitting in the waiting area. Millie motioned for Carina to join the Harrises and introduced her, "This is Carina Svensson. Carina, these are my parents, Rhonda and Leroy Harris."

"I am glad to meet you. Millie has told me all about you and your furniture store. We have an exciting story to tell. I am sure you know some of it already."

Millie was holding her father's fingers with one hand and her mother's with the other. Millie said, "We'll tell you everything on the way back to Crafton, but Carina and I are both hungry. Can you please take us to dinner?"

The nearest restaurant was in the terminal and the foursome had a quick but relaxing meal before starting back to Crafton. On the three and one-half-hour trip, the girls told the entire story of the scary ordeal concerning the crash and over two days after with Rocky and Jerry. Mr. Harris did all the driving in the dark while the women talked like former classmates recalling old times. The girls raved about how Rocky and Jerry helped get them out of the plane and into the unfinished lighthouse.

Mr. Harris was beginning to feel a bit drowsy, so they stopped for coffee about an hour from Crafton. He pulled the Pontiac into a burger joint, shut off the engine and turned to ask the three women, "Coffee for everyone?"

Carina nodded, "Yes, please." Rhonda and Millie gave affirmative nods. Rhonda reminded Leroy, "One sugar and one of those packets of cream, please."

Millie and Carina said in unison, "Black, please."

Mr. Harris entered the lobby and placed the order. Five minutes later he returned with four coffees on a tray which he hooked to the driver's window. As he distributed the coffee, he asked, "Millie, tell me more about Rocky and Jerry staying with the Schneider family. Why did those boys not come home with you and Carina?"

"Professor Schneider needed their help to recover some gold bars from a miniature submarine sitting on the bottom of the ocean not far off the island where the lighthouse is situated. He told Rocky and Jerry he would pay them each a thousand dollars if they would help him recover the gold. Rocky told me that it was deeper than thirty feet." Millie sipped her coffee.

"So, they would need diving equipment. Did you see it?"

"Uh-uh, we left the Point Basilleton Lighthouse before we saw any diving gear. But Rocky wouldn't risk diving in the ocean without the proper equipment, neither would Jerry."

"And you said the Roman coins Doctor Schneider gave you are all fakes?"

She took another sip and nodded, "Yes."

Mr. Harris gulped down some of his coffee, took a deep breath, and remarked, "This whole thing makes me very suspicious. What are you going to do about the parchment? And where is it?"

"Oh, we don't have the parchment, only a photograph. The film's in Carina's camera. We'll get it developed at the pharmacy in Crafton. I've been thinking we'll show it to Aaron, maybe it's some kind of code, not just some old writing by Norsemen."

Carina had been listening closely and commented, "Hearing you and your father talk has made me a little suspicious, too. Tell me about Aaron."

"I guess I didn't explain who he is. Lieutenant Nesbitt, Aaron, was in the Navy. He's my stepsister's husband. He's an expert with codes. He's really smart, so is Elena, my sister. I remember when Rocky was ten, he told me he never thought Elena could be in the FBI because she was too pretty."

Corina finished off her coffee and said, "I thought you were joking with Stewart. Your sister really is an FBI agent?"

Millie took another sip, "Not really, she works for an agency that sometimes carries out operations for the intelligent service.

Rhonda chipped in, "Wait until you see her, Carina, you'd never suspect she does secret activities. She doesn't tell us much about her work. It's kind of hush-hush." She gave her empty coffee cup to Leroy and said, "Let's get back on the road, dear. I think we're all getting tired and need to get some sleep. Aren't you getting tired, Mil?"

"A little, but I'm worried about Dad. Why don't you drive the rest of the way?"

Rhonda replied, "No, sweetie. Don't you recall that I don't like to drive at night?"

"I guess I forgot. I can drive the rest of the way if Dad is getting too tired."

Rhonda scooted over closer to Leroy and rubbed his neck and

shoulders. "Would you like Millie to take over, dear?"

"Nope! I'm fine. The caffeine has done its job." He flashed his headlights and a girl came from the restaurant and removed the tray from the driver's window. Leroy backed the Pontiac away from the hamburger joint and moved into the spotty highway traffic. "Let's see how far away from Crafton we are when we see the lighthouse beam. The first person that observes the light gets an extra pillow." He grinned and the women laughed.

Rhonda won the extra pillow, but she had an advantage over the girls since she was in the front seat. Millie told Carina not to bother, it really wasn't a competition. The clock on the dash read ten twenty seven when they pulled into their driveway at the side of the big renovated two story home. Mr. Harris let the women out and drove to the garage in back.

Rhonda unlocked the front door, turned off the burglar alarm, checked for mail and sat down on the sofa in the living room. "I'm going to relax for a few minutes and then go to bed. You girls can do whatever you want. Millie, show Carina the guest room."

Millie took Carina upstairs to the extra room where Carina left her backpack. After showing Carina the bathroom where they freshened up, the girls went downstairs to the kitchen. Leroy had just opened a beer and was sitting on a stool next to the kitchen sink. He hesitated a moment and then asked, "Would you girls like some beer, tea, or something else?"

Millie took a look at Carina, who shook her head. "No thanks, Dad, but thank you for coming to Boston to get us. I think we'll go to bed and tomorrow we'll visit with Linfields and Morgans to tell them the whole story of the crash and why Rocky and Jerry wanted to stay in Labrador to help the Professor."

"Okay, girls. I'm glad you are safe and home Millie. I don't know what we'd have done if we'd lost you. Next time you go to Europe, come home on a boat or a modern passenger plane."

Millie and Carina grinned. "Good idea, Dad. We're going to bed. See you in the morning. Good night."

CHAPTER 21

Recovery Barge

Rocky woke up to a dark and extremely cold morning. His sleeping bag was keeping his body warm but his face was cold, and he thought feeling the frigid air was like sticking his head inside a refrigerator. He remained still with his eyes closed until he heard the professor moving around, starting to prepare breakfast and lighting a fire to take off the chill.

Jerry spoke softly, "You awake, Rock? I'm damned glad we have these sleeping bags. I think the professor is starting the fire. Has he said anything to you?"

"Nope. We'd better get going though. I think we'll be able to punch through the rocks today. I was just wondering what the girls are up to. I'll bet they're at Millie's in Crafton. They'll probably visit with our parents today."

"I hope they talk with my mom at the hospital. She'll want more information than we provided when we talked over the relayed radio. She'll want to meet Carina, too."

"What'd you say about Carina?"

"Just that I was interested and that she's from Sweden."

Rocky chuckled, "Your mom will know more about her in five minutes than you found out in a month. Your mom should work for the police, she'd make a great detective."

Jerry laughed, "My mom does know how to get information

from people. She gets the funniest stuff from patients at the hospital, especially when she's drawing blood. Some of the roughest toughest men are afraid of needles."

"Time to get out of those bags, gentlemen. Get your shoes and jackets on and let us get busy. I would like to get that hole through the rock wall completed today." The professor was cooking some eggs and had made oatmeal topped with maple syrup. We ate quickly and sipped scalding hot coffee. He sent us ahead to work below ground. He said he would join us in a few minutes, but he was gone for more than ten. Jerry and I figured he had to go to the bathroom.

We knocked a large piece of rock loose and could see some water leaking through cracks in the wall separating us from the ocean. Jerry warned, "Let's wait for him, what if water pours in and the place floods?"

I agreed and we put down the tools and sat on the floor for about five minutes before the professor appeared. He didn't volunteer what he had been doing and we didn't ask.

I looked at the professor and informed him, "Water started leaking through cracks in the rock. What should we do?"

He came over where we worked, inspected the rocks and commented, "Go ahead and break through. Good work!" His enthusiasm was evident and he stepped away from the site to let us get back to work. Jerry held the drill rod and I hammered it three times before I felt the rock crumble. We could see daylight through the irregularly shaped fist-size hole. We were surprised that water didn't pour in, so we continued making the hole bigger until it was almost large enough to crawl through. The opening was about three feet above the ocean and the cold air from above the water brushed over our bare faces and hands in a gentle breeze.

Jerry glanced at me and commented to the professor, "So what's our next step?"

I looked at Schneider and asked, "Don't we need the winch?"

Professor Schneider gave us a sly grin, "Hannah is on her way with the parts."

Jerry stepped next to me and inquired, "How do you know, Professor?"

"Earlier, when I sent you to work, I climbed to the top of the lighthouse, courtesy of the grooves you fellows carved in the concrete and I saw a signal from Rocky Point. Hannah should be here within thirty minutes."

Jerry and I both said, "Cool," almost in unison. Jerry shrugged his shoulders and whispered, "I guess he wasn't taking a dump." We put the hammer and drill in the toolbox and removed the chunks of stone from the floor. With the box full of rock as before, we carried it up the ladder and transferred it under gray skies to the other end of the island. As we returned to the lighthouse, we heard the cabin cruiser approaching. We spun around and watched Hannah wave to us as she piloted the boat closer to the tower where her father waited. Jerry and I ran the last fifty yards.

We expected Sunny to be with Hannah, but she was alone. With the boat anchored, she wrestled the dinghy into the water, transferred several small, wrapped packages plus what looked like a heavy odd-shaped burlap bag into the rowboat and started towards shore. I could see that she was adept with oars. I grinned as I imagined her skill was developed during her years chained in the hold of a Spanish galleon. Schneider was impatient, waiting for the arrival of the parts necessary to construct the winch. He was almost standing in the frigid ocean water.

Jerry nudged me, pointed at Hannah and said, "Jeez, strong back and shoulders."

I nodded and replied, "Yeah, I think she worked out with the Canadian Olympic rowing team."

Jerry was serious, "Possible, but I don't think so."

I explained, "That was a joke, Jer."

Jerry glanced at me and grinned, "No kidding?"

The little boat ground to a halt a couple of feet from shore and Hannah tossed the packages to her father. She said something to him and he called us over to help with the burlap bag. Apparently it was very heavy and she couldn't handle it without straining or breaking something. Jerry and I leaned over the gap of water, pulled the dinghy onto shore and hauled the heavy bag out of the boat.

Hannah gave a big sigh, "Thanks, guys. It was too heavy for me to carry or throw." She then said, "I have to tell you, father. There are some visitors coming. Two seagoing tugboats are bringing a large barge along the coast at about ten knots. I expect it to be here shortly. Before long, you will probably hear the tugs, their motors are noisy."

Schneider acknowledged, "Thank you for the warning, Hannah, and thank you for the packages. The boys just broke through the rock wall earlier today. The winch parts arrived just when we needed them. Give your mother a hug for me."

He pushed the dinghy away from shore and said goodbye. We watched her row to the cruiser and climb aboard, stow the little boat, then guide the fancy craft into deeper water. As the cruiser headed toward the southern horizon, we began to hear the approaching tugs. I was interested to see what the barge looked like and how many men would be present to extract the plane from the ocean.

Jerry commented, "I wonder how the bodies are going to be recovered?"

I mused, "After being in the ocean for about a week, I wonder how they will look."

"I don't think it will be a pleasant sight," Jerry remarked.

The professor commented, "I agree with you, Jerry. I'd rather not think about it. Lat's get the things Hannah brought us into the lighthouse."

Jerry and I had already picked up two of the boxes and were walking toward the tower when Schneider gave us instructions, "We need a story to tell if anyone from the recovery team asks questions about why we are here. When Hannah observed the tugs and barge from Rocky Point, she put a camera in one of the boxes. She suggested we say we are here taking pictures of the Aurora Borealis for a scientific study. I believe it is a good idea."

"Very clever of Hannah to think of that," I said. Jerry nudged me and whispered, "She's smarter than she looks." I had to agree. She was all right, but not any kind of beauty. Nothing like Carina or Millie, that was for sure. But she was pleasant enough, she was good at helping in the kitchen and she could pilot a boat. I was looking forward to see if there was anything to eat in those containers she delivered.

Jerry and I each retrieved another box and together we lugged the heavy burlap bag into the tower. When we opened the packages, most of the contents consisted of metal parts for constructing the winch we were to use to drag the submarine out of deep water. According to the professor, Jerry and I would have to dive below thirty feet to attach ropes. But first, the winch had to be assembled and attached to the floor of the cavern. Then the lines would pass through the hole and into the ocean depths. I hoped the ropes were strong enough to withstand the pulling force. Jerry and I had been estimating the dead weight of the sub to be more than a ton, but the water would have some buoyant force to give it a slight amount of lift.

We nearly dropped the burlap sack down the ladder because of its weight and irregular shape, but we were able to get it into the cave without breaking anything. Bones were the only things Jerry and I worried about breaking, the metal parts were impossible to damage, just various shapes and lengths of angle iron. We opened the bag and dumped the contents on the floor. Schneider looked at the pieces and said, "We will need a wrench to tighten all the bolts. I will get it for you." As he started up the ladder, he said, "I will be right back."

When the professor was out of earshot, Jerry said, "Rock, I've been thinking about Hannah."

"You mean you've had an attack of testosterone?"

He chuckled, "No, not that. I think Hannah should be about five years older than I am, so she's twenty-three. But I think she's older than that, like a lot older, maybe in her thirties. What do you think?"

"It hadn't occurred to me, Jer. But now that you mention it, you could be right. She does seem older than twenty-three. Jeez, maybe she's really not Schneider's daughter."

"Zip it, Rock, he's coming down the ladder."

We waited for instructions with our hands in our pockets to keep them warm. Schneider gave me the wrench and I dropped it on the floor. The cold metal was going to turn my fingers to icicles, so I hurriedly slipped on my gloves and picked up the cold steel tool. Schneider unfolded a drawing of the winch and we started assembly. Twenty minutes later, the winch was nearing completion. We had to attach the handle and ropes that wound around a wide central pulley. It had a brake and a position lock to maintain tension on the ropes.

We heard two slightly different horn sounds. We decided to watch what was going on above before we ventured into the cold ocean water. Professor Schneider suggested we watch the divers on the barge and perhaps learn some techniques to apply to our project. Jerry and I were happy to go above ground to get out of the cold underground dampness. Doctor Schneider came up with us and opened the smallest box Hannah had delivered. It was packed with sandwiches and a six pack of Canadian beer. We sat on a folded blanket and had a cold weather picnic while watching the tugs maneuver the barge into the approximate position where we had last seen the DC-3.

Jerry stood up suddenly and started toward the other end of the island. Following closely behind him, I assumed he wanted to get a closer look at the activities on the barge, as I did. Jerry and I stopped when we got to the high point close to where the plane crashed. There were two divers sitting at the edge of the barge talking to a man standing over them. They gave him a wave, adjusted their face masks and dropped over the side into the ocean. I looked back at the lighthouse to see where Professor Schneider was and saw him coming slowly toward us. He seemed to be very cautious where he was placing his feet, as if he had fallen on the rocks before.

The three of us watched the surface of the barge for at least ten minutes before any interesting activity took place. One of the three men we could see on the deck suddenly ran to the far edge of the rescue raft and knelt down. We couldn't see what was going on, but I assumed one or both of the divers had surfaced, having located the sunken aircraft. Another fellow joined the first one kneeling and the third man waved at one of the tugs. The tugs maneuvered the barge slightly and dropped anchors.

A crane was raised above the deck and I could see a cable with hook attached being lowered into the water. There was some yelling going on but what was being said was unintelligible. I figured one of the men was giving directions. The distance was too great to understand the voices and the tug noises drowned out the words.

Professor Schneider said, "If any of those men comes ashore, do not mention you were survivors. I would not like to open a can of fish that would be hard to explain."

Jerry and I nodded.

"You boys may stay and watch if you like. I will go back and make sure the winch works properly." The professor walked away as he had arrived, carefully watching where he stepped.

We watched him for a few more seconds before Jerry said, "That expression he used was kind of strange, wasn't it?"

"Yeah, but maybe in Canada a can of worms or a kettle of fish is a can of fish."

Jerry replied, "I don't think so. I lived in Canada for a while and a can of fish is just that . . . a can of fish is like tuna in a can."

I didn't say anything more, but I began to wonder about a few things.

CHAPTER 22

Visiting with Parents

Back in Crafton, Leroy and Rhonda Harris had gotten up at 7:00 a.m., prepped for the day and had a quick breakfast. They discussed last week's sales at their furniture store and piled their dirty dishes in the kitchen sink. As Leroy picked up his car keys from the entryway table, he asked his wife, "Should we wake the girls or just leave them on their own?"

Rhonda replied, "The girls can fend for themselves, dear. Come on, let's get to the store and open up. Holiday season is approaching and we've got a lot to do to get ready. That dinette set needs to be in the window and decorated for Thanksgiving."

"You're right. I'll put the keys to the Fairlane on the table. Mil is used to driving the Ford."

They left the house from the kitchen, entered the garage, locked the kitchen door and drove to downtown Crafton in the Pontiac.

Millie woke to a soft thump on her bedroom door. She rolled over, a bit groggy and sat up. She said, "Come in, Mom."

"Isn't it time to get up?" It wasn't her mother's voice.

"Oh! It's you, Carina. Come in. What time is it?" Carina pushed open the bedroom door and said, "It is a bit after nine o'clock. Are we going to have breakfast?" Bare footed, Carina was dressed in long gray slacks and a white sweater. She wiggled her toes and asked, "Should I wear shoes on your rugs?"

Millie grinned, "Sure, shoes are okay, we don't care but thanks for asking. Don't worry about getting the rugs a little dirty. Mom will have the rugs cleaned before long, usually after every two weeks or so. I'm sure your shoes aren't dirty." Millie started to peel off her pajamas and said, "You can go down to the kitchen and get whatever you like. I'll be down in a few minutes . . . after I get dressed and brush my teeth. Do you have a toothbrush?"

Carina shook her head, "I think I left it at the Point Basilleton lighthouse."

"We'll get you a new one at the drug store when we take the film in for developing."

Carina found Wheaties cereal in the cupboard and was eating it dry when Millie joined her.

"What are you eating?"

Carina pointed at the cupboard. "It's from a box up there."

Millie smiled and said, "You need to add milk and some sugar. It will improve the taste and make it softer . . . much easier to swallow. What do you have for breakfast food back home? We didn't eat cereal when in Sweden."

"Our cereal is made of oats and mixed with yogurt, but I am trying different things now."

Millie got a quart of milk from the refrigerator, added some of the liquid to the Wheaties and set the sugar bowl next to Carina. Carina sprinkled sugar on the cereal and cautiously took a spoonful, chewed for a moment, swallowed and grinned, "That is much better."

After the girls finished eating, Millie drove the '55 Ford to Pfann's Drug store, about two blocks from the Linfields' craft store. They left the roll of film, bought Carina a toothbrush, then walked to the pier and entered Crafton Crafts. Millie introduced Carina to Lee Linfield, Rocky's father, the proprietor of the store.

As the girls browsed the aisles, customers entered the store and Lee busily waited on shoppers. After about ten minutes, Carina and Millie moved to the entrance and waved to Mr. Linfield, "We'll see you later when you're not so busy and tell you all about our experiences."

Linfield waved and said, "Later, girls, thank you for dropping by."

As they walked back to the car, Carina remarked, "Mr. Linfield is genuinely nice and his shop is wonderful, so many things! I could spend hours in there buying presents."

They took a few steps when Millie said, "Let's visit with Mr. Morgan and tell him what Jerry is up to. I'm not sure what he told his parents on the radio."

Back in the car, Millie changed her mind and said, "I think we should see Mrs. Morgan first. As supervisor at the hospital laboratory, she should have some time to talk. Then we'll go to Mr. Morgan's machine shop. It's on the south edge of town, close to the nearest highway."

At the hospital, Millie asked the receptionist at the front desk if Mrs. Morgan was available. He answered immediately, "I'm afraid she is busy until noon. What do you want to see her about?"

"We have information about her son. He's in Labrador, Newfoundland, Canada."

The aide thought for a second, "One moment, please." He grabbed the phone and dialed three numbers. The girls overheard him say Labrador and he asked, "What are your names, please?"

Carina leaned over the desk and spoke loudly, "Carina Svensson and Millie Harris."

The aide hung up and looked at the girls. "She will be right out. Please have a seat in the waiting area." He pointed across the hall where a half-dozen chairs lined the wall.

Mrs. Morgan, dressed in a white lab coat with a pencil stuck in her hair, came through a set of double doors walking rapidly. When she saw the girls, she ran about ten steps and threw her arms around Millie, stepped back and said, "You look fine, dear." She glanced at Carina and said, "And you must be

Carina. Jerry described you very accurately. I'd know you anywhere." She gave Carina a hug and said, "Please tell me more about Jerry. We didn't get much about him from the radio call. Is he doing all right in Labrador?"

Natalie Morgan listened to the girls' tale with great interest. Carina pointed out the actions of Jerry that helped save them. Millie related how Rocky and Jerry climbed to the top of the lighthouse to watch for distant lights. Millie explained how all four of the survivors escaped from the plane and lived two days on the island with little food. Carina told about the rescue and the reason the boys stayed to help the professor.

"Those boys . . . that sounds just like Jerry and Rocky, helping someone and earning money for college at the same time."

Millie inquired, "I'm wondering if we should visit with your husband. Is he terribly busy these days without his son's help? I know Jerry's very clever with mechanical things . . . similar to his dad's ability."

"Steve is busy these days, repairing snow blowers, snow mobiles, and truck motors. He probably would take time off to listen to you, but I can tell him all about Jerry tonight at home. Maybe you should visit with Sandra, Rocky's mom. I'm sure she would appreciate all the information you can give her about Rocky. Mrs. Makler might also be interested."

"Oh, thank you, I almost forgot about Mrs. Makler. She'd be happy to hear everything about Rocky." There was a pregnant pause, then Mrs. Morgan got to her feet saying, "I'm so glad you girls came by. I have to get back to work now, lab supervision never ends."

Carina said, "It was so nice meeting you. Bye."

Millie followed with, "Bye, Mrs. Morgan."

Mrs. Morgan gave a last second wave and disappeared from the main hallway as the double doors swung shut.

The interior of the Ford had grown cold while the girls were talking to Natalie Morgan, so Millie ran the engine a few minutes and got the heater going before driving to the Crafton lighthouse. Sandra Linfield was like a second mother to Millie and as she drove, she anticipated receiving a big hug from Rocky's mother.

Carina saw the lighthouse looming above the rocky coastline and the keeper's home. She felt a strange longing to climb to the top and observe the ocean. She whispered to Millie, "I want to go all the way to the top. When does the light come on?"

"Not until this evening, about six o'clock when the sun's about gone. I'll climb the winding stairs with you. Rocky and I have been up there several times and the evening sights are wonderful, especially when there is a ship on the eastern horizon. It's kind of magical when the ship disappears into the dark blue water and then the light flashes on. Of course, those things are not related."

"That sounds cool . . . really cool."

Millie turned on the path leading to the lighthouse, stopped in the parking area and shut off the engine. The girls got out and proceeded to the dark-green front door of the keeper's home. Millie rang the bell and Susan opened the door.

She squealed, "Oh! Millie! And you must be Carina, the girl from Sweden." Susan gave the girls a hug and said, "Come in, Mom's on the phone with Granma. Have a seat, she'll be right with you. I'm sure you want to talk about Rocky and I want to hear all about the crash. I bet that was really exciting."

Millie introduced Susan to Carina and Carina asked, "Do you like living next to a lighthouse?"

Susan giggled, "It's okay, the lighthouse is kind of like having a big room where people come to visit, but we don't have to vacuum. I don't like to go to the top, it's kinda scary up there." She pointed at the ceiling in the direction of the tower. "I'll go up there with Rocky though, as long as it's not windy."

The girls heard the telephone being put back in its cradle and footsteps on the linoleum floor. Sandra Linfield appeared and rushed to the visitors giving the two a big hug simultaneously. She stepped back and shook hands with Carina, saying, "This is a first for me. I've never met anyone from Sweden before." They sat down and Sandra explained, "I was on the phone with my mother and recognized Millie's voice. My mother is coming over, can you two stay for lunch?"

Millie and Carina traded glances and nodded. Millie said, "That would be every nice, Mrs. Linfield, we have lots to tell you. It might take a while."

The girls heard the crunching of tires on gravel and Susan remarked, "That's Granma in her old Desoto. She loves that old car." Then a car horn sounded two beeps. Susan added, "Yep, that's Granma. She always announces her arrival."

Sandra commented, "Mother drives over here although it's only a short walk. She's having problems with her balance and doesn't want to chance falling."

Millie observed Mrs. Makler through the window facing the parking lot as the elderly woman approached the front door. She was going to greet Rocky's grandmother at the door but Susan raced ahead and flung open the entryway.

"Come in, Grandma. Millie and her friend from Sweden are here."

Susan had surprised Mrs. Makler. The matron grabbed the doorjamb to steady herself, paused for a second and stepped unsteadily into the room. She closed the door behind her, leaned against it, peeled off her heavy coat and tossed it at Susan, who laughed and hung it on the coat tree next to the door. Except for Susan, Millie was closest to Mrs. Makler, now in her middle seventies, and said, "It's so nice to see you. I'm so glad you came over. Carina and I were going to visit with you at your home after talking to your daughter."

Mrs. Makler said, "Let's sit down so we can talk. Sandra, do you have something to warm my hands?"

"Sure, Mom, I'll get you some coffee. Is that all right?" Sandra started for the kitchen.

"That would be fine. I want to meet this young person." She pointed a wavering hand at Carina and added, "So you are the young lady from Sweden. I visited Stockholm with my husband in 1938, before the war. That was a wonderful city. How is it now?"

Carina moved from an overstuffed chair, sat beside Mrs. Maker and shook hands. "It's a great city. I've spent my entire life there. This is the first time visiting the United States. I want to see New York City, the Statue of Liberty and the Empire State Building. I've heard much about them."

"Perhaps Rocky and Millie can accompany you before the holidays, if that boy would ever return from far off places." Mrs. Makler looked at the girls and added, "Now, tell me all about the accident and why my grandson is staying in Labrador."

Sandra returned with a tray of coffee mugs, a small pitcher of milk and a little box of sugar cubes. When everyone was served, Millie started relating the story about the doomed airplane ride across the Atlantic. Mrs. Makler sat quietly without commenting as Carina occasionally took over from Millie to accentuate some of the major events.

CHAPTER 23

Visit with Mrs. Makler

When the girls had finished their story and the remaining coffee was cold, Mrs. Makler said, "May I see the coins you took to the Harvard professor?"

"Yes, I have them." Millie stood, opened her purse and handed the folded envelope to Mrs. Makler. With arthritic fingers, Mrs. Makler opened the envelope and picked up one of the coins. In a few seconds she stated, "This one is an imitation. It's obvious. It can't be more than a few years old." She pushed them around with her fingers and said, "It looks to me that they are all like this. What did the Harvard professor say?"

Carina replied, "She said they are all fakes, just what you are saying."

Sandra suddenly interrupted, "Millie, will you please help me in the kitchen? I'm almost ready for lunch. Five women having lunch together should be fun. I think Mom will have lots more questions for you and Carina."

Sandra was correct, her mother had many more questions for the two girls, mostly about the rescuing family, especially Doctor Schneider. She asked Sandra to get her a pencil and paper. Marty Makler was still thinking like a covert agent and seemed very suspicious about the professor that was absent from Harvard, Dr. Simmonds. Mrs. Makler made a number of notes and stated, "When I get home, I'm going to make some calls to Washington. I've still got a few important contacts at the capital."

Millie commented, "Oh, Mrs. Makler, we forgot to tell you about the parchment. We have a photograph of it at the drug store. We took a roll of film there for developing a little while ago."

"Now that is something I would really like to see. When you get the photograph, please bring it by my house so I can take a look. I've seen some real doozies in my time. This might be another."

Millie wondered if her stepsister was home with her husband, Aaron. "Do you know if Elena is home? We'd like to show the parchment to Aaron to see what he thinks."

"I haven't seen her or the lieutenant for several days, but I have her work number. Lieutenant Nesbitt, Aaron, is out of the Navy now and works for some intelligence company. He and Elena are planning on starting a family soon. Did you know about that, Millie?"

"No. Really? I can't imaging Elena wanting to stay home from working undercover. I'll bet she wants a baby before she gets too old. It would be cool if she had twins, then I'd be Auntie Millie times two!"

"And since I live next door, I'd volunteer to babysit the little ones." Mrs. Makler smiled and after a second of meditation suddenly saddened, "But when they get older, I wouldn't be able to chase them around . . . unless my balance improves. I guess I could take them for rides though. I can still drive." Her smile returned.

Following lunch, Carina and Millie climbed the Crafton lighthouse winding stairway to the gallery. Millie poked her head through the access door to scare any birds away and then climbed through the opening to the elevated floor. She hadn't been up there since she was fifteen and grabbed the metal railing before standing erect. Carina showed no fear and moved to the rail and looked straight down at Millie's car.

"Your car sure looks different from up here, doesn't it? It looks longer and thinner from so far above. It almost looks like four people couldn't even fit in."

Millie looked down and commented, "You're right, it does look small. When you see a ship out on the bay, it looks like a toy in the bathtub." Millie and Carina strolled around the circular platform and returned to the access door. "Let's go to Pfann's, get your film and see how the parchment photo turned out. Then we'll go over to see Mrs. Makler." Millie grinned and said, "Mrs. Makler sometimes makes a cupcake into a five-tiered wedding cake, so don't be surprised."

Carina chuckled, "That sounds like my mother. She tends to over exaggerate."

Suddenly Millie remarked, "Oh, how many pictures were on that roll of film, twenty?"

"I think so. I took lots of pictures when we were in the Scandinavian capital cities. Mostly you, Rocky and of course, Jerry." She looked Millie in the eyes and questioned, "How old is Jerry?"

"I thought you liked him. He's eighteen, almost nineteen. His birthday is in February. I'm not sure but I think it's on the twelfth."

"Do you think I'm too old for him? I'm twenty."

"No, I don't think you're too old for Jerry. He has lots of world experience and is a nice guy. He and Rocky have been best friends for seven years and if Rocky and I like him, he's got to be a good guy." Millie grinned and added, "I'll guarantee it."

"Okay, let's get those pictures. I want Mrs. Makler to see what that goat skin looks like. I am very curious to get her evaluation."

Ten minutes later, the girls entered Pfann's Pharmacy and went to the back to pick up the developed film. Carina had requested two copies. She paid for the pictures at the front counter where cosmetics and magazines were sold. That's when she noticed the earrings and wrist watches. "Gosh, Millie, these are so cheap compared to prices in Sweden. I must come back to get some gifts before I return home." She surveyed the corner drugstore from the interior and added, "This is a really nice store."

Millie took Carina by the arm and forced her outside to the Ford. "Quick, get in! I want to see all your pictures. Then we'll drive over to Mrs. Makler and show her the parchment photograph. I'm wondering what she's going to say."

The girls sat in the car for nearly fifteen minutes studying the pictures and laughing at some of them. When they had seen all of the shots, Millie commented, "There are several of those that I would like copies of. I'll pay you for the ones I want."

"Oh, no you will not. I got two of each so I could give you one set. You don't have to pay me; you can consider them a gift. Maybe you can mount them in a book to save them as your Scandinavian trip."

"That's a great idea. I'll do that. Thank you." She gave Carina a hug and announced, "Next stop, Marty Makler's home. It's next door to my sister's house." She started the car, checked in her rearview mirror, pulled away from the curb and pointed the car toward the lighthouse.

Carina frowned and questioned, "We are going back to the lighthouse?"

"No, but close by. Mrs. Makler lives close to the Linfields, only a few blocks away. Rocky used to pull his sister in a wagon from the Makler house to the lighthouse. That was when he was only ten years old."

The girls drove a little past the tower, turned at the first right and saw the green Desoto parked on the front lawn of the Makler home. Millie wondered why the car was not in the driveway close to the garage as usual. She concluded Mrs. Makler must have been in a hurry. Maybe she had consumed too much coffee.

Millie turned into the driveway and parked where Mrs. Makler usually placed her Desoto. As the girls got out of the Ford, Mrs. Makler appeared on the front porch. "Oh, I didn't think you would be coming over so soon. Please come in and show me the parchment photo. I'll move my car later."

Mrs. Makler entered the foyer leading the girls. Millie suddenly stopped when she noticed a big black cat sitting on the back of Marty's reading chair. Carina almost walked into Millie.

"Mrs. Makler, when did you get the cat?"

"About a month ago at the animal shelter. He's a good mouser. I forgot to feed him this morning and when I got home he was in the window waiting for me. I just had to feed him right away. Animals like a strict routine, you know. That's why I parked funny. His name is Hunter."

Millie chuckled, "We noticed you had parked on the grass. I thought you were in a rush to get to the bathroom."

She chuckled, "Good assumption, young lady, but my bladder is doing fine. Now show me the picture of the parchment."

Millie and Carina sat next to each other on the sofa. Mrs. Makler dragged a dining chair across the living room rug and sat in front of the girls. Carina extracted the envelope of developed photos from the pocket of her slacks and began to search through them. Just as she spotted the parchment picture, Hunter jumped on the couch between the girls. Carina handed the picture to Mrs. Makler and began to pet the cat.

"Do you like cats?" asked Marty.

"Oh, yes, we have three of them at home. They are all indoor cats. My mother loves them and I play with them sometimes."

Marty silently viewed the picture from all angles before commenting. "I believe this is gibberish. It's not a message but maybe a signal of some sort. I think Aaron Nesbitt should take a look. He's an expert with codes and written documents of all kinds. He's a really smart young man." She thought for a moment and continued, "But you know all about him, Millie, he's your brother-in-law."

"We talked about doing that, but we thought you might give us some suggestions as to what it might mean. We'll show it to Aaron when we see him. We don't know where he is right now."

"Well, he can't be too far from your sister. I see them together all the time, coming and going from their home. Millie, you know they live next door."

"Sure, I remember, but they aren't home very often are they? They both work in Washington."

"Oh, I see them every other weekend, usually. They seem incredibly happy." Mrs. Makler raised her arm as if she suddenly remembered something very important. "When I got home and fed Hunter, I phoned my old contact and asked about Professors Schneider and Simmonds. I should be getting some info on them tomorrow morning. I'll phone you, Millie. Is that okay?"

"Please do. Carina and I will stay home so we can talk to you. We don't have any plans for tomorrow, do we, Carina?"

Carina shook her head, "Nothing I can think of."

Millie held Hunter and stood up. The cat bolted from her arms and scurried into the kitchen. Carina remained sitting for a moment and got to her feet just as Mrs. Makler said, "When are you girls plan to return to Labrador?"

Raising her eyebrows, Carina glanced at Millie and said, "I do not think we will be going back. That place holds only bad memories for me." Millie nodded in agreement.

CHAPTER 24

Raising the Plane

Jerry and I watched the recovery crew for about a half-hour before becoming bored with the seeming lack of progress on the barge. "Let's go back to the lighthouse, Jer. Nothing is happening here."

"Yeah. I thought the Canadians would move a little faster than in the states. I guess not."

When we arrived at the other end of the island, Professor Schneider was leaning against the lighthouse wall shading his eyes with his hands and squinting. "I can't see what is going on down there. Have they begun to raise the airplane?"

I answered, "No, we couldn't see any progress. There must be some problems. Maybe the weight of the plane filled with water is too much for their crane." That was the only reasonable thing I could suggest.

"I don't think that's a difficulty, Rock. I'm thinking the divers are having to fight currents while attempting to get belts around the fuselage or the engines. That's assuming they're going to lift the entire plane as a unit."

Doctor Schneider commented, "I believe that is the plan. They will lift the plane up slowly, letting the ocean water drain out and lighten the load, then swing the plane onto the barge."

The only thing we could see was the top of the crane but if I climbed to the top of the lighthouse, I could watch the recovery activities. That idea was shot down before I had a chance to grab the rope and put my foot in the first notch in the wall when Schneider said, "I want you boys to get into your wetsuits and make a dive. I would like to know how deep the sub is and if it has decomposed in the salty water."

Jerry whispered, "Here we go, Rock. Let's suit up and take a dip in the ocean."

Jerry and I spent about a half hour to get our suits and equipment ready. The professor stood by and wanted to help, but there was little for him to do. Jerry and I had been diving in the bay at Crafton for the last two summers and followed a routine for two divers. We politely declined Professor Schneider's offers of assistance. The wetsuits fit well and we adjusted weights a few yards offshore before beginning our first attempt to locate the minisub. Jerry had to add a pound more than I did, because he displaced a bit more water.

We roped together and walked away from shore dropping below the surface where the bottom dropped off to a depth of about twelve or fifteen feet. There was a nearly level shelf that extended about twenty feet farther into the ocean and then a sudden decline, but we could see the bottom sloping down at a steep angle. We had to swim against the current; without our swim fins we would have been forced to the southern end of the island. As it began to get difficult to see with light from above, we turned on the bright underwater lamps.

Moving against the current was forcing us to expend quite an effort as we descended, ever on the lookout for the submarine, scanning the drop off to the north. We tried to maintain a depth of thirty feet with our lights shining deeper into the sea. Jerry gave me a hand signal that we should go lower, another ten feet and I agreed. I assumed we were just east of the lighthouse, but the current might have carried us south of where we had entered the water.

We dropped another ten feet, where the current was getting slightly stronger and we would be running out of air in a few minutes. Still no submarine detected. We had to surface or run out of air so I jerked on our connecting rope and we began to ascend. Although we had been at depth for only a few minutes, we rose slowly while fighting the current. When we broke the surface, Jerry and I were surprised to discover we were nearly fifty yards from our entry point, the current and our swimming had been very deceptive.

As we removed our facemasks and realized what had occurred, Jerry commented, "Look where we are, Rock. I had no idea we were so far south of the lighthouse."

"I'm just as surprised as you are, Jer. I think we better figure out a way to stay east or slightly north of our entry point. Any ideas?"

"I'm too cold to have any reasonable thoughts. Let's get out of these suits and warm up. Maybe I'll think of something when I'm not shivering."

Professor Schneider met us as we exited the water and began removing our swim fins. "Did you find the sub?" he asked excitedly.

I shook my head, "We didn't see anything but the bottom and a few fish but we were drifting south all the time. We both thought we were moving north and slightly east."

"Yeah, we went down to forty feet, but didn't find the sub. We're going to need a better way to tell our position underwater. We thought we had countered the current but we were forced backwards."

Schneider sat on the ground, crossed his arms against his chest and said, "Hmm. Another problem to solve. They never seem to end." We watched him sit there motionless for at least a minute. Jerry and I waited patiently for him to react and after another thirty seconds, he suddenly exclaimed, "I've got it! Hannah will be here tomorrow and there are two anchors on our boat. One will be dropped where I think the sub is and the rope attached will be tied to the winch. That will give you a line to follow to where I believe the sub is located. You should be able to see it with those high intensity lights." He rose to his feet and walked swiftly to the lighthouse. We trudged after him, removing our rubber suits as we entered our temporary island home. There wasn't an abundance of water available but we washed our bodies with cold water-soaked rags to remove ocean water residue. Memories of escaping from the DC-3 flashed through my mind, images brought on by the cold water bath. Standing there naked was not fun but Jerry and I both laughed when I commented about everything shriveling up in the frigid weather. We hastily donned dry clothes, then rinsed the salt water from our wetsuits and hung them up to dry.

The cold had stimulated our appetites and luckily the professor had anticipated our hunger. We scarfed up some peanut butter sandwiches and hot chocolate hardly uttering a word. When Schneider saw us relaxing he said, "There is a storm coming down on us from the north so Hannah will probably be delayed for a day or two. We will plan your dive details while we are waiting. We can also take another trip to the recovery sight to see what progress has been made to lift the airplane. That should be done first before the onset of bad weather. There will be plenty of time to plan your next dive before Hannah returns with the anchors."

I commented to Jerry, "Let's check out the recovery activities. Maybe they've got the plane out of the water and on the barge. They can't let it hang over the water when a storm blows in."

"You're right, and when the storm hits, those ocean tugs will have their work cut out for them keeping that barge in tow. I don't think they'll try to move the plane in rough water conditions."

The professor set off toward the recovery barge and we followed slightly behind. His long stride kept him moving at a fast pace. He no longer moved carefully as before. Jerry and I didn't even try to keep up with him. Besides, we were tired from the dive. It's surprising how much a dive in very cold water saps one's strength. The wetsuits kept us from suffering hypothermia.

Professor Schneider stopped at the highest point at the southern end of the island and sat holding a small tablet and pencil. I think he planned on sketching how the seamen on the barge had attached cables to lift the plane. As the plane came into view, we could see a cable had been attached to the left wing tip and a cradle of sorts was slung under the fuselage directly behind the trailing edge of the wings.

The wing was rising above the surface and water was pouring from the cargo and passenger doors. Divers must have opened the cargo door from inside the plane. With all the loose boxes of furniture tumbling through the water, it would have been a dangerous undertaking.

We watched the water gush from the plane for about five minutes and then the crane began to rotate the plane and slide it onto the barge. When the cables slackened, two figures entered the plane, each carrying a black package the size of a small sleeping bag. Jerry said, "Body bags. That's going to be a gruesome sight."

As we sat there observing, one of the men on the barge walked to the deck edge closest to us and yelled, "We need to talk to you gentlemen. Stay where you are."

We glanced at the professor and he advised, "Remember, we are here to photograph the aurora. If they get too inquisitive, let me do all the talking. You are undergraduate students from the University of Washington, working on theses under my direction. One other thing, don't give them your real names."

Jerry stuck out his right hand, "I'm Stan Bafus. Glad to meet you."

I shook hands with Stan while grinning and said, "Happy to meet you, Stan, I'm Richard Gordon."

Schneider chuckled and gave us one more instruction, "If our visitors come to the lighthouse, tell them you understand the trap door leads to an abandoned cavern for geothermal heating and cooling. The installation was planned but never completed."

I kicked at a loose stone and sent it bouncing across the rocky surface into the water. I was a little nervous about saying something wrong, so I told Jerry, "I'm gonna keep my mouth shut unless it's to answer something really simple."

Jerry nodded, "Good idea, me too."

We were keeping our eyes on the barge activity when a small craft came from behind the far tug and headed directly for us. As it came closer, I could see three figures in the boat, all wearing heavy cold weather clothing. The outboard motor pushed the small boat rapidly through the calm sea water to a grinding halt on the desolate island's rocky shore.

Two of the men got out of the boat and approached us, the third fellow remained sitting beside the engine. He patted his lefthand breast pocket, probably checking for a pack of cigarettes. I don't know why I thought of that, except I had seen similar looking guys around boats back in Crafton, cargo inspectors. They always seemed to have a cigarette hanging from their lips, sometimes unlit.

Professor Schneider met the two guys a few paces from their boat. The bigger, chunkier one said, "I'm Max Webber, National Transportation Safety Board." He shook hands with the Professor Schneider, who said he was Assistant Professor Brad Anthony.

Mr. Webber stated, "I wouldn't be here normally for a wreck investigation in Canada, but the plane was licensed in the United States. It looks like there were two fatalities, the pilots. Did any of you see the accident?" He removed his sunglasses and began squinting, although the northern sky was darkening, the sun hiding behind a cloud formation.

Professor Schneider answered, "No, we didn't know of the accident. I'm not sure we were on the island when the plane crashed. When did the plane go down?"

"The plane crashed during the last nor'easter, more than a week ago."

"I guess we were at the Point Basilleton Lighthouse when the storm struck. It is also called Rocky Point Lighthouse. That is how most people refer to it. We depend on the keepers to bring us supplies."

The other man, a bit taller and not as chubby as Mr. Webber, stepped forward and introduced himself. "I'm Daniel Cooker, Transportation Safety Board, Canada. We have information that the Rocky Point lighthouse keepers rescued the four passengers following the crash. You didn't see them when you were at the lighthouse?"

"I am afraid not. The boys and I had been there the day before the storm and had gone inland to hike to Cartwright, but we were not prepared to go so far and turned back after two days. We returned to Rocky Point after the rescued people were gone. I believe they were flown out the day before we returned. Then we began setting up our camera to record the aurora."

The two inspectors seemed to be satisfied with the professor's lies. The inspectors glanced at each other, shrugged, and Mr. Cooker said, "Well, thank you for the information. I suppose we should go back and prepare for some rough seas."

I was somewhat shocked at what the professor told them, "If you pull your barge ahead about four hundred yards, you will have more shelter from the current. The island is shaped like a crescent, so you could drop your anchors in the bay."

What was Professor Schneider thinking? It seemed to me the tugs and barge moving closer to the lighthouse would encourage the workers and inspectors to make visits to the lighthouse, just what we didn't want. I figured Jerry had the same thoughts, but after a moment, he said, "Do you think Schneider was trying to indicate that he was a nice guy and was concerned about their well-being, trying to discourage any ideas of suspicion?"

I guess Jerry had considered Schneider's comments more deeply than I had. Maybe he was right. I nodded and said, "That's probably the answer."

Upon reaching the lighthouse, Jer and I climbed the tower and watched the tugs move the barge into the shallow bay to the west of the island. With the wind increasing as the front approached and before the rain began to fall, we watched from the tower as the workers on the barge cut the wings off the fuselage with torches. That's when Jerry and I knew they weren't planning on restoring the DC-3. It was going to be used for parts. We concluded the wings were going to be trashed but the motors would be salvaged. As the wings were being removed, cables from the crane to the motors kept them from falling haphazardly to the barge's deck, they were let down gently. The wings with motors attached were lashed to the deck, as was the fuselage and tail section. The workers were preparing for the ensuing storm. Just as we felt a few rain drops strike, we dropped to the ground and sought shelter in the lighthouse to ride out the bad weather.

The wind gusts carrying sheets of rain couldn't be felt hitting the tower wall, but as I watched the tugs and the barge sandwiched between them, I was happy to be standing inside looking out the door. When lightening flashed, I shut the door and withdrew to the interior where Jerry was talking with Professor Schneider. I joined them and commented, "I think this storm is going to be stronger than the one that caused our plane to crash."

CHAPTER 25

Visitors From the Barge

The professor had started the propane burner and was warming something for us to eat. Four candles provided most of the interior lighting. Millie gave me the novel she had on the plane when she finished it but I had only read the preface. I had finished my book. I should try to get some reading done so Millie and I can talk about it when we're back together again. The book was written by a mountaineer climbing in the Swiss Alps.

I wondered what Millie and Carina were doing back in Crafton, hopefully they were having better weather than we were. They were probably going out for dinner tonight, Millie told me that her mother wasn't much of a cook, nothing like my mom. Millie ate dinner at the Crafton lighthouse more often than she did at home, at least that's what I thought. I always enjoyed walking her home from an evening at my home. Recently those twilight journeys had ended with a kiss, but that was over a month ago. I glanced at Jerry and wondered how often Millie had eaten dinner at his place. I had never asked.

Jerry interrupted my thoughts, "The professor thinks Hannah won't show up until late tomorrow if this storm lasts through the night."

"That's okay by me. I'm not looking forward to going back into the ocean, especially if we have to go below forty feet. I lose confidence below thirty, it's so damned dark and we have to think about stopping as we come up if we stay down very long. I don't relish having the bends or running out of air."

I gave Jerry a serious glance and said, "How much do you think the professor knows about scuba diving?"

"Well, he did get us all the necessary equipment, even if it wasn't exact fits."

"Yeah, I guess you're right. Maybe I'm just being overcautious."

Two hours later, we had eaten and were settled for the night when we heard a loud knocking at the lighthouse door. Professor Schneider made his way to the door in the semi-darkness dressed in a bathrobe under his coat and carrying his pistol. It was pretty obvious he wasn't expecting anyone. I was sure Hannah hadn't arrived with the extra anchor; she wouldn't make the trip at night in a raging storm.

Two men entered, one leaning against the other, kind of stumbling. At first I thought the one being supported was drunk, but then I recognized him. It was Mr. Webber, the inspector from the United States. If he were to be caught soused, he would undoubtedly lose his job. Even in the poor lighting, he looked extremely uncomfortable. I heard the professor ask, "What is wrong with this man?"

The upright gentleman announced, "I'm Doctor Warner. Mr. Webber is not an experienced seaman. The pitch and roll of the tug was too much for him. I've given him some medication, but he can't seem to keep anything down. Would we be able to spend the night? Don't worry about accommodations, a crewman is coming with some sleeping bags and food for a couple of days. We won't stay long, just until the storm blows itself out."

Jerry whispered to me, "Schneider can't say no, can he?"

"Nope, we're stuck with some visitors. If he says no, they will wonder what we have to hide."

We heard another rapping at the door and before the professor could get to it, it swung open and a crewman barged in carrying three sleeping bags and what I guessed was a sack of groceries. I guess we were going to have three guests for at least one day. The bags were covered with a dusting of white material. Jerry said, "Damn, that's snow, Rock."

I wondered what else would happen due to the storm and I had to grin, "We'll have to have a snowball fight tomorrow against the barge crew."

Jerry laughed and replied, "Yeah, if tomorrow ever arrives. This storm is worse than the one we lived through after the crash. I think the ocean is pouring through the hole we made from the chamber. The white caps in the bay are nearly three feet high and on the eastern side I'll bet they're even higher."

While Jerry and I were whispering, I watched the barge doctor scratching his chin and looking around for a good place for three men and their sleeping bags. I said to Jerry, "Let's move to the trapdoor and let these guys have more room away from the entrance. It's damn cold over there."

Jerry remarked, "Yeah, just as I was getting nice and warm. Okay, let's do it."

In our underwear, we slid out of our zippered bags and dragged them onto the trapdoor, repositioning them. The professor's area was about two yards from us on the right as we faced the outside door. He had moved our diving gear, probably into the cavern below us. I couldn't see any of our wetsuits or any place he might have stored them above ground.

We crawled back into our still warm bags, zipped them up and watched the three men from the tugs get situated. I got this strange feeling, I wanted to pull out Millie's novel and read but all I would have from that pursuit would be eyestrain and a headache. I would have to fight to extract words from the pages in such poor light. I decided to close my eyes and instead think about Millie.

Morning arrived in darkness but the wind had diminished to what I estimated as a few miles per hour. I could tell by the quiet conditions.

The doctor and Schneider were drinking coffee, sitting quietly beside the propane burner. The aroma permeated the lighthouse and reminded me of the mornings in Crafton. I imagined having hot chocolate with those little marshmallows floating on top, but that was only fantasy. I doubted if there were any marshmallows within five hundred miles.

Jerry said, "Morning, Rock. How much snow do you guess is out there?"

"I don't know but I'll find out in a few minutes. As soon as I'm dressed, I've got to take a pee."

"Me too."

We dressed inside our sleeping bags, except for heavy coats and shoes, crawled out of our warm cocoons and pulled on our windbreakers and shoes. Mr. Webber and the crewmember, still reclining quietly in their sleeping bags, didn't look up as Jerry and I went outside. We opened the door, moved quickly to the outside and shoved the door closed. The snow was about eight inches deep and the air was bitterly cold.

Even though we were in the shelter of the lighthouse, the slight wind still hurt our skin. We stepped away from the entrance, opened our flies, and with our backs to the wind, turned some snow yellow. We hustled back inside where it was at least twenty degrees warmer. I could see Jerry's breath when he exhaled. We picked up our metal cups from our sleeping area, joined the professor and doctor. and filled the cups with coffee.

I knew the brew was going to be hot enough to burn going down, so I took a few sips and waited a minute before the first big swallow. Jerry was using the coffee to warm his hands as he held the cup under his nose and inhaled deeply. I grinned, thinking his nose was going to run like after eating soup, but surprisingly, nothing happened.

Doctor Warner went over to Mr. Webber and the crewman, knelt and had a short conversation. The crewman rummaged through the sack he had brought with him and handed the doctor two cans. I heard him say, "The stuff in one of those cans will warm us up." Mr. Webber and the crewman both chuckled. The doctor returned to Professor Schneider, tossed the cans to him and said, "Eggs and pork and beans. Mr. Webber is feeling much better. He's hungry. I recommended that he stay away from coffee for a day or two."

We had our own supplies and the professor surprised me by warming the contents of the two cans for the visitors. I thought the barge doctor would have done the cooking for our guests, but he didn't make an offer to assist with breakfast. Professor Schneider didn't go out of his way to offer the three men any of our provisions. I assumed he was beginning to hold them in contempt but he also didn't know when Hannah would be bringing groceries for us. We didn't have food for more than two days if she were delayed past her normal visit to the distant lighthouse. I figured she would be at least one day late. If the storm had struck Rocky Point with the same severity that we had experienced, she wouldn't be travelling alone. Sunny would be with her.

After breakfast, we talked with the visitors for nearly an hour. Jerry and I were very careful what we said and didn't ask them much about the airplane recovery. I suppose it was mid-morning when we all heard horn blasts from the two tugs.

Doctor Warner had just asked about the trapdoor, but before Professor Schneider had begun to start his story, the doctor stood and said, "That was our signal to return to the tugs. We're shoving off on our return trip to Square Island Harbour." He stepped over to Mr. Webber and asked if he needed any assistance with walking. The inspector shook his head, buttoned his coat, and wrapped his scarf around his neck.

They thanked us for our hospitality and went out into the cold, leaving their bag of provisions with us. The doctor said, "Keep the bag's contents, we have plenty on board."

The professor said, "Thank you. Have a nice return trip. Please sound your horns when you pass by Rocky Point."

We followed the men to their skiff, helped clear off the snow and gave them a shove off from shore. They didn't have far to go, only about forty- or fifty-yards, so the crewman rowed the skiff to the barge. I imagined the outboard motor would have been difficult to start after being exposed to the cold overnight, therefore he didn't attempt to start it.

Jerry asked me, "Did they say why they were leaving so soon?"

I shook my head, but Professor Schneider said, "The sea is calm to the south and there is little wind and no snow. They said the snow we received was a local phenomenon and didn't extend to the south more than half-a-mile."

"How did you get that information?" I asked.

"The crewman had talked with the captains of the tugs and that is what they said last night. They wanted to give Mr. Webber a bit of time to recover before heading south. They planned on leaving today no matter what."

We remained outside about ten minutes watching the tugs move the barge several hundred yards to the west, turn their bows to the south and give a horn blast. We waved, but I doubted anyone on the barge or tugs was watching us. We hustled back for shelter in the tower and to wait for Hannah. Until she arrived, there was no reason to continue diving. We had to have that extra anchor.

I warmed my hands, settled back and started reading Millie's book. Two pages into the first chapter and the professor said, "Let's take a look in the chamber to see if water came in during the storm."

Even though I was a little annoyed that we had to move our belongings from the trapdoor, I thought it was a good idea. If water had gotten into our work area, we would have to bail it out. It would be freezing cold, just what I didn't want to do. I probably wouldn't get to read without interference until I got back to Crafton.

We tossed our stuff in piles on the floor and the professor used his magnet to unlock the door. He lifted the hinged door and shined a beam from his flashlight into the hole. That was the first time I could remember hearing him cuss, "Damn! There must be two hundred liters of ocean water down there." He gave us a scowling look and said, "We have to remove the water and dry our tools and ropes . . . anything that got wet, especially the winch."

Jerry and I took a look and could see water at the bottom of the ladder. Jerry suggested, "What about tossing the water out through the hole we just made to the outside?"

I countered with, "It'll be hard to do that, Jerry, we'd have to toss the water four or five feet to get it through the hole. Half of it would just flow back in. I think we should fill a bucket, lift it up and dump it outside."

"Okay, I'll go down and fill the bucket, you pull it up and dump it. We'll do a few loads and then change places, lifting the bucket is going to be tiring and our feet will get wet and very cold."

I grinned, "Don't fill that five gallon bucket to the top, just half full. Okay? That'll be about twenty pounds of water."

"Right, I wouldn't want to strain your arms."

I joked, "Be careful down there, don't get your feet wet."

"All right . . . gentlemen, no more jokes. Would you get busy and get something accomplished? As soon as Hannah arrives, you will be very busy."

As I hoisted the first bucket, I hoped our promised pay would be worth all this trouble.

CHAPTER 26

Another Schneider Family

I had raised the half-full bucket eight times before Jerry wanted me to take his place. My arms were beginning to feel a little burn, so I agreed. I pulled on my wetsuit, descended the ladder and started scooping up ocean water. I gave a tug on the rope and the half-bucket of water banged into the ladder a couple of times as it rose through the hole in the floor. A minute or so later, the bucket came hurtling down from above for a refill.

At the rate we were removing ocean water, it was going to take us another hour and then more time to dry the tools, maybe another half-hour. I couldn't think of a more boring job to earn money for college tuition. As I scooped up water, my mind wandered. Millie and Carina were probably rising from a warm comfortable bed and getting ready for breakfast. I wondered what Millie looked like when she got up. I had never seen her when she didn't look great, except once, at the time of exiting the upside-down DC-3. But I think that was mostly from shock, fear and being soaking wet.

It was eight o'clock in Crafton when Millie threw back her sheet and covers, opened her door and called to Carina down the hall in the guest bedroom. "Ms. Svensson, time to get up! We have things to accomplish this morning."

A minute later, Carina, fully dressed, stuck her head into Millie's bedroom and said, "I wondered when you would get up. Are we going to eat something? Your parents left for work an hour ago. Do you normally sleep in like this?"

Millie laughed, "Only when I have a guest. When do you normally get up?"

"About five in the morning. I used to milk the cows, gather the eggs, feed the chickens, and water the horses before breakfast. I grew up on a family farm. We moved to the city when I was fourteen."

"Wow. That's an intense but productive morning. I kinda wish I had those experiences. I grew up on boats and in different cities and various oceans all over the world. My parents used to deliver yachts to very rich people. It was fun to see all those places, but I didn't have any real friends until I was ten years old. Rocky was my first real friend, and then Jerry."

"No girl friends?"

"Oh, one or two. I had one here in Crafton, but she moved to Norfolk, Virginia, last year. I had a friend in Manila, but I wasn't there very long, only three months. What about you? You must have friends in Stockholm, haven't you?"

Carina snickered, "They have all gotten married and have started families. I have been travelling for my father for the past two years. I like to travel. I've been to almost every European country, but I have avoided Russia. Jerry said he was born in Russia."

"Yeah, his father was killed in the war by Germans. Mr. Morgan is his stepfather."

"You would never know that. Jerry talks about Mr. Morgan like he is his real dad. Say, are we going to have some breakfast?"

"Sure. Go ahead to the kitchen. I'll be just a minute."

Millie dressed quickly, rushed to the kitchen and found Carina staring at a page in Rhonda's cookbook. "What are you looking for?"

"A recipe for pancakes or is it so simple no one writes it down?"

"Look under hotcakes." Millie got milk and an egg from the fridge, a five-pound bag of flour, already opened, and a large bowl from the cupboard. "It probably says for a dozen, but let's make two-thirds of that."

"Four each? That's too much for me, Millie."

"I always figure one will be burned, so that will make three each, and they won't be very big."

Carina followed the recipe and before long was standing over the stove flipping pancakes. She used all the batter, had two stacks four pancakes high and a big smile as she gave Millie the dinner plate with the hotcakes. She stood over Millie and asked, "Where is the pitcher of reindeer blood?"

Millie was startled for a moment and broke out laughing. "The maple syrup is in the cupboard." She pointed to the shelves to the right of the sink. Millie jumped up and grabbed the butter dish from the countertop. She sat down observing one very dark pancake and three light-brown pancakes on her plate. Using her fork, she pushed the nearly black pancake to the edge of her plate.

Carina had already poured syrup over her stack and had taken a big bite. "I love pancakes!" She waved her fork like a little kid and stabbed it into her pile of hotcakes a second time. Millie took her time, spread butter and syrup on her stack and took a bite just as the phone rang. With her mouth full, she answered on the third ring.

"Hewwo." She swallowed and said, "Hello. Oh, hi Mrs. Makler. Sorry, Carina and I are eating. We'll be over in a-half-hour. Is that all right?" She listened for a moment, said, "Bye" and hung up.

Carina asked, "Did Mrs. Makler say anything about the parchment?"

Millie shook her head and responded, "She didn't want to say anything over the phone, someone might be listening to her conversations."

"Do you think she is paranoid?"

"I don't think so. She's a retiree from a secret service company and is just cautious. She knows all about listening devices and is especially careful when she talks with people at the capital. Rocky says she's still a crack shot with a pistol."

"Are we going to walk to her home?"

"No, it's too far when it's this cold. Let's finish eating and drive over. It's not far from the lighthouse."

Mrs. Makler was waiting at the door for the girls and almost pulled them out of the cold into the house.

"I'll make some hot chocolate for you, then I'll tell you what I have found out about those people in Labrador and Harvard."

Mrs. Makler helped Millie and Carina with their coats and asked them to sit on the sofa. She went in the kitchen for a few minutes and returned with a serving tray containing three mugs of steaming hot chocolate. She sat across from them with her feet on a footstool. She sipped some of her drink and said, "I couldn't get straight information from the feds but Professor Simmonds is being watched by the FBI. He is masquerading as a professor, but he is suspected of being a Russian spy. He came to Harvard from Vancouver, British Columbia."

Millie offered, "He probably came to Canada by way of Alaska and Siberia. Those Russians are a sneaky bunch. They worry about us attacking them but what would we want Russia for, more mouths to feed?"

Carina smiled and said, "I agree with you. They don't seem to realize Communism doesn't work. Freedom and democracy are the best."

Mrs. Makler was nodding her head. "Let me tell you about the Schneider family. They came to Canada in 1937 from the Netherlands, before the war started in 1939. They have a thirteen-year-old daughter named Hannah. She had polio and wears a brace on her left leg. Does that sound like the Hannah you met?"

Millie and Carina were shocked, the Hannah Schneider they knew was approximately thirty years old and looked to be as strong as a bull elephant.

Millie said, "Are you sure, Mrs. Makler? The woman we know as Hannah has no leg brace and is about thirty years old."

Mrs. Makler replied, "I thought there must be some mistake. I wonder where the real Hannah Schneider is. What about Mr. Schneider? Is he tall, nearly bald, overweight and is a retired professor of languages?"

Carina said, "Professor Schneider is tall, has a full head of hair and is an expert with explosives used for mining. He looks to be in very good shape physically and he is mentally sharp."

Millie added, "And Mrs. Schneider is about five-six, chubby and wears glasses."

"That sounds about right for her," said Mrs. Makler. She gave Millie an intense look and said, "I think we should have a talk with your sister and her husband. Jerry Morgan and Rocky might be in some deep water, very deep murky water."

Her telephone gave two short rings and then a normal ring, then was silent. Mrs. Makler slowly rose, got her balance and moved to her phone. She lifted the handset, replaced it and then dialed three numbers. She held the phone to her ear for several seconds and then said, "Ninety-eight."

Millie looked at Carina and grinned, shook her head, shrugged, and whispered, "Telephone code."

The electric wall heater fan and the refrigerator motor were competing with Mrs. Makler's voice, so the girls couldn't hear any of the conversation, but it lasted less than a minute. When Mrs. Makler rejoined the girls, she said, "I have some good news, the legitimate Schneider family has been located in the Bahamas. They are taking a one month vacation."

Carina inquired, "Then who are the people at the Rocky Point lighthouse?"

Mrs. Makler replied, "The Canadian authorities are working on that, but they haven't shown much interest. It's a low priority item as long as the lighthouse is functioning properly and there are no reports of injury."

"Now I'm worried about Rocky and Jerry. What are the imposter Schneiders up to? I don't think it's a coincidence that they are using the Schneiders' names. What are they trying to hide?" Millie glanced at Carina and asked, "Do you think we should have someone travel to the Rocky Point lighthouse to tell Rocky and Jerry what we have discovered?"

Carina frowned, "I wish I could help, but I cannot do anything, Millie. My father wants me to visit two furniture manufacturers, one in Illinois and another in Oregon, then I have to return home. He is sending me more travel money. I am to receive it at the Crafton bank. Where is the bank? I will walk to it."

"You don't need to walk; I'll take you to the bank. Since you have other obligations, I'll get my sister to go with me to Rocky Point. Maybe her husband will be able to go too. I need to have a talk with them anyway, to see if I'm going to be an aunt before long."

The girls thanked Mrs. Makler for her help and told her they would keep her abreast of the developments at the distant lighthouse in Labrador. As they stood on the Makler porch saying goodbye, Mrs. Makler said, "Rocky and Jerry probably don't realize they might be in real danger. Make sure Elena and Aaron are given all the facts about the situation. Have a good day, girls."

Millie responded, "I'll make sure they know everything we've found out. Thank you."

Following a visit to the local bank, where Carina proved her identity and signed two thousand dollars of traveler's checks, the girls went to the Greyhound Bus Terminal. Carina didn't want to impose on the Harrises to drive her to Boston to book a flight to Chicago. She had traveled throughout Europe extensively and was no beginner to bus travel. She was scheduled to leave for Chicago via Greyhound the next morning at ten o'clock.

Shortly after dinner and following dessert at the Harrises', unexpected visitors rang the doorbell. Millie jumped up and ran to the door, anxious to see who was calling. Her initial thoughts were that the Linfields had come with news about Rocky and Jerry. She was surprised to see her sister, Elena, and her brother-in-law, Aaron, carrying luggage and exhibiting gigantic smiles.

"Come in! Come in! I'm so glad you are here. How are you guys?"

Millie almost dragged the Nesbitt couple into the living room, hugging Elena as they entered the foyer. Carina watched as the elder Harrises greeted the couple and took their suitcases. Mr. Harris said, "Carina, this good looking couple of VIPs are Elena and Aaron Nesbitt. I believe you and Millie have much to tell them." He stepped back glancing at his older daughter and her husband as they shook hands with Carina and said, "This young woman is Carina Svensson, from Sweden. She was with Millie, Rocky, and Jerry on the plane that crashed off the coast of Labrador. Her father owns a furniture manufacturing company."

Rhonda asked Elena, "Would you guys like something to eat, some dessert, hot chocolate or coffee?"

Elena responded, "Hot chocolate would be great, but don't go to any trouble." Aaron smiled and said, "Coffee would be fine, Rhonda, black. I take it with one lump."

Millie followed Rhonda into the kitchen and helped prepare the drinks for everyone, five hot chocolates and a coffee with one cube of sugar."

CHAPTER 27

The Nesbitts Arrive

While consuming the beverages, Millie and Carina related everything they knew about the incomplete lighthouse, the two Schneider families, the phony coins and the parchment. It took refills of the chocolate drinks before all the details were covered. Aaron declined a second cup of coffee, he wanted to get a good night's sleep.

When the girls had completed their story, Aaron said, "The coins might have come from the lighthouse construction workers. Perhaps they were used as ante for a card game, something they might have carried in their pockets. I'd like to see the photo of the parchment, though; it sounds interesting but might not have any credibility as evidence of early visitors to North America from Europe."

Carina excused herself for a moment and returned with the photo of the parchment. Aaron studied the photo for a minute or so, examining it from side-to-side and top-to-bottom. He shook his head, scowled, and commented, "I don't think it's old. There's no diffusion along the edge of the markings. It looks more like a kid's doodle. I could be wrong. I assume it could be a signal to someone."

Elena had listened attentively to the girls' tale and was interested in the gold bars the professor had mentioned as payment for his work with the Third Reich. She knew that gold was used during the second world war to finance the war effort, but she suspected that few if any officers were paid with gold.

Perhaps gold confiscated from prisoners or persecuted people could have been used as payment for other activities and might have become available to officers associated with mining. She had been mulling over the ideas as the others were talking. She suddenly became aware of a question from her father; he had been looking outside for their car.

"Elena, how did you and Aaron get here? I don't see a vehicle."

"A friend drove us from Boston. He lives on a farm north of Crafton, just outside of Edgewater. He asked if we wanted to go home, but we decided it would take him even longer to get to his place. So, he dropped us off here. That's why we have luggage with us. Aaron and I need to bum a ride from you or Millie, we were told she drives now."

"I'll take you to your place. Millie is going to help Carina pack for her trip to Chicago tomorrow. Right, Mil?"

"That's right, but you can take the Ford if you want. I'll pick it up early in the morning."

"No thanks, Dad will take us home. I think we should head home; we've had a long day."

Mr. Harris and Aaron carried the suitcases out to the garage while Elena said goodbye to Carina and followed the men. Aaron returned to the living room to say goodbye to the Harrises' guest and gave Carina his best wishes for her continuing trip.

Mr. Harris drove Aaron and Elena to Aaron's old home, which had been temporarily owned by the Harrises and next door to Mrs. Makler. Aaron had purchased his old home from the Harrises when it was vacant after the Harrises bought the big house on the hill where they currently live. It was rented out by the month to vacationers while Elena and Aaron rented near Washington. Mrs. Makler took care of the property when the Nesbitts were in the capital. It was usually vacant from November through February, so Elena and Aaron used it on occasion when they got away from the seat of government during the winter.

Elena's dad stayed with the young couple for a few minutes to make sure they were settled and returned home. Elena and Aaron discussed their views of the story Millie and Carina had told them earlier. After turning up the heat, changing the sheets and unpacking, Elena checked to see if Mrs. Makler's lights were still on. They were, so she put on her jacket and hurried next door.

Elena jumped the three steps to the porch and reached for the doorbell, but before her forefinger could press the button, the door flew open. Mrs. Makler was pulling on her coat and coming outside.

Both women blurted out, "Oh!" and took a step back from the doorway.

Mrs. Makler said, "Elena! I was just coming over to see if it was you and Aaron. I saw the lights come on a short time ago but I hadn't been notified of any new tenants. I was hoping it was you."

Elena stepped closer and said, "I came over to tell you that Aaron and I have time off for Thanksgiving and we're going to take a short fishing trip up north before the holiday. We'll be leaving early in the morning. How would you like to come over for a few minutes? We can bring each other up to date on recent events."

"Well, only if your house is warm. My rooms are nice and comfy. Why don't you two come over here while your furnace does its work."

"Uh, all right, that sounds good. I'll get Aaron. Be right back." Elena jumped to the ground and sprinted across the lawn separating the two homes.

Mrs. Makler thought, 'I wish I were that flexible and could move that fast. Getting old is no fun at all.' She stepped back from the door waiting for Elena and Aaron to appear on the porch. She wanted to ask the couple where they were going to fish, she knew of some good spots at lakes, rivers and along the coast of Maine. She and her husband had investigated most of northern Maine when they were younger.

The professor, Jerry and I waited all day for Hannah to show up with the extra anchor but she never arrived. We were anxious to locate the little submarine and recover the gold bars. Jerry and I had two goals in mind, get paid for our efforts and head back to Crafton for a warmer environment though still winter weather. We were getting tired of constant exposure to the freezing north winds, cold hands and feet, and plagued with the uncertainty of hidden dangers of diving in frigid waters. It was difficult to not think of a warm bed and homecooked meals.

As soon as the sun disappeared in the west, we began our usual preparation for dinner in the lighthouse. The professor said we were on our own and could select anything from the groceries we were given by the barge crew. But before we opened any cans of food, Professor Schneider had another task for us. We were asked to inspect the below ground floor to see if any more water had accumulated in the cavern, so, armed with flashlights, we went below and checked for seepage or spray blown in from the ocean waves. Fortunately, there had been little wind all day. Therefore, we didn't expect to see any accumulation of water on the irregular rocky floor.

When we reached the bottom of the ladder, I asked, "See any water, Jer?" We scanned our flashlight beams around and except for traces of moisture we hadn't been able to get into buckets, I didn't see anything new.

Jerry answered, "Nope. Let's get out of here, it's colder down here than it is outside."

We shut off our lights, climbed the ladder to the ground level of the lighthouse and closed the trapdoor. Professor Schneider was eating something from a metal bowl and he paused to look at us.

"Any more water down there?"

I answered, "No sir, nothing new. It's just as we left it."

"Good. You'd better get something to eat and go to bed. Hannah should be here tomorrow after it is light enough to navigate safely. I hope we will locate the submarine by noon tomorrow."

Jerry sorted through the dozen or so metal cans and picked out two cans for dinner: mixed vegetables and chicken noodle soup. We alternated cooking and it was his turn. As he opened one of the cans he whispered, "He always says we when you and I are doing all the work. He's gonna get most of the benefit."

"I just want to finish the job and get the hell out of here. I'm tired of living on this piece of rock. This sure isn't my idea of camping, either. I'm starting to wonder if half of what he says is true."

Jerry and I had a hot meal, which I guess was better than expected, burned our used paper plates and got ready for bed. As I lay in my sleeping bag, I hoped Hannah would show up and we could find the sub and the gold bars. I didn't want to waste another day freezing my butt off.

What I expected to be another routine day started at six o'clock. The professor was punctual; I can say that was one of his favorable traits. The odor of coffee greeted my cold nostrils. Jerry and I built a small fire in our old fireplace to burn up some of the accumulating garbage and cooked some oatmeal with strawberry jelly left by the barge crew. Only one can remained of the donated provisions, a large metal can of corn. A picture of an ear of corn decorated the label.

The professor donned his heavy coat and went outside. I watched him walk south for a few moments before I returned to check out our diving gear with Jerry.

Jerry asked me, "Where did Schneider go?"

"He's walking to the other end of the island, probably watching for Hannah."

After twenty minutes or so, Dr. Schneider returned, futzed around with his notebook and ate something, then went back to walk again.

Jerry and I puttered around for at least an hour before the professor came back and suggested we get into our wetsuits. I had read another chapter from Millie's book while the professor was gone. I used my flashlight when reading and removed my gloves to turn pages. I was getting so frustrated with our inactivity, I didn't care if the batteries ran down.

Jerry and I helped each other slither into our suits and attach weights that would allow us to drop to sixty feet or even deeper if we adjusted our buoyancy further. We hoped forty feet would be as deep as we would have to descend. We would see.

We all heard the engine on the cabin cruiser at about the same time. Schneider said, "Hannah's here, boys. Let's get the rope attached to the spare anchor and show her where to drop it."

I checked with Jerry for any comments, but he shook his head indicating he had nothing to say. We followed Schneider outside into bright sunlight and not a whisper of wind. The boat was approaching slowly from the west and Hannah was waving her right arm. The professor indicated the boat should come closer and I could hear the engine noises come in spurts as the distance from the boat to shore lessened. When the vessel was ten feet from the rocks, Hannah silenced the engine, the bow drifting another few feet before striking bottom. Hannah tossed a line to Jerry and he held the boat stationary.

Professor Schneider called out to me, "Get one of those coils of rope and throw it to me. I'm going on board to position the boat and drop the anchor where the sub is." Schneider stepped into the water holding onto Jerry's line, the water extending a bit past his knees. Hannah gave him a hand and he clambered aboard The Commuter with some difficulty.

While Jerry kept the boat steady, I hustled to the lighthouse floor and picked up a hundred foot coil of rope. When I got back to The Commuter, I saw the professor waiting, so I used a discus throw and tossed the rope. I was surprised when the professor caught the coil without stumbling and falling overboard. He yelled at Jerry, "Release the line and watch when I drop the anchor east of the lighthouse."

We walked about forty yards to the other side of the island east of the lighthouse to observe the spot where the professor estimated the probable site of the sub. We had a short wait before The Commuter came rapidly around the northern tip of the island and moved closer to shore. The boat jockeyed position and after a minute or so, I saw the professor shove the anchor over the side.

I imagined the professor's hands were going to be sore by the time the anchor hit bottom. The rope was being let out slowly as the heavy weight dropped from the boat. I should have warned him to wear gloves. Too late now. He probably wouldn't have paid attention anyway, I'm a peon.

It looked like about half the rope was remaining when it suddenly went slack, but I estimated The Commuter was still eighty to ninety feet offshore; the rope was too short. I guess at least another twenty to thirty feet would be necessary to reach the winch through the hole we had knocked in the cavity wall. As if he heard what I was thinking, the professor yelled, "I need more rope, this coil won't make it to shore."

Jerry gave me a crazy look and said, "We can't throw a hundred foot coil of rope that far, it's too damn heavy and I'm not gonna swim it out to him."

I had the same assessment and I had an idea. If I took a hundred feet of rope to the top of the lighthouse and unraveled about half, I envisioned tossing the fifty foot coil about ten yards, enough distance to get to the boat if it came as close to land as the anchor rope would allow. I mentioned what I was considering to Jerry and he thought a moment, "Yeah, that should work. Good thinking, Rock. Do you think he knows how to tie a sailor's square knot?"

I replied, "If he doesn't, we might have to retie the ropes underwater."

CHAPTER 28

Finding the Sub

I couldn't climb to the top of the lighthouse in a wetsuit, so I took it off and dressed in my regular clothes, but without my heavy jacket. I had to have mobility. Jerry had prepared the second coil of rope for me, tying it into two connected coils with pieces of twine from our original boxes of equipment. Luckily, we hadn't burned the short lengths of cord.

The professor couldn't see me climbing to the top of the tower and I heard him yell at Jerry, "What is the problem? Where is Rocky?"

Jerry yelled back, "He's at the top of the lighthouse. He will throw you more rope."

The toss went as planned. The coil of rope twisted through the air and landed on the bow of The Commuter with a loud thump. Fortunately, the professor didn't have to catch the rope, it might have knocked him down or maybe off the boat. As soon as I saw the professor untying the coil, I dropped the loose end to Jerry and returned to ground level.

With my wetsuit back on, I exited the lighthouse and asked my buddy, "Where did The Commuter go? Are they going to the west side?"

"The professor didn't say anything. He dropped the rope into the water and the boat backed away and went north. I assume they're coming around to let him off. It's quieter on the western shore and is shallower." Jerry chuckled, "You know that."

A few minutes later, we heard the engine and the boat came into view with Hannah at the helm, as usual. As The Commuter approached the rocks, the professor threw us a line and we pulled the boat to shore. He waved at us and called out, "We have some things to unload."

Jerry passed the line to me and waded into hip-deep water to receive a medium size wooden box that I guessed by Jerry's grimace to weigh about thirty or more pounds. He carried the box away from the water and set it down beside me. He said, "There's another one, about the same size. I think the crates are full of canned food. I hope they don't have plans to keep us here more than a week." He sloshed back to the boat and carried the second box to shore.

When the professor joined us, he turned toward the boat and waved to Hannah after throwing her the bow line. The boat backed away, turned and Hannah gunned the engine and accelerated, leaving a small rooster tail wake trailing from the stern.

Professor Schneider didn't take any time watching the boat speeding south. He said, "Let's get these crates into the lighthouse. I hope you boys are ready to dive." Jerry and I each grabbed a box and moved the crates to the floor next to the propane stove. Schneider was watching us and said, "Have you got the rope passed through the hole into the cavern?"

I forced a quick, short laugh, a bit irritated, "Hardly. Have you any idea how to do that?" Jerry and I had talked about the problem, we knew our arms weren't long enough to reach the rope through the hole in the rocks. We needed something or someone to grab the rope through the opening in the rock wall.

Jerry whispered to me, "One of us is going to get wet and feed the rope from the outside."

I whispered back, "Yeah."

Schneider asked, "Where is the free end of the rope now?"

Jerry answered, "It's looped around a rock at the base of the lighthouse. Rock or I will have to feed it through the opening so you can attach it to the winch."

I informed Schneider, "We enter the water together for safety, the buddy system. You will have to pull the line through the opening and fasten it to the winding spool."

Jerry finished my next thoughts to Schneider, "When the line is taut we will follow it to the anchor and locate the sub. We'll give two tugs on the rope to let you know we've found your craft. Then you'll have to give us some slack so we can attach it. We'll signal again and you can start pulling in the sub. We'll stay with it so it doesn't get tangled on anything."

I had to give one last instruction, "It the winding stops, don't pull any more, the rope might break and one of us could get injured. Let us fix the fouled line. We'll signal when it is cleared."

The professor agreed, "All right, I will go below and wait."

Jerry and I completed dressing for the dive, checked our air supplies and entered the water together. Now we were dependent on hand signals, but underwater, we were following our prearranged actions and functioned as an integrated unit. It was much like our training dives back at the wharf in Crafton.

Jerry had secured the rope so the twine was easily removed. Once we had ten feet of the free end in our hands we had to bob up from the surface and insert the rope through the opening in the wall. We were able to push two yards of the loose end of rope through the opening before we felt the professor pulling on the line. We waited about a minute before we could see the line disappearing into the cavern at a rapid rate. We assumed he was using the winch. So far, the professor had followed our instructions.

I motioned to Jerry to start following the rope down to the anchor. The current wasn't strong enough for us to have difficulty since we grasped the line as we descended to thirty feet. When the seeing became difficult, our lights illuminated the anchor, but the submarine was still out of sight. At least we had a fixed location where we could begin searching.

I motioned to Jerry to let the current take us south, so we released our holds on the rope and drifted away from the anchor. Jerry saw it first. The nose of the sub was pointed at the lighthouse and at thirty five feet but had rolled about ten yards from our rope line. It was bigger than I originally imagined, nearly three feet tall and longer than the Harrises' Pontiac.

Jerry pointed toward the anchor and we swam back to the rope and jerked it twice. It slackened immediately. I held the light so Jerry could undo the square knot. When I saw the knot, my respect for the professor slightly increased, he knew how to tie a line so it wouldn't slip. Jerry had the line removed from the anchor easily, despite the rope being wet and having been stretched by the anchor's weight. As he was untying the rope, I saw his air was getting close to the red line, so I motioned toward the surface. He nodded and we started up. I figured Schneider was going to be pissed.

Near the surface, we removed our swim fins and walked ashore toward the lighthouse. Schneider met us at the entrance, hands raised up, scowling, "What is the problem!?"

I exhaled through pursed lips and said, "We're out of air."

The professor paused a moment and relaxed, "Oh, I forgot to tell you, the crate with the blue tag contains more fully charged cylinders. There should be enough for you to complete your job. How does the sub look?"

I answered, "It's bigger than I thought, but our initial quick inspection didn't show any damage."

Jerry added a little humor, "It looks like an upside down pregnant torpedo."

The professor turned and went inside. We followed and watched as he pried open the two crates. The first one opened was full of canned goods, the second had four small bottles of compressed air and some small cans numbered one through four. I wondered what those contained but didn't bother to ask. I just grabbed two of the compressed air supply bottles.

I gave one bottle to Jerry and he removed the empty from my back and installed the full one; I did the same for him. We were ready to return to the sub and attach the line to the bow ring. I wondered if the rope was strong enough to withstand the force the winch would exert on the sub. I told that to Jerry as we got ready to dive.

He mentioned something I hadn't noticed, "That sub hasn't been underwater fifteen years, it's too clean. I'll bet it hasn't been in the ocean more than a year or two."

I thought momentarily and replied, "You know, I think you're right."

We moved through the water to the rope, grabbed on and let the current carry us to the submersible. We inserted the line through the metal ring at the nose of the torpedo-like craft, tied it securely and gathered in the slack until it looked straight toward the lighthouse. I gave two mighty tugs for the professor to start pulling the sub toward shallower depths and the rope started moving, rapidly at first and then more slowly as the slack vanished. We kept our lights on the sub as it started to move against the current, the bottom sand rising into a small cloud but drifting away and partly hiding the sub from our light beams. I was surprised the rope didn't break.

Maybe since our efforts were paying off we were feeling stronger, but without much effort, we swam against the current, keeping our eyes on the rope and the sub. As the strange looking underwater craft skidded slowly across the sandy rock-strewn bottom, the sounds from metal scraping the rocks made me nervous. I expected the rope to break at any minute. Jerry and I stayed far enough removed from the taut line so if it did break, the ends wouldn't hit us.

After a couple of minutes, we doused our lights. The sub had been pulled into shallower water, but the sandy bottom had diminished and was rockier. Although it was only five more minutes, it seemed longer, maybe because I expected something tragic to happen any second. Perhaps that anxious feeling originated from the metal on rock scraping noises. I don't remember being worried for so long when underwater.

Jerry signaled when our depth was at ten feet and I struck the rope twice, hoping the professor felt the signal and stopped the winch. Fortunately, the professor had reacted correctly. I stayed with the sub and Jerry surfaced. I was getting more nervous as time passed, but all of a sudden Jerry returned with a cylinder of compressed air. At first, I thought it was for me but he shook his head and pointed at the sub. He showed me a screwdriver and mimed opening a tin can.

I nodded and we found a small panel held in place with four screws. I removed the screws as Jerry watched. It was slow going, but the panel fell off and drifted to the rocks below after I removed the last screw. Jerry had me move away from the opening and inserted a small diameter, two-meter-long hose attached to the cylinder. He opened the valve and we waited, as we swam against the current which had lessened closer to shore and nearer the surface. I noticed a few tiny bubbles escaping from the hull of the sub and motioned to Jerry. He nodded. He had seen the same thing.

I moved to the nose where the rope was tied and put my hand on the blue-gray painted metal surface. I occasionally used my fins to hold my position but wanted to feel the instant the sub began to rise. My analysis of the situation wasn't good. If the rope broke and the sub sank back to the bottom, it might crush Jerry. Just as I dismissed the possibility, the sub rose about a foot and then kept moving upward toward the surface. The bulge must have completely filled with air, expelling most of the water.

We went up with the ugly looking craft and broke the surface almost simultaneously. When Jerry's head came above water, he pulled off his facemask and called out, "Get another line on the tail end and pull it onto the rocks, I'll keep air flowing so it doesn't sink."

As I ripped off my fins and facemask, and stepped out of the water, I realized the only other rope we had was wound around the spool on the winch. I had to get to it fast. I hoped Schneider had a knife handy. I realized I had my diver's knife strapped to my leg and had to chuckle.

I almost slid down the ladder and yelled at the professor, "We need some rope, fast!" He gave me a dumb look and pointed at the coil in the winch. "It is wrapped tightly. There is no loose rope."

I flipped the winch lock lever and pulled ten feet of the wound rope out, cut it off and tied it to the winch to hold the sub in place. Then, I unwrapped another forty- to fifty-feet of wet line and hacked it off. I coiled it quickly and went up the ladder.

CHAPTER 29

Gold Bars

Jerry was standing in the water beside the sub holding the gas cylinder and said, "What took you so long, Rock?" We both started laughing and I tossed a length of the coiled rope to him. I estimated the sub was about half above the water so attaching the line near the propellor would be easy. Jerry tied the rope to the tail end and I began to pull the craft toward shallower water as Jerry removed his fins and walked ashore.

Jerry turned off the air flowing from the cylinder and dropped the container beside me. He said, "It's almost empty." He could see I was struggling with the rope, so he grabbed on and we wrestled the sub close enough to shore to reach the interior.

The professor approached us carrying a hammer and a metal rod about a foot long. Without a word, he knelt and pounded the rod into a groove in the rocks. We understood the rod's purpose, made a small loop in the rope and pulled the line tight to the metal post to keep the sub in position.

The professor asked, "Do you have the screwdriver?"

I nodded, pulled it from my belt and gave it to him. Jerry and I were surprised when he stepped in the water and began removing screws below the hump. He tossed five screws to the rocks at our feet before getting out of the foot-deep water. Then he said, "Your turn, Rocky," and gave me the screwdriver.

I assumed I was to remove screws from the other side in deeper water, so I waded in and swung my legs over the nose rope. It was obvious which screws to remove. When I had thrown the fifth screw over the sub, the professor said, "That is enough. Now we must lift the projected portion free. Pass me the screwdriver."

I wasn't sure if I should toss it to him, so I said, "Catch, Jerry," and flipped the implement to my buddy.

The professor gave me a little scowl and said, "Well, all right. Jerry, insert the screwdriver into the back hole and lift. It will be tight."

I couldn't see what Jerry was doing, but when I saw a grimace, I noticed the bulge rising away from the body of the sub, so I lifted the closest edge and the bulge swung up like a car hood hinged at the front. The interior looked cramped; the professor would have been very uncomfortable crammed into such a restricted space. I noticed the escape mechanism at the top of the extended bulge cover, only accessible from the interior. I couldn't see any gold bars. Was the professor's assertion a hoax?

Jerry scanned the interior of the sub and said, "I don't see any gold bars." We glanced at the professor. He smiled and commented, "The bars are out of sight at the bottom. There is a metal plate that slides forward. If you can reach them, hand them to me."

Since Jerry was a foot higher than I was, it was easier for him to reach into the sub and slip the light sheet metal forward about half-a-foot. A dozen shiny metal bars, each imprinted with a small swastika were arranged in a three by four array. Jerry and I looked at each other in disbelief, our suspicions were wrong, the professor had told the truth.

Professor Schneider gave us some instructions, "Remove the bars two at a time and put them in the lighthouse in the same orientation they have in the submarine, a three by four array. I like them in that order, they are easy to keep track of. Do not drop them, I want them as they were prepared, no dents or scratches."

I thought his request was a bit strange, but Jerry picked up two of the gold bars and headed for the lighthouse. I went to the other side of the craft, picked up two more bars and followed Jerry. As I carried the gold, I had a sudden thought, I wondered if the bars were made of pure gold or some type of alloy. The shiny gold-colored metal might not be pure gold. It wouldn't surprise me if the Third Reich compensated the lower officers with something cheaper than pure gold. When Jerry and I passed outside the lighthouse, I mentioned the idea of an alloy.

He said quickly, "I had the same idea, Rock. How can we tell?

"We'll talk later."

When we finished moving the metal bars to the lighthouse, the professor told us to cut the lines and push the sub back into deeper ocean water. I felt like objecting to adding junk to the ocean, but kept my mouth shut. As we followed instructions, Jerry commented, "I hope this is getting near the end of our job. What else are we going to do?"

I said, "I'd like to get paid and return to Crafton. Isn't Thanksgiving next week?"

Jerry replied, "I don't know. I've lost track of the date and the day of the week."

The professor met us as we pulled the metal tie-down rod from between the rocks. We had to kick it several times to get it loose.

"The next thing I would like you to do is bring everything up from the cavern . . . and I mean everything."

We considered it an order, not a request, so changed out of our wetsuits into our normal clothing. It felt good to have shoes on again.

I didn't know what the professor was going to do while Jerry and I cleaned out the cavern and I was surprised when he came down with us and began dismantling the winch. He wound the rope around the spool first and then asked us for the appropriate tools, a hammer and a wrench.

I started to move the tool chest to the ladder and decided it was going to be awkward carrying it up the ladder with one hand while gripping the ladder with the other. It was too heavy. I dumped the contents out and repacked the chest with half the tools. My decision required me to make two trips.

Jerry helped the professor load the winch parts into the original bags. The sackss stunk from being in the water and never really drying out. I was familiar with decaying kelp that washed up along the rocks below the Crafton lighthouse; the bags had a similar odor. As they worked on the winch, I took the heavy hammer and the rock drills up. I thought of measuring one of the gold bars, but it wasn't obvious where they were. The professor must have moved them. I didn't want to rummage through his things.

The batteries were next and then the half-bicycle. I had to take it apart, but that was easy. All I did was take off the rear wheel and pulley, the frame was constructed of cheap metal, not made for extended use. The generator was heavy, so it required a separate trip. I carried the bike pieces up and piled them out of the way of our normal living areas.

Jerry and the professor lugged the damp canvas bags loaded with metal winch parts to the base of the ladder. The professor started up the rungs and told us to finish cleaning out the cavern. I grabbed one of the bags, Jerry the other and we pulled them up to the lighthouse floor. The last thing remaining was the wiring and lights. The only illumination below was from the open trapdoor but I remembered the locations of the lights. I coiled the wires, put the bulbs in my pockets and climbed the ladder in near darkness the last time.

When I appeared at the top of the ladder, the professor inquired, "Is that everything?"

I nodded and said, "Yes sir, it's completely empty."

I was surprised when he said, "Good job. You fellows have earned your payment." I hadn't expected him to say anything.

Jerry was quick to ask, "Do we get paid with gold bars?"

Schneider didn't answer immediately. He just stared at Jerry and then shifted his glare to me. "No, I will pay you with American dollars. They will be arriving in a short time." He turned away and began moving toward the door but suddenly did an about-face, almost like a practiced military move, and came back a few steps. "Do you think those girls delivered the parchment photograph to Professor Simmonds?"

I knew Millie would have delivered the photo almost as soon as she arrived in Boston, since the Harvard Campus was only twenty minutes away from the airport by taxi. I answered, "Millie and Carina probably reached Boston the day after leaving here, so I'm sure Professor Simmonds saw it then."

"You are sure about that?"

I glanced at Jerry and he gave me a thumbs up. I said, "We're sure. We've known Millie for the last seven years. She's highly dependable."

Schneider reversed direction again and went outside where the sky was turning gray.

I looked at Jerry and said, "I wonder what that was all about?"

He shrugged, "I don't know, Rock, but it has me thinking."

"Yeah, me too. Why would Hannah be bringing two grand in dollars up here? Wouldn't the Schneiders pay us when we returned to Rocky Point?"

Jerry nodded in agreement, "And what is so important about Millie delivering the parchment picture to that professor guy at Harvard?"

We stood there pondering for a few seconds and Jerry said, "I'm goin' outside to get some fresh air, the sun's going down. It'll be dark in half an hour."

I wasn't tired and aside from talking with Jerry in near darkness, evenings in the lighthouse were not entertaining. I really wanted to read more of Millie's book. Since I had dismantled the cavern lights less than an hour ago, I felt I could reassemble the bicycle generator and have good lighting to read by tonight. In less than fifteen minutes I had the system working. When the professor and Jerry returned, I surprised them with the bright lighthouse interior.

Professor Schneider didn't comment but Jerry grinned and said, "Good idea, Rock, now we can stay up until midnight."

Schneider cleared his throat, "That I do not recommend."

I was glad to have the lights working for reading and it was going to be a welcome change from the usual, having to eat dinner in the dark. Who knew what was contained in the those cans we opened? We read the labels with the aid of flashlights, but there were no guarantees.

When the professor began cooking his dinner, I mounted the bike seat and began pedaling to charge the batteries to give us lights. Surprisingly, Schneider acknowledged my efforts and waved to me, although I was only ten feet away. He didn't speak.

I continued the stationary ride while Jerry cooked our dinner, spaghetti and meatballs. While I pumped the pedals, I read more of Millie's book, starting another chapter. I was getting to an interesting part when Jerry called out, "Come and get it! Get off your seat and come eat."

I chuckled and tried to think of something that rhymed but couldn't come up with anything. As I marked my place in the book, I thought of Millie and Carina, wondering what they were doing. Maybe they were out shopping for a turkey.

Half a can of spaghetti and meatballs wasn't enough for me, so I made a peanut butter sandwich and had some coffee. Jerry joined me with coffee and we talked about the girls. We were both anxious to get back home to eat real meals and sleep in our own beds. We assumed Carina would still be staying with Millie. Jerry wanted to double date and maybe spend a day in Boston before Carina left.

It must have been about nine o'clock when we decided to turn out the dimming lights. The professor hit the sack about an hour earlier after doing some calculations. We didn't know what he was figuring. Whatever it was, when finished he put his pencil in his zippered notebook and stuck what might be a diary in his sleeping bag. Obviously, the writings were private.

I was awakened by the sounds of a motor and it took me a moment to figure out it was from a boat. We had slept in . . . even the professor, but we all dressed quickly. It was a quarter after eight. I turned on the lights, even though they were dim. The batteries needed more charging, they didn't have much capacity. We didn't bother going to the door to greet visitors. It couldn't be Hannah, the engine noise was completely different, higher pitched. So, we just waited to hear a knock on the door. I imagined inviting them into our luxury apartment and had to laugh as I climbed on the bike seat.

CHAPTER 30

Partial Payment

The lights brightened as I pedaled and Jerry came over and stood beside me. "Who do you think that might be?" he asked.

I shook my head and replied, "If it's not Hannah, I haven't a clue. What do you think?"

He shrugged, saying, "Someone bringing our money?"

I guess Jerry was a better businessman than I was. He was probably correct. We'd find out before long. How long would it take for visitors to tie up and come ashore? I kept pedaling for at least five minutes before someone pounded on the lighthouse door.

The professor got up from sitting on his sleeping bag and walked to the entrance. When he moved slowly toward the door, I quit pedaling and got off the bike seat. When the door opened, Jerry and I heard, "Are you Professor Schneider?"

"Yes, yes. Come in."

I saw a blond-haired, fairly tall man, six feet or more, and a woman, five or six inches shorter, both dressed as if they were on an Arctic expedition. The tall guy had a crooked nose, like it had been broken in a fight. Schneider was leading them into the lighthouse and introduced Jerry as Stanley Bafus and me as Richard Gordon. I was surprised that Schneider remembered those names, I had trouble recalling them. Those were the names we were to use if the crewmen from the barge asked our names. I didn't know if Jerry had forgotten his assumed name.

The professor broke the silence, "These people are Mr. and Mrs. Clarence Atwater. They are here to pay me for the gold bars."

Clarence had a handshake like a limp rag and his wife's wasn't much better. It was almost like they had never shaken hands with anyone before. I guess they weren't aware of the impression it created.

I asked Mrs. Atwater her name and she said, "Gloria," and smiled. Then she said, "My middle name is Bea, so I go by Glory Bee, Bee like in honeybee." and tittered. "You probably go by Dick; Richard is so pedestrian." She forced another smile and brushed her long black hair from her right cheek over her ear to reveal a dark mole near her earlobe. It resembled an unattractive earring. I noticed her face was misshapen, her left cheek bulged out like she had an infected tooth or something similar.

"No, Richard or Rick, but not Dick." I knew I did not care for this woman, the Atwaters were a strange pair and I hadn't even talked with Glory Bee's husband. He appeared okay, was very quiet and had a dead fish handshake. I wondered how they became couriers. But I would keep my opinions to myself until they were gone. Jerry and I would have a big laugh, he usually had thoughts similar to mine.

The professor ushered the Atwater couple to the propane stove and asked if they would like some coffee. He followed up with, "We have sugar, but no milk or cream, sorry." Then he asked Jerry and me to join them. I had mounted the bike seat and was pedaling to keep the lights at full brightness.

Jerry joined them and Schneider nodded to me that I should stay where I was. I was less than ten feet away, so I could clearly hear the conversation.

Schneider inquired abruptly, "How much did you bring me?"

Mr. Atwater answered, "Ten thousand." That's when I noticed the scar from his hairline across his left eyebrow to his eyelid. I wondered if he had been in a knife fight or had a car accident of some sort. Perhaps I would never know, I would probably never see the Atwaters again.

Professor Schneider became angry and shouted, "That is less than half of what Professor Simmonds agreed to! I will only sell four of the bars for ten thousand. He promised me twenty-five. You should know that!"

"Simmonds told us to make the payment immediately, but we couldn't get twenty-five thousand without arousing suspicion. We decided to bring what we could get. If you can prove the genuineness of the material, we will come back with the other fifteen thousand. However, we would like to meet at the Rocky Point Lighthouse. It is more convenient there," said Mr. Atwater.

Professor Schneider sat quietly staring at the roof of the lighthouse for about fifteen seconds before saying, "All right. I will show you." He got to his feet and went to the table where his various instruments were kept. He returned with the yellow gadget Jerry thought was a radiation detector. He said, "You boys stay here." He motioned to the Atwaters, "Come with me."

Schneider and the Atwaters went outside. Jerry and I followed to the door but just watched. We stayed inside the tower as the professor had asked.

I was amused and stated, "So he hid the gold bars where we couldn't find them."

Jerry remarked, "I can't believe he worried that we might steal some of them. Where would we take them? We're stuck on Crescent Island with no way off."

I grinned, "We could swim to the mainland in our wetsuits."

Jerry looked at me, frowned and said, "You're full of it, Rock."

We couldn't see what was going on, but they were huddled together about fifty yards from us. The professor was on his knees, the Atwaters standing. They remained in that position for nearly a minute, maybe longer, before Mr. Atwater reached down and helped the professor to his feet. Apparently the Professor handed Atwaters gold bars and they started back to the lighthouse.

Jerry and I waited next to the propane stove where I said, "I wonder if they paid Schneider for the gold?"

"We'll know soon. If he doesn't get some money, he's gonna get pissed off. Think of all the trouble he has been through." Jerry was right, Schneider had gone through a lot to secure his gold.

The Atwaters and Schneider came in the lighthouse and gathered at the stove. The professor turned on one burner and they warmed their hands. The professor commented, "Those boys have done a lot of work, pay them first, one thousand each. I will take the remainder."

We were close enough to see the stack of hundred dollar bills come from Mr. Atwater's inner coat pocket. I couldn't keep my eyes off that pile of money, a hundred one-hundred dollar bills. Clarence counted off ten of them and handed the little stack to his wife, who stepped closer to Jerry and counted them out into Jerry's palm of his right hand. I could tell he had never gotten that much money before. He seemed frozen in place as if his heart had stopped beating and he had turned to stone.

I was next. I swallowed hard as she started counting the bills in a harsh but quiet voice, nearly a whisper: one, white; two, from; three, the; four, right; five, if; six, you; seven, want; eight, to; nine, fight; ten. She quickly moved her right index finger to her lips and stepped away from me. I was being overloaded with the sight of ten one-hundred dollar bills and a rhyme only one other person I knew would be aware of, Elena Harris Nesbitt! She had taught me the rhyme when I was ten years old. I recalled the second line: black from the back if you want to attack. That was when I had white and black marbles to shoot with my slingshot.

I was about to explode but I couldn't tell Jerry who Mrs. Atwater really was until we were alone. I could hardly wait. He might not believe me. I was having a hard time believing Glory Bee was Elena, her disguise was so good. If she hadn't said those words, I would never have recognized her. Mr. Atwater must be Aaron, Elena's husband, Lieutenant Nesbitt a navy veteran. His appearance was significantly altered, too, and I couldn't recognize their voices, either. I wondered how they altered their speech, maybe with a drug.

The Atwaters were buttoning up their coats while Schneider counted the stack of hundreds. When he reached eighty, the Atwaters were about to exit the lighthouse. Clarence said, "We'll be back with the rest of the money in four days, as long as the weather holds. We'll deliver the funds to Rocky Point, so be sure you are there."

"Don't worry, I'll be there, along with my wife and daughter."

The professor's last comment bothered me. He hadn't included Jerry and me being at Rocky Point. But then I thought about Elena and Aaron. Would they be leaving to get more money to pay for the rest of the gold or stick around.

We followed the Atwaters out to their boat, The Ocean Wave, and watched them climb aboard. They had forced the boat onto the shoreline, so it must have a sturdy bottom. It was a sleek looking cabin cruiser painted an aqua color and flying a Canadian flag. The craft backed off the rocks about twenty feet and turned south. Glory Bee waved as they gradually picked up speed. They were out of sight in a couple of minutes. Jerry and I watched them leave but Schneider went back into the lighthouse. I wondered what was next for us.

We slowly walked toward the tower. After taking a couple of steps, I said, "Did you recognize the Atwaters?"

"Nope. Never saw them before. He had a wimpy handshake, didn't he?"

"They're friends of ours, Jer. The Atwaters are Elena and Aaron Nesbitt."

"You're crazy, Rock. Your mind is playing tricks on you. We've been on this crappy island too long."

"Believe me, Jer. Glory Bee recited part of a rhyme Elena and I had back in the Bahamas seven years ago. No one else would know that. I know it's her, it has to be."

When we were a few yards from the entrance, Schneider came out and asked me, "What did Mrs. Atwater say to you when she counted out your money? I heard her say something, what was it?"

I had figured he might ask about it so I had something prepared. I looked him in the eyes and said, "She told me I should only use the money for education."

He must have believed me. I was relieved when he nodded, turned away and went back inside the tower. When Jerry and I entered the lighthouse, the professor gave us new instructions, "I want to repack all the boxes from Rocky Point, except for the food. Don't waste any space in the boxes. Don't bother with the parts to the winch, they should remain in the burlap sacks."

We had to ask about some of the items. Did he want the gas cylinders packed? The answer was no. He told us to just leave them loose. They would be tossed into the boat after the boxes were loaded.

I wondered when Hannah was returning to transport the accumulation of items on the floor of the lighthouse. I heard Jerry inquire, "How do Rocky and I pack our things? We don't have much."

"Keep your belongings separate. We will hand carry them. Hannah should be back later today. We will begin loading when she gets here with Sunny."

Jerry commented as we began packing one of the boxes with various articles that aligned like puzzle pieces so little dead space remained. It was a challenge to get as much in each box as possible, almost like attempting to get ten pounds of flour in a five pound bag. The professor watched us move around searching for just the right items to fill the available spaces. When the first box was full, he said, "You will need small box labeled with number four to complete that job."

I remembered box number four was labelled poison in capital letters and reminded Jerry, "That's the one with poison written on it."

We scanned the area for the container but didn't see it. The professor said, "It is over here."

He pointed at the four small containers next to his sleeping bag. We never went near his personal belongings before, expecting a lecture about intruding on one's personal space. I ventured over to the can and was surprised at its weight. I cautiously lifted the lid and discovered it was full of nails. I chuckled and called to Jerry, "It's filled with nails."

He smiled and said, "Bring a hammer, the smaller one. We'll close this box up tight."

We filled two more boxes but realized we had way too many items to pack. The professor had gotten off his duff and helped us finish off the third box. The cooking apparatus and canned goods were yet to be packed, but since the professor was ignoring those objects we concluded we would be having at least one more meal on Crescent Island. That turned out to be correct.

After we had eaten, Hannah and Sunny showed up and backed the cabin cruiser to within four feet of the shore. Sunny jumped off and secured the boat while Hannah tossed several wooden boxes ashore.

Sunny was talking to Hannah but in a foreign language. As Jerry and I watched, Jerry poked me in the stomach and said, "They're speaking Russian."

I replied, "Not German?"

Jerry shook his head, "Nope, it's Russian."

Jerry and I picked up the boxes and carried them inside the tower. The professor went out to welcome Hannah and Sunny. He said something to them and Jerry said, "More Russian."

"Jeez, Jerry, I'm really getting suspicious. We'd better watch each other's backs."

CHAPTER 31

Explosion

All five of us packed the newly arrived boxes. Hannah carried out the sleeping bags and returned empty handed. I assumed she tossed them onto the boat; her feet weren't wet.

We hadn't packed the lights, wires or batteries yet and when I started to pick the wiring and lights up, Professor Schneider said, "You can leave those for now, Rocky, we will take care of those things later." So, the remainder of the materials were packed in the last empty carton leaving little room for the lights, wiring and batteries. Sunny, Jerry and I carried the stuffed and sealed boxes to the boat and put them on board. Hannah was on the deck rearranging things, apparently to balance the load.

The professor waded out to the stern, climbed aboard and was talking to Hannah. As soon as their conversation was over, Schneider raised his right arm into the air. I figured he was stretching to relieve a cramp. Jerry said, "We'll get the rest of the materials now. We'll toss them to you."

Jerry and I turned to go back to the tower and were surprised by Sunny; he had a gun pointing at us. He ordered, "Fork over the cash. You won't need it. Put it on the ground and move away."

We could only follow orders. Jerry and I glanced at each other with forlorn looks. What could we do against a gun? Sunny looked like he was ready to use the pistol. Then he waved the handgun toward the lighthouse. "Into the tower, boys. Quickly!"

I didn't look back for fear of getting shot. He must have picked up the two thousand dollars. Maybe that was his pay for working with the professor.

We had little choice but follow directions; he stayed about ten feet behind us. There was no way for us to rush him and get the gun without one or both of us getting shot. That would be our finish. We'd have to play along. I don't know what we were thinking, but we moved slowly hoping for a miracle that never came.

Sunny had us open the trapdoor and go down the ladder. When we reached the bottom, he commanded, "Step away from the ladder."

I guess we didn't move fast enough, because a second or so later, he fired a bullet into the rocks to get us away from the ladder. The noise reverberated through the rocks. We moved quickly, afraid the next bullet would ricochet off the rocks and into one of us. We watched the ladder rise and disappear through the opening above. Then the door banged shut leaving us in darkness.

All I heard next was from Jerry. "Son of a bitch! I didn't see this coming."

My evaluation of our situation wasn't worth much. All I could think of was Elena and Aaron returning with enough money to buy the rest of the gold bars, if that was what they were going to do. I now had big doubts. That would be four days before they discovered Jerry and I were missing. They would return to the lighthouse to search and find the bodies of two young men that passed away from hypothermia.

I commented to Jerry, "If you move around, say something so I know where you are, I'll do the same."

We maintained our positions for some time, maybe fifteen minutes, before Jerry said, "I'm going to sit on the floor, I'm tired of standing in the dark. Have you got any ideas, Rock?"

"Only two, but we'd need tools. I was thinking we could make the hole larger and escape, but we'd fall in the ocean and freeze our asses off.

There's no way to get to the trapdoor, it's at least twelve feet over our heads and there's no way to climb."

Suddenly the trap door opened and Sunny called to us, "How are you boys doing? I have decided to give you some nourishment." Cans of food started dropping from above and I moved farther into the cavern to avoid being hit in the head. There was a slight pause after five or six cans fell from above, then a burlap bag hit the floor. I could tell it was heavy by the thud and sound of metal clanging.

I rushed to see the contents of the bag but couldn't open it before the trapdoor slammed shut leaving us in darkness again. Jerry saw the bag and heard the noises as I had and hurried toward the bag. We banged into each other, bumping our heads. Jerry said, "Damn, Rock, I understand why your name is Rocky, your head is as hard as a rock."

I could hear him rubbing his head, I was doing the same. He commented, "I think that bag is full of metal parts to the winch. Feel in the bag to see if any bolts are in there." I knew what he was thinking, if we could fasten the bolts into the rocks, we might climb to the trapdoor and escape.

"I got you, Jer, but it still would be a tough climb to the top."

"I know, but at least we'd have a chance. Those cans of food won't last long."

"The foul odors might be a bit disagreeable. We'll have to dispose of things through the hole in the wall."

Jerry observed, "Number one won't be bad but number two will create lot's of gagging if we don't toss it out."

I laughed, "The low temperature will give us some assistance, maybe freeze it solid."

I completed searching the bag for bolts and found half a dozen that might help us. They were two inches long. I told Jerry what I found but before we could say anything more, we were knocked to the floor by an explosion.

My ears were ringing and when I called out to Jerry, I couldn't hear myself. I was deaf. I assumed the same thing had happened to him. I wanted to say, "What was that?" I crawled to Jerry's last position and found him laying on the floor. He wasn't moving but he still had a heartbeat and was breathing shallowly. He would be okay, hopefully in a few minutes. I sat beside him with my hand on his chest. I wondered why I wasn't knocked out too.

I sat there hoping he would come to quickly since his respiration and pulse seemed normal. My eyes had adjusted to the dark and I began to see there was a source of dim light in the cavern. The hole in the rock wall was allowing some light from outside to enter the cave, like a porthole in the side of a ship. I could make out Jerry's body on the floor. I had never been alone with anyone unconscious before. All I could do was wait. I wanted to get his thoughts of what had happened. It didn't take me long to form an opinion, Sunny had blown up the lighthouse. Several hundred pounds or more of lighthouse fragments would keep the trapdoor sealed, maybe forever at least for us. Another obstacle to overcome if we had any hopes to get out of the cavern. The only way through that wooden door would be by chipping away with Jerry's pocketknife. If we could get a hand through a hole in the door, we could probably tear boards away.

Jerry was unconscious for about ten minutes and when he became aware that I was sitting beside him, he thought he was blind.

"Jesus, Rock, what happened, was there a cave-in?"

"No cave-in. I think Sunny blew up the lighthouse. You were knocked out by the blast but for some reason, I wasn't."

"Oh, that's right. We're in the cavern below the tower. Any new ideas of how to get out?"

"Nope, nothing new. I guess we'll just have to sit in the dark and pray the Nesbitts are watching out for us. If they don't come back, we're on our own."

"Have you investigated the rock walls to see if there are any cracks we can use to fasten bolts or where we can wedge metal pieces to climb up to the door?"

"I explored the walls where the ladder used to be but didn't discover anything. Maybe you should feel around, I might have missed something."

"Okay, I'll do that, but I have a headache. I'm gonna sit here a while."

"Yeah, don't exert yourself after being knocked out. Just take it easy. I'm not in any hurry. You'll notice there is a little bit of light from outside. Your eyes will adjust before long."

The Atwaters had cruised south a mile or so past the southern tip of Crescent Island before turning east and sailing four to five miles farther from the coast of Labrador, then cruising north. They were staying out of sight from the lighthouse, although they didn't expect anyone to be looking across the ocean to the east.

The Ocean Wave sailed north at a slow rate for thirty minutes. They cut the engine and rode the three-foot waves while eating sandwiches and drinking coffee.

Glory Bee asked, "Clarence, when should we start back toward the island. Have we given them enough time to vacate?"

"Well, Glory," he grinned, "I think we can reclaim our regular names now, we're out of earshot. Let's turn back. I'd like to take a look at that unfinished structure. I'm wondering if it has any chance to be completed by the government. Maybe the Schneiders left something."

Elena said, "It was kind of fun using fictitious names, wasn't it?"

Aaron started to say something when they heard a large explosion. Cracking a big smile, he said, "Do you think the French are attacking a British settlement on the coast?"

"I know you're joking, that happened about a century ago, didn't it?"

"That's about right. Let's head back to the lighthouse to see if something happened on the island. For noise to be that loud, it didn't come from the mainland. I hope that wasn't the Schneiders' boat that blew up."

Elena put the binoculars to her eyes and watched the western horizon as they traveled across the waves. The boat remained fairly steady for minutes at a time as Aaron guided the cruiser through the swells to the west. As soon as she saw the lighthouse, she would give Aaron a more accurate heading.

Elena tired of watching the horizon and gave the glasses to Aaron. She took over steering the boat, changing directions slightly every minute or so. After ten minutes, Aaron pointed and said, "Five degrees starboard, Elena."

She frowned and replied, "Right or left, Aaron?"

"I'm sorry. To the right."

Aaron had spotted the southern tip of the island, rising above the ocean about twenty feet. They were slightly south of Crescent Island about a mile away. He kept the binoculars pointed straight ahead for a few seconds and then gave the glasses to Elena. He had seen enough. Aaron slowed the boat and steered farther north. They were still a quarter mile from shore.

All of a sudden Elena screamed, "Good God, the lighthouse is gone! It looks like the remains of a German city after the Allies bombed it flat during the war. We have to go ashore!"

They beached their boat fifty yards from the wreckage. Aaron was concerned that more explosives might be present and unexploded. They separated and moved slowly, trying to see if anything looked dangerous. Elena scanned the mess with the binoculars.

"I don't see anything dangerous, Aaron, just piles of rubble."

"Okay, let's get closer and see what remains . . . see if anything left is useful. Our report will have to specify anything of value."

Cautiously approaching, they exchanged comments concerning what they saw. Aaron worked his way to the trapdoor, moving large chunks of concrete by hand and kicking brick-size pieces out of the way. Elena joined him as he surveyed the trapdoor covered with sand, rock, and a few broken pieces of wood. He picked up a brick, didn't have a good grip and dropped it on the slightly damaged trapdoor.

Elena heard something. A sound from below ground caught her attention. "Aaron, there's someone down below!"

"I didn't hear anything, are you sure?"

"Shh! Listen!" Elena got to her knees, wiped debris from a small area and put her ear to the dusty door. She heard a voice and stood up quickly. "Somebody's down there! We have to open this door!"

The Nesbitts cleared the entire trapdoor of debris and saw there was no fixture in evidence for opening the door made of heavy planks. Aaron stepped back and said, "I think I'll have to break through the wood with a heavy piece of concrete."

Elena pointed at a chunk she thought Aaron could lift and said, "Try that one."

Aaron picked up the wedge-shaped chunk, lifted it as high as he could and dropped it on the center of the door. The concrete bounced but the wood made a cracking noise. He tried again and could see a crack developing. The center board snapped on the third attempt, creating an irregular hole with the projectile lodged halfway through the door. He tried to pull the battering cement piece from the board without success.

Elena suggested, "Stomp on it, Aaron."

"Okay, after I get my breath." He sat on the piece of trapped cement for thirty seconds, taking deep breaths of cold ocean air while Elena rubbed his shoulders.

He stood up, balanced himself on his left leg and brought his right foot down as hard as he could. The wedged shaped piece of rock and cement nearly went through the door.

Elena encouraged, "One more like that and we'll be able to talk to whoever's down there."

"Here goes!" Aaron mashed his foot against the concrete and it went through the wood creating a gap about four inches wide and a foot in length. The remaining shorter length of wood was pushed into the hole. Aaron reached down, grabbed it and tore it free, tossing it aside.

Elena crouched down over the opening and asked, "Who's down there?"

She was surprised by the answer, "Rocky Linfield and Jerry Morgan, who are you?"

Excitedly, she turned to Aaron and said, "Did you hear? It's Rocky and Jerry." She answered back, "It's Elena and Aaron, Rocky. How far down are you?"

"I'm standing on that hunk of concrete you just dropped down here. I think it's about twelve feet from top to bottom. Drop some more of those pieces of rubble. We'll build stairs and climb up unless you have a rope to pull us out."

Aaron looked down into the opening and commented to Elena, "I think it's going to take about ten more like the one I just dropped down there. See if you can locate more concrete about the same size, but not too big and not too small."

Elena smiled, "Goldilocks pieces, eh?"

Aaron laughed and replied, "Are you trying to sound like a Canadian?"

"Ah! You do listen to what I say. Here's more concrete of the right size." She pointed at a pile of rubble a few feet away.

CHAPTER 32

Rescue

Less than an hour transpired before faint noises were being transmitted through the rocks surrounding the boys. Jerry was the first to hear some scraping from above.

"Hey, Rock, hear that?"

"What?"

"Listen! Somebody's moving around up there."

Rocky reacted when he also heard sounds, thumps and scratching noises. "You're right, Jerry. Someone is up there!" He yelled, "Hey! There are two of us down here! We're trapped!"

The next thing they heard was a loud thump on the trapdoor surface. Something heavy had struck the door. A few seconds later another crashing noise. The trapdoor was being broken open.

"It looks like we'll be getting out of here soon, Jer."

The third crushing noise caused sand, small rocks and wood slivers to cascade into the cavern and a ray of light penetrated the darkness. Rocky stepped farther back from the hole and crouched beside Jerry.

"Whoever it is up there, they're strong. That chunk of concrete must be heavy," said Rocky.

There was another thump, then a large piece of concrete fell to the cavern floor, followed by a woman's voice asking who was in the hole.

Rocky replied, "Rocky Linfield and Jerry Morgan. Who are you?" He moved directly below the hole for better communication. When he heard who it was above, he almost wet his pants. It was too good to believe. He turned to Jerry and said, "It's Elena and Aaron! We're getting out of this hell hole."

Jerry commented, "Well, I guess it pays to pray! You were right about Atwaters being Elena and Aaron, they're the only ones that would be near enough to save us. I was thinking they would be returning in four days. All that time we'd be in near complete darkness and living off the food in those cans."

Following a short discussion with Elena, Rocky stepped away from the shaft and another chunk of concrete fell to the floor. When it was in place, Rocky said, "We're ready for another one," and backed farther into the cavern to avoid being struck by falling concrete.

It took nearly half an hour to build steps that would reach within eight feet of the remaining lighthouse floor. When Aaron rested a moment, Alena asked, "See how high you can reach, Rocky."

He stood on the pile of makeshift concrete steps and extended his hand to within a foot of the lighthouse floor. Elena said, "Take off your belt and make a loop, we'll pull you up, then Jerry."

After widening the hole in the trapdoor, Rocky was pulled up into the bright daylight. Rocky looked at Elena, still disguised as Glory Bee, and gave her a big hug. He commented, "You sure you are Elena? You had me fooled for a while."

She said, "I wasn't sure you remembered that rhyme, that was seven years ago and you were just a little boy."

"Oh, I remembered everything. You were my first love."

He likewise gave Aaron a hug and thanked them both. After Rocky's eyes adjusted to the daylight, Aaron and Rocky lifted Jerry from the cavern. Jerry gave both Elena and Aaron a kiss on the cheek and said,

"Thank you very much. We were starting to worry . . . just a little. But Rocky told me who was behind the disguise. We figured we would see you again at the Rocky Point lighthouse. We didn't think they would try to get rid of us."

Aaron spoke up, "This is a dangerous place now, let's drop more debris in the hole so if someone falls in they can get back out without assistance."

With three people working and Jerry relaxing because of being knocked unconscious, it took about thirty minutes to throw enough debris into the cavern hole to get it within three feet of the surface. While the group gathered material, they found Rocky's and Jerry's backpacks, dirty but still intact. When Rocky handed Jerry's container to him, he replied, "Thanks Rock, Carina's address and phone number are in there, very important information."

Rocky responded, "Thank Elena, she found it right next to the water. Sounds like your mind is working fine, you're thinking about a girl."

"Yeah. I feel good and I'm hungry. Do the Nesbitts have something to eat on their boat?"

Elena heard Jerry's query and responded, "We've got food in the boat's galley. Let's get out of here and start back toward Goose Bay. It's a bit longer than a five hour trip. You can clean up, eat, and get some sleep. The Canadian authorities are going to have something to say when they read our report. Lots of questions."

Jerry and I said good riddance to Crescent Island and what remained of the distant lighthouse. We didn't need any help getting aboard The Ocean Wave. We found the galley and were preparing hot food as Aaron backed the cruiser off the beach and headed north. I could tell The Ocean Wave was a much faster boat than the Schneiders' shuttle vessel, having additional power and feeling more solid as we skimmed over the waves. Elena joined us and said, "When we reach Lake Melville, we'll pick up speed. This thing really goes in quieter water."

Jerry looked at me, swallowed, raised his eyebrows and remarked, "We're already going much faster than the Schneiders' craft ever did. I don't think it's only due to the pilot, either. This is a classy boat."

Elena quipped, "It's a loaner from the Canadian Navy. Aaron still has some connections." She grinned and continued, "Bye the way, those gold bars are not pure gold, they are about ninety-five percent uranium. The gold is just an outside coating. We'll get them analyzed when we reach Goose Bay."

I stated, "You were right, Jerry. That instrument the professor had was for radiation, not gold. But we never needed to use it."

Elena asked, "Did you guys ever come in contact with the uranium?"

Jerry answered, "No. We just handled the outside covering, the gold part."

"That's good. You won't have to be decontaminated. The people at the base will probably make you shower and check for any residual radiation on your bodies. I won't be surprised if they check all of us."

I couldn't resist staring at Elena and finally asked, "Who did your makeup?"

"Aaron and I put these rubber cosmetic accessories on each other. Don't you think we did a pretty good job?"

"Very good. How did you change your voices?"

"A pill causes us to be hoarse, it changes how our vocal cords work. We don't use it very often."

I woke suddenly and said, "Uranium." I must have conked out and been dreaming. Elena was gone but Jerry was leaning back, almost reclining, and asleep a few feet away. It took me a moment to recall we were on a boat, the hum of the engines reminded me of flying in that DC-3, but that seemed long ago now. I checked my diving watch. We had been on the

Ocean Wave for a little bit more than four hours. As I watched Jerry, he blinked, sat upright and rubbed his eyes with his fists.

"What's goin' on, Rock?"

"How are you feeling, Jer? Any headache?" I asked.

He exercised his neck muscles, briefly turning his head in all directions. Then he moved his shoulders around and replied, "I feel great! Sleep sure helps with headaches, doesn't it?"

I grinned and replied, "I usually take aspirin, because I get them during the day, but I guess I could sleep during the day on weekends."

"Yeah, and then you wouldn't have time for Millie."

"No, Jer, that's for the evenings."

Elena popped into the galley to get some coffee for Aaron and asked, "Are you guys discussing anything important?"

I grinned, "Yes, headaches."

She frowned and said, "I thought I should give you a heads up about questions from the Canadian authorities. You'll be talking to them instead of the armed forces personnel. Labrador and adjacent islands are part of Canada." She carried a mug of coffee from the galley and returned a minute later, sat next to me and gave us some advice. "Whatever you say, make it the truth, without embellishments. Be as specific as possible. Make sure you tell them about the submarine and the gold. Let them know you knew nothing about the radiation. I'm sure they will want to recover the sub."

We arrived in Goose Bay after four hours and fifty-three minutes, faster than Elena had estimated. The boat had ridden high on the water making good time while on Lake Melville. Jerry suggested the name on the boat should be The Ocean Flash, a minor change but probably requiring a stack of paperwork. We were met at the pier by a small contingent of Canadian officials and escorted to the air terminal.

Following an hour of questions, our party of four was treated to dinner and provided accommodations for the night. In the morning, Jerry and I met with the Nesbitts for breakfast. While enjoying our meal, two Canadian officers joined us and requested our presence at an official meeting.

I asked Elena, "What's this all about?" as we were led down a corridor to a living room sized space containing tables and chairs to accommodate about two dozen people. I was happy to see Elena had removed her disguise makeup, as had Aaron. She looked beautiful as usual. We were seated together at a large table with officials that had questioned us the day before. When the door closed, a uniformed officer stood and stated, "I am Lieutenant Colonel William Blanford. I will be leading an armed unit to remove the current inhabitants at Rocky Point Lighthouse. We are going to take four individuals into custody: Professor Konrad Schneider, Ingrid Schneider, Hannah Schneider and an individual going by the name Sunny. They are all Russian agents and are not related. At this time, they will be charged with possession of enhanced uranium, attempted murder, and destruction of Canadian Government property. They may be charged with other crimes at a later time. If any of the suspects resist with weapons, do not shoot to kill. We will be travelling to the site in helicopters. Civilians, please dress warmly."

"Are there any questions?" Colonel Blanford asked. We all looked around and nobody stood or raised their hand. He scanned over the group and said, "All right, we will depart in thirty minutes."

I guess I was a bit confused with what Colonel Blanford said, so I asked Elena, "He wants all four of us to go?"

"That's right, Rocky. I believe he wants us along to positively identify people and gold bars."

Jerry and I made good use of the short time available. We changed our underwear, rolled on some deodorant and put on cleaner shirts from our backpacks. I think we still smelled a bit musty but we felt a little bit better. We didn't have enough time to shower and looked forward to that activity when we returned from Rocky Point.

As we boarded the flying bananas, a soldier provided us with earplugs. Aaron and Elena were on one helicopter, Jerry and I were on the other. All soldiers carried some kind of firearm and there were two medics, just in case. Jerry and I left our backpacks at Goose Bay. What would we need them for?

The choppers were in the air for slightly over two hours and set down about a hundred yards from the lighthouse. When we got closer to the tower and adjoining buildings, I glanced out to sea and saw a seaplane landing about two hundred yards from shore. The Schneiders were not going to get away by boat.

The soldiers raided the lighthouse and in ten minutes the Schneiders and Sunny were in custody.

When the four suspects were handcuffed and sitting in the living area, Colonel Blanford asked Jerry and me to join him outside the main entrance. We took a short walk to the largest building. He stepped inside and motioned for us to enter.

He exhibited a big smile and said, "I would like to introduce you to the Schneider family."

CHAPTER 33

Finally Back Home

When we stepped into the room there was a hush. The Schneiders had been speaking in Russian but suddenly became quiet. The professor, in handcuffs, stood up and said, "Where have you boys been? We couldn't find you when we started back to Rocky Point."

I wanted to punch him in the mouth when I heard that obvious lie. I noticed Jerry's fists were clenched. He was thinking the same thing but we knew the soldiers wouldn't allow us to beat the crap out of Schneider. I glanced at Jerry and remarked, "Can you believe that garbage?"

Colonel Branford spoke to the suspects, "Currently there are three charges against you: destruction of government property, transporting enhanced uranium without a license, and two counts of attempted murder. The first two actions carry significant fines, but the third offense will carry incarceration for a minimum of seven years."

Sunny and Professor Schneider began conversing in Russian. Jerry was listening and interpreted for us. I didn't think they knew Jerry spoke Russian. "They are going to request help from the Russian Embassy, they aren't worried if those are the only charges."

Elena and Aaron had their heads together, but I couldn't hear what they were saying. When they parted, Aaron stepped adjacent to Colonel Branford and said, "We have a Professor Simmonds in protective custody in Washington and he has volunteered information about a plan to explode a dirty bomb in New York City at Christmas time. The Schneiders are involved, supplying enriched nuclear material. Simmonds was the contact man to arrange payment and to take possession of the uranium. He used an assumed name. This Professor Simmonds does not exist. He is an FBI agent; his information is highly reliable."

The colonel said, "The prisoners will be transported to Ottawa for trial and then extradited to the United States for further charges. Perhaps they will be used in some sort of prisoner exchange. They were trained for this mission in Russia and are Communist sympathizers."

Four soldiers were left in charge of the lighthouse until the original lighthouse family returned from vacation. The prisoners were flown to Goose Bay in one of the choppers. Colonel Branford didn't want to mix accusers with suspects, so Elena, Aaron, Jerry and I returned to the base in the other flying banana.

The eight gold-covered uranium bars remained at the lighthouse to be claimed by an atomic energy cleanup team. The bars purchased by the Atwaters were transported to Ottawa. Ten thousand dollars of US currency was returned to Arron and Elena to be refunded to the CIA. The Schneiders hadn't had time to spend any of the money or disperse it to another country.

Following the hour on the ground at Rocky Point, the helicopters were back in the air, returning to Goose Bay. Though it was dark when they boarded a plane to Boston, the four Americans were looking forward to seeing friends and families in Crafton. They arrived in Boston a few minutes after midnight and spent the early hours of the next day in a hotel at the airport.

The first thing Jerry and I did when we were situated in a hotel room was take showers, something we hadn't done it seemed like forever. Jerry stripped and was in the shower before I had even thought about it. I turned on the TV and watched the end of the late news. There were old western movies and wrestling on, but I didn't want the government paying the rental fee and I really had no interest. I was so tired and wanted Jerry to get out of the shower so I could clean up. We both slept in our underwear and woke up when someone knocked on our door.

At the same instant, the phone rang and Elena told me to meet them in the restaurant for breakfast, it was eight o'clock. We did our best to be presentable and ate pancakes, bacon and I had the best coffee ever. Jerry had a mug of hot chocolate. When I saw what he ordered, I thought I would have some too, but then I remembered the last time I had a chocolate drink for breakfast, I threw up in the back seat of the car. I stuck with coffee and water.

There was a large clock on the restaurant wall where nearly everyone had a clear view of it. I assumed it was there for travelers to be aware of arrivals and departures. We ate and talked for an hour and left the hotel at nine o'clock. Aaron rented a station wagon for our return trip to Crafton. The car was parked outside the hotel entrance and we all climbed in. Aaron drove, Elena sat beside him. Jerry and I hadn't ridden in a car since we were in Scandinavia a month ago. It seemed strange at first, but when the heater warmed us up, I leaned back in my seat and closed my eyes. I could hear passing cars, the heater fan and a few murmurs from the front seat. I pictured going to the Harrises' home and anticipated a big hug and a kiss from Millie.

It had started raining and I could hear more sounds, the monotony of the windshield wipers and the tires occasionally splashing through puddles on the blacktop. I kept my eyes closed and remained in a state of limbo as the car slowed to a stop for a few moments and then accelerated. Voices came from the front of the car, but I couldn't recognize the words, they were just another background noise.

Elena watched cars turning in front of the station wagon. The third car looked familiar, a silver over blue four-door Pontiac. She turned toward Aaron and asked, "Did you see that Pontiac?"

"I did. Your father was driving and Millie was in the passenger seat. Should we tell Rocky?"

Elena made a split-second decision, "No! I think I know where they are going and the reason why. Weren't you going to say something about seeing them?"

"I was, but I was trying to figure out why they were on the road."

"I'm pretty sure I know why." She turned around and noticed both boys still had their eyes closed. She moved closer to Aaron and whispered, "I think Dad and Mil are going to the airport to pick up Carina. I believe her trip was cut short and she's on her way back home."

"Yeah, but why would she fly into Boston? Why not New York?"

"To say good-bye to friends, especially Jerry."

"You think?"

"That's what Millie told me. Carina and Millie had a heartfelt discussion. Carina thinks Jerry is the real deal and Rocky told me Jerry really likes Carina."

Aaron asked Elena, "Did you call ahead to let everybody know we're coming home?" Her answer surprised him.

"Nope. I thought it would be more exciting for the families if we show up unannounced."

"What about having the Linfields, Harrises, and Morgans meet with Mrs. Makler for dessert and have Rocky and Jerry show up?"

"Great idea! That will give Dad, Millie, and Carina time to return from Boston. We'll go home and pay a visit to Marty. I think she'll go along with it 'cause Rocky is her grandson. The boys will stay with us until their unexpected appearance at Marty's for dessert. What will Marty use as her excuse to get everyone to come to her house?"

Aaron suggested, "How about her birthday."

"No, that won't work. I believe her birthday is in March. The Linfields will know that's not right."

Aaron thought for a second and said, "I know, let's tell Marty you're pregnant. She'll spread the word and say she has invited us over for a mini celebration."

Elena grinned sheepishly and said, "That should do it."

When the station wagon was about fifteen minutes from Crafton, Elena turned around with her knees on the seat, reached back and touched Rocky's leg. He blinked a few times and asked, "Are we home?"

"Not yet, we're about fifteen minutes from Crafton. I need to talk to you and Jerry."

When Jerry heard his name, he rubbed his eyes, straightened up and leaned forward. "What's goin' on?"

I got his attention, "We're almost home. Elena wants to tell us something."

She spoke over the car noises, "Aaron and I have come up with something and we wanted to see if you will agree to do it. It will be a big surprise for your families."

Elena explained the plan to Jerry and me and we immediately agreed to it. No one would be expecting us to show up, everyone would think we were still in Labrador. I thought about it as we entered the Crafton city limits and decided to say what was on my mind.

"I think we should let Granma in on the plan. You know it's her house and she might want to clean up or order some food."

Elena didn't have to think at all, "You're right, Rocky. Thanks. We'll stop at her house first. Besides, if she sees a strange car arrive at our house, she might call the police. No telling what might result."

Aaron made the turnoff from the lighthouse road and pulled the station wagon into Granma's driveway. Jerry and I got out of the back seat after Aaron and Elena were on the porch ready to knock.

We closed our doors quietly and sneaked behind Aaron and Elena, squatting down so we couldn't be seen from the front door. Elena knocked three times and we waited. I could hear Granma's steps as she approached the door. She invariably wore black shoes with one-inch heels. They always clunked on the hardwood floor.

The door swung open and Granma said, "Oh! Elena and Aaron, you're back from your trip up north. Did you get any fish?"

Elena chuckled, "We sure did, two big ones." She stepped sideways toward Aaron and I popped up to my full height. "Hi Granma!"

She stood there open mouthed and then lunged forward, arms circling me. We hugged and she spoke into my right ear, "Rocky, you scallywag! Does your mother know you're home from Labrador?"

Before I could answer, she said, "Jerry is with you, too. You both look fine, I guess Canada agreed with you."

Then I answered, "Nobody knows we're home. We just got back to Crafton; we came here first. We have a plan and need you to help us. It's kind of sneaky."

"Well, you've certainly come to the right place, I love surprises. Come in, all of you. Tell me what you're thinking of."

The living room was just as I had last seen it after graduation and right before we had traveled to Scandinavia. I could smell coffee. An unfinished crossword puzzle and ballpoint were on the middle cushion of the sofa. Granma scooped them up and had us all sit down.

"Are you hungry? You must be, after that long trip from Boston. How about a sandwich and some chips? Elena, come in the kitchen and help me." Without waiting for an answer, she walked across the room and into the kitchen. Elena gave us a shrug and followed.

From the kitchen, I heard Granma say, "You men, better wash up . . .

and turn on the TV, I want to see the afternoon news."

I knelt in front of the TV and rotated the channel selector switch while watching Aaron and Jerry. I didn't care what was on and waited until I saw an eyebrow twitch on the others' faces before I went to the bathroom and washed up. My peach fuzz beard was showing, so I needed to ask Aaron if he had a razor I could use. Jerry's beard was heavier than mine, so I figured he would need to shave, too.

By the time the three of us were scrubbed, Granma and Elena had a large serving tray of sandwiches, carrot and celery sticks, and potato chips in the center of the dining table. Granma had a large pitcher of lemonade and a carafe of hot coffee ready on the counter near the sink. We sat down, snacked and talked about our celebration plan. Elena got up and poured drinks for us while

Granma made a list of items she needed to get at the grocery store. When we were finished planning, Aaron gave Granma two twenties. She refused, but Aaron insisted. Jerry and I didn't have any cash or we would have contributed. I would give Aaron a twenty when I got some cash.

Granma dismissed us to the Nesbitts' when she said she had to make some invitations and go to the grocery store. Elena suggested we needed a chocolate cake. Aaron nodded and added, "Better get a vanilla one, too."

On the way across the lots to Aaron and Elena's house, I asked if I could borrow Aaron's electric razor. Elena heard what I said and commented, "You and Jerry need to wash your clothes, too, you're getting a little gamey." I sniffed my underarms and had to agree. The showers we had were great for our bodies but our clothes needed soap and water . . . lots of soap and water. Jerry and I were given free rein of the house while Elena and Aaron went to the Sheriff's Office to send reports to Washington. They wanted secure telephone lines; their home phone didn't meet high enough standards.

Jerry and I were shocked when we opened our backpacks to wash our stinky clothing. Jerry pulled a wadded up sock from one of the inside pockets of his knapsack and out popped ten one-hundred dollar bills. He yelled, "Rock! Look in your backpack, in one of the inside pockets!"

I opened my pack and found the same thing, ten one-hundred dollar bills. "Geez, Jer, Elena and Aaron must have given us a reward! I hope the CIA doesn't give them any crap."

The washer and dryer were put to good use that afternoon and Jerry found an ironing board and steam iron in the hall closet. I had to laugh when I saw Jerry standing in his underwear at the ironing board pressing his shirt and pants. I said, "Sorry I laughed," when he offered to press my clothes. I thanked him but did the job myself. I needed some practice at domestic duties before going to college.

We both could have used a haircut, but neither of us wanted the other to brandish a pair of scissors anywhere near our heads for fear of a humorous trim. We played a series of chess matches while waiting for Elena and Aaron to return for dinner. Jerry won most of the games, but I was getting better, extending one game for a half hour. I was beginning to realize the power of pawns.

Elena and Aaron arrived home with dinner at five thirty. As soon as they came in the house, Jerry and I thanked them for the money. When we asked if they would get in trouble, they said no, their department heads thought we deserved a reward.

The Nesbitts had stopped to get a half dozen burgers and four servings of fries at the new McDonald's restaurant. We ate and talked while watching the six o'clock news. Every five to ten minutes, Elena got up and looked out the kitchen window. I figured out what she was doing, so didn't ask. After the fourth peek, she said, "Time to go. Marty just gave the signal."

Jerry gave me a puzzled look and I said, "Granma signaled it was time to go when she raised the kitchen shade." He grinned and said, "I wondered why Elena kept getting up. I should have known."

Elena gave Jerry and me instructions: "Put on your coats and wait outside Mrs. Makler's front door. Aaron and I will go in first. It should only be a few minutes. I'll open the door for you." We stepped outside and waited for Aaron to lock his entrance door, then Jerry and I waited until the Nesbitts reached Granma's front door before we started across the lawn. When we got to the door, we could hear a commotion inside, lots of applause and a few whistles. Elena must have just announced her pregnancy and many noisy congratulations were given. The voices calmed and I heard Elena say, "Whew, I need some fresh air."

She opened the door; Jerry and I stepped inside and all hell broke loose. Millie flew into my arms and Carina launched herself at Jerry, almost knocking him over. We kissed and hugged and then the rest of our families joined in to smother us with hugs, kisses and backslaps.

The questions seemed endless, but after the initial onslaught had died down, Aaron took the floor and said, "Elena and I are sorry to have used a ruse to get you all here, but we wanted to surprise everyone."

Mom said, "You aren't really pregnant, Elena?"

Aaron answered, "That's right, Mrs. Linfield. It was just a bit of deception."

Elena stood up in the middle of the room and said guiltily, "Aaron, didn't know, but there really is a new Nesbitt in the oven."